A REAL COWBOY ALWAYS COMES HOME

A Wyoming Rebels Novel

STEPHANIE ROWE

Authenticity Playground Press

COPYRIGHT

A REAL COWBOY ALWAYS COMES HOME (a Wyoming Rebels novel). Copyright © 2022 by Stephanie Rowe.

Print ISBN 13: 9798829467975

Cover design by Kelli Ann Morgan, Inspire Creative Services.

All rights reserved. No part of this publication may be reproduced, disseminated, or transmitted in any form or by any means or for any use, including recording or any information storage and retrieval system, without the prior written consent of the author and/or the artist. The only exception is short excerpts or the cover image in reviews. **Please be a leading force in respecting the right of authors and artists to protect their work.** This is a work of fiction. All the names, characters, organizations, places and events portrayed in this novel or on the cover are either products of the author's or artist's imagination or are used fictitiously.

Any similarity to real persons, living or dead, is purely coincidental and not intended by the author or the artist. There are excerpts from other books by the author in the back of the book.

CHAPTER ONE

"Caleb! Caleb! Wake up!"

The voice was distant, penetrating the fog trying to claim his brain.

"Caleb!" Someone shook his shoulder, and the move sent sharp pain knifing through his side, jolting him back to consciousness.

He opened his eyes and saw a man leaning over him, shouting. The man had dark skin, a shaved head, and a cut bleeding profusely from above his right eye. "Caleb!" The man was shouting at him, calling him Caleb.

Was that his name? He didn't know.

He couldn't remember anything. He felt like a thick fog was wrapped around his brain, drowning out his ability to think. He sat up, gritting his teeth at the pain in his side. What had happened? There was smoke all around them. Flames licking at the remains of a charred building. "What's going on?"

"They found us, and they got Gabrielle. I'm going after her." The man shoved a small bundle in his arms. "Take Zach. Go! If Gabrielle and I don't make it, you know the deal. You know where the fake paperwork is that says he's your son." He met Caleb's gaze. "Tell Zach about us when he gets older. Make him proud of his mom and dad. And be the dad he deserves. You'll be all he's got."

Caleb looked down and realized that he was holding a baby. A baby? He didn't know anything about babies. Or did he? "What—"

"I got enough supplies to last a couple weeks, but that's all I could grab." The man shoved a stuffed duffel bag at him. He looked around at the carnage. "They clearly found you, too. You need to get out of here. I'll draw them away from you. They want Zach. Keep him safe. Go deep under. Never let him be found."

Caleb tightened his arms around the baby and slung the duffel over his shoulder, grimacing at the pain that the action created. "How will you find him?"

"He's my son. If I live, I'll find him." The man kissed the top of Zach's head, and then took off in a sprint toward a truck that was parked askew by the side of the road. He jumped into it, then hit the gas, taking off down the street and leaving Caleb behind in the darkness.

Caleb swore and looked around.

The night was dark. There were no streetlights. No houses around. Just the flickering light from the lingering flames surrounding him. It looked like there had been an explosion, but he didn't know how he knew that. He had no idea where he was. Who he was. What had happened. Who the man was who'd just handed him a child to protect.

Zach squirmed in his arms, and Caleb looked down at the baby. The big brown eyes were staring up at him with absolute trust. Zach smiled at him, and Caleb realized that Zach knew him. This kid was someone he'd spent time with, which meant the man probably was, too.

A friend? More than that. A brother? Someone who trusted him with his own son.

Protectiveness roared through him, and Caleb forced himself to smile at the baby. "Uncle Caleb's here, Zach. We're going to have some fun, okay?"

Zach continued to smile at him, those big brown eyes unwavering with trust and vulnerability.

In the distance, Caleb heard sirens approaching. Threat or help?

He didn't know. He couldn't take the chance until he figured out what was happening.

He stumbled to his feet, then swayed as dizziness hit him. He put his hand on his side, then swore as pain shot through him. His left knee. His hip. His head. His side. He felt like he'd been run over by a tank. Or knocked down by an explosion.

Then his hand hit the butt of a gun, and he looked down.

He was armed.

His side was bleeding profusely.

His jeans were torn and charred.

His brain was foggy.

He quickly searched his pockets, but found no ID. No wallet. No cash. Nothing. The watch on his wrist was cracked and wasn't working, so he didn't even know what time it was.

He had no idea what had happened, or how he'd gotten there. Or who he was. But he knew one thing: a baby was counting on him for survival.

The sirens got closer, stealing time from him.

He looked around. The road in front of him. Darkness and woods behind him. A baby in his arms that was depending on him.

Without hesitation, he turned away from the road and headed into the darkness, fading from sight with an instinct born of many years of training.

Training he didn't remember.

∼

Ten hours later, Caleb was desperate. He was pushing his body beyond exhaustion, and he needed a place to lay low, recover, and make sure Zach was safe.

He was on edge, not trusting anyone he passed. He had no idea who to look for, who would be coming, what they'd do.

All he knew was that he had to keep Zach safe from a person who had apparently blown up the building he'd been in, and kidnapped Zach's mother.

Public transportation was out of the question, obviously.

He had no idea what resources he had in his life to go to for help, since he couldn't remember a single thing about his life or who he was.

But apparently, he had no morals, because when he saw a pickup truck parked along the side of the road with the engine running, he stole it. He'd then swapped different vehicles four times over the course of the drive, trying to obscure his trail from whoever was hunting him.

Caleb's head was pounding as he drove. He still couldn't believe he'd stolen multiple vehicles. Who stole trucks? He also, apparently, carried a gun. He was hunted by people who blew up buildings, kidnapped women, and hunted babies. He stole trucks and even knew to cover the license plate of the truck with mud to make it more difficult to track the vehicle.

Who was he? He wasn't sure he wanted to know.

But he'd kept driving. Because there was a baby who needed his help.

He'd made one stop for food, baby supplies, medical supplies, assorted gear, and a car seat, and then they were on the road again. How had he known he'd needed a car seat? Guns and diapers. He knew it all...but he knew nothing.

The landscape changed from town to fields, and as it did, he felt himself relax.

When he drove past a field of grazing horses, something inside him settled. It felt right being out in cowboy country. Horses. Fields. It was familiar to him. His past, maybe? Because he doubted that explosions and guns were a part of cowboy life.

Exhaustion fought to consume Caleb as he kept driving, following a map he'd bought, toward unpopulated woods. He found a dirt trail and drove along it, getting farther and farther from civilization. He passed house after house, but none of them were right. Cars in the driveway. Signs of people living there.

He knew what he needed to find, and he knew where he was likely to find it.

Survival. He had survival skills. He knew how to survive when he was being hunted.

What the hell?

It started raining after that, the onslaught battling his wipers for supremacy. He drove past a sign that said Hart Ranch. It was a massive property, and he could see some huge houses from the road. Rich cowboys. Imposters, probably, because no real cowboys were that rich.

After another few minutes, he found a heavily overgrown dirt road, and he turned onto it. He was so tired that he was having trouble focusing, and Zach was growing restless in the car seat. He had to find a place to stop soon.

He emerged out of the woods and found a small cabin. It was dark. Shingles were falling off. Shades were down. Bushes were partially blocking access to the front door. It looked abandoned.

Relief rushed through him. "We're home, Zach," he said,

keeping his voice in the singsong tone that made the infant smile. "Hang on, buddy."

He jumped out of the truck, quickly jimmied the front door of the cabin, and checked it out. Small, dusty, definitely unoccupied, but it had a kitchen, a couple bedrooms, and it was fully furnished. *Perfect.*

Chatting with the baby as he did so, Caleb quickly unloaded the truck, then swung back into the driver's seat. "We're going on an adventure," he said as he turned the truck around and drove back toward the main road. "You like hiking in the rain, right?"

Zach giggled and babbled nonsense, which made Caleb grin. Blissfully unaware, which was fantastic. Hell, who knew what Caleb was blissfully unaware about, right? He had no idea what his life was, or anything about it.

All he knew was that his body hurt, and he was running on fumes. He needed to sleep. Eat. Probably stitch up some body parts. Then figure out what the hell he was going to do next.

He reached the main road, and then drove another few miles before parking along the edge of a ditch. It was closer to the cabin than he wanted it to be, but he knew he was at his limit. Both for himself and the baby. "All right, little man, time to have some fun."

He wiped his prints off every surface of the vehicle, then tucked two extra blankets around the baby and fastened a waterproof cover over the carrier. After making sure Zach was secure, Caleb got out of the truck, hooked the car seat over his arm, then leaned into the driver's seat.

He shifted the car into drive, then jumped back, as the truck eased forward, off the road, and down into the ditch. It landed with a clunk, off the road, out of sight for now.

He was surprised that no guilt flashed through him for stealing and crashing someone else's truck, but he gave the vehicle a nod. "Thanks, Gus," he said, meaning it. He'd written down the registration info, and if he had a chance, he'd pay Gus Stevens back for the trouble he'd caused by stealing the truck.

Tell the man he'd helped save the life of a baby. And maybe his own life, though he was beginning to wonder if that was a life worth saving.

"All right, Zach." He checked on the baby, and Zach blinked at him with sleepy eyes. "Let's go, then." He shouldered the infant carrier, then turned and hiked across the road. He stepped off the far side and into the rainy woods.

Within moments, the road was out of sight, and he and Zach were invisible from the world once again.

But this time, they had a destination. An abandoned cabin that would give Caleb the chance to recover, to figure out what the hell was going on, and maybe remember who he was.

He better remember fast, because he knew they were in danger.

Big danger that he needed to see coming if there was any chance of them surviving.

CHAPTER TWO

"Here comes a puddle!" Jenna Ward floored the truck so that the tires bounced in the muddy puddle at the edge of the dirt road. Water flew up, spraying the windshield.

Her thirteen-year-old daughter, Gracie, who had been sitting with her arms folded over her chest, couldn't quite hold back the giggle. "I'm too old for puddles."

"No one is too old for puddles." Her headlights reflected off another little pond pooled by the side of the dirt road. "Here's another!" She swerved the truck again, and the tires splashed through it, drowning the truck in water.

Gracie finally laughed. "Mom, you're so weird."

"I know. You're welcome. Every kid deserves a mom who is too weird for words." Jenna let out a breath of relief. Gracie had been so annoyed to be dragged off to Gram's cabin for a week-long mother-daughter bonding trip with no Wi-Fi, no cell service, and no neighbors, let alone stores.

Honestly, Jenna hadn't really been up for it either, but her grandma, Gram, had basically forced them out the door. She'd claimed it was because the cabin hadn't been aired out in five years and they owed her a spring cleaning of it in exchange for all her free babysitting of Gracie for the last few years. But Jenna knew that it hadn't been about that.

It had been because she'd been worried about them. She'd pulled Jenna aside and practically ordered her to take the trip.

So, she'd taken a week off and dragged her reluctant kid off for a six-hour drive into the middle of nowhere Oregon, armed only with cleaning supplies, a week's worth of groceries, and gas for the generator.

The first five hours had been tough for both of them, but in the last hour, with the dark of night settled around them, Jenna had started to feel the tension ease from her neck and shoulders, and they had finally started talking like the friends they had once been...before everything had fallen apart. "We're almost there. Another couple minutes."

She peered through the rainy windshield, looking for the dirt driveway that would be coming up any moment. It was so dark and overgrown that it was hard to see, but she knew they were close.

Gracie yawned. "Mom?"

"Yeah, baby?"

"I missed you."

Jenna's throat tightened up and she looked over at her daughter. Gracie had her feet up on the dashboard, and her arms were wrapped around her torso, hugging herself. She didn't look at Jenna. She was just staring out the windshield, as if mesmerized by the rain splattering on the glass. Her skin was lighter than Jenna's but still a beautiful brown, and her kinky hair was in tight braids, just like Jenna's. "I missed you, too, Gracie."

Gracie looked over at her then. "If you missed me, why did you take that job? Why are you always gone? Why do you work so hard?"

Jenna let out her breath. She'd hidden so much from her daughter about how hard the last couple years had been. It wasn't Gracie's burden to bear. But keeping the weight off Gracie's shoulders had created a wall between them.

She wasn't sure what the right answer was. "I hate leaving you every time I walk out of the house," she said.

"You're not answering the question." Gracie's jaw jutted out. "You never do." She turned her head to stare out the passenger window. "I was so stupid to think this week would change anything."

Jenna took a breath, trying to ignore her sudden weariness. "What do you want to change?"

"You."

Jenna glanced over at her daughter, guilt flashing through her. "Gracie—

Gracie screamed suddenly and pointed at the road. "Animal!"

Jenna hit the brakes, and the truck skidded in the mud. Gracie shrieked as the truck shot off the road and down into a ditch, landing with a jarring clunk.

Jenna caught her breath as the truck stopped and immediately looked over at her daughter, relieved when she saw Gracie with her hands braced on the dashboard, apparently fine. "Are you okay?"

"Yes." Gracie sounded scared, but not hurt. "Did you hit the animal?"

"I don't think so." The angle of the truck told Jenna that she wasn't going to be getting it out by herself. "But the truck is stuck."

Gracie turned around to look behind them, then sighed. "Mom. Really?"

Jenna tried to summon positivity she didn't feel. "I felt like an adventure."

"I don't. You could have consulted me."

"Next time I accidentally drive off the road into a ditch, I'll definitely check with you first." Jenna checked her phone just to make sure that cell service hadn't magically appeared since the last time they'd been here, but she had no bars.

She sighed and leaned back, trying to figure out what to do. Movement caught her eye, and she looked to the right. Her heart softened. "It was a dog. She looks fine." Dogs were her happy place, and just the sight of one made her feel better.

"A dog?" Gracie looked over. "Where? I don't see her?"

The dog had already scooted out of range of the headlights. "It's gone." But she realized that the dog had been standing on a packed dirt road. Relief rushed through her. "But that's our driveway up ahead. We can hike in."

Gracie's jaw dropped. "Hike? You want us to *hike* to the cabin?"

"Yep. Pack what you need for now. If the ATV is still there, I'll drive it out and get the rest of the stuff in the morning. It's cold enough that the groceries should hold."

Gracie didn't move. "It's pouring."

"Yep."

"It's muddy."

"Yep."

"The driveway is about a mile long."

Jenna grinned. "I know, right? Every teenager's dream. You can thank me in your Grammy Award acceptance speech, you know, after you get a record deal and an award-winning single, and buy me a mansion as thanks for all the great experiences you had as a teenager."

The corner of Gracie's mouth quirked. "I am definitely not going to buy you a mansion. Maybe a tiny cabin in Siberia."

"I love Siberia. I hear it has beautiful nature." She grinned. "Ready?"

"How about you hike in, get the ATV, put a roof on it,

then drive back and get me? Then I don't have to get wet or muddy, and you do all the work. I'll wait here."

Jenna reached over into the back to grab her raincoat. "Absolutely. That's a great plan. You know I live to serve you and help you become a lazy, indolent diva with no ability to care for yourself. That's a mother's job right there."

Gracie sighed. "You're incredibly annoying." But she began to lace up her boots with just a few huffs.

"It'll be fun. Remember when we used to go hiking? You loved it. Hand me that flashlight from the glove box."

"I loved it when Dad hiked with us, and you were happy," Gracie said quietly, muttering under her breath, just loud enough for Jenna to hear her, as she retrieved the flashlight.

Jenna pressed her lips together as she took the flashlight from her daughter. "You think I'm not happy now?"

Gracie looked over at her. "You haven't been happy since he died. Not even for one minute. No matter what I try."

Jenna stared at her daughter, shocked by the words. By all of them. That she wasn't happy. That her beautiful, sweet baby girl had taken upon herself to make her mom happy... and felt like she was a failure at it.

Suddenly, Jenna understood with complete clarity why her grandmother had insisted on this trip. It wasn't about her. It was about her daughter. She leaned in toward Gracie. "You don't need to do anything to make me happy. You make me happy every second of every day simply by being you."

Gracie shook her head. "Nope. You're not happy. I know it. Gram knows it. Everyone knows it." She reached in back and grabbed her coat. "But whatever. That's life, right?" She grabbed her backpack, opened the door, and stepped outside into the rain. She slammed the door shut before Jenna could respond.

A crushing feeling of guilt tried to take over, but Jenna lifted her chin.

She was going to fix this. She had a week without work, without a phone, and now, without a truck. All she had was time, and her beautiful kid, who deserved to know that she was perfect exactly as she was.

But as she grabbed her bag and opened the door of the truck, she couldn't help but wonder if Gracie was right. Was she always unhappy? She worked so hard at life that she never paused to think about being happy or not.

No. She was happy enough...at least she could fake it enough to take the pressure off her daughter. This week, she was going to bring the joy back into her daughter's eyes and heart. Create smiles again. Laughter. Girl bonding. Enough to hold them together when they went back to real life.

"Mom? Are you coming?"

Jenna took a breath, then plastered a smile on her face and in her voice. "You bet, Gracie. Let's go have some fun." She sloshed around the truck, and saw Gracie standing next to a deep puddle, looking annoyed.

"I'm already wet," Gracie announced. "And we haven't even started walking yet."

"Well, then, you know what that means, don't you?" Jenna headed toward her.

"That I should wait in the truck?" Gracie asked hopefully.

"No. It means that there is no sense in trying to stay dry, then." As she said it, Jenna jumped forward, landing with both feet in the puddle next to her daughter. It was a brilliant move, except that her backpack knocked her off balance, and she fell backward, shrieking as she flailed with her arms, trying to grab onto something to keep her balance.

There was nothing to grab, and she landed on her butt in the mud, her hands sinking out of sight while cold water rushed over the lower half of her body.

Gracie started laughing. "That was literally the worst execution I've ever seen in my life."

Jenna grinned. "I get an A for creativity, though, right?"

"It was a total fail." Gracie was laughing so hard that she went down on her knees in the mud. "You didn't even get me wet! I saw you coming, and backed up and then your hands were flailing through the air and—" Gales of laughter bust out of her. "You're sitting in mud!"

Gracie's laughter was so contagious that Jenna started laughing as well. "It's down my jeans actually. I can feel it sliding between my butt cheeks."

"Mom! I don't need that visual. Oh, my God."

Jenna held out her hand. "At least help me up. The mud is like a suction cup."

"Fine, but seriously. I can't even with you." Gracie grabbed Jenna's hand, and Jenna immediately gave a hard yank.

Gracie shot forward with a squawk and landed in the puddle next to Jenna. "Mom!" She came up spluttering and laughing. "I can't believe you did that!"

Jenna couldn't hold in her own laughter. "Really? I feel like that was pretty predictable. You definitely should have seen that coming."

Gracie sat back on her hands, grinning as water and mud streamed down her face. "I'm going back home." But she was laughing so hard that her words were barely intelligible.

"Me, too." Jenna stood up and held out her hand to help Gracie. "But first, let's go hike a mile in the rain, the dark, and the mud, to a nearly abandoned cabin that might or might not have a working generator to provide electricity and running water. Cool?"

Gracie beamed up at her. "Cool."

She put her hand in Jenna's, and Jenna realized it was the first time she'd held her daughter's hand in much too long. "Bring on the mud, baby cakes. This week is going to be great."

Gracie hopped to her feet, hope lighting up her face. "No more mud, though."

"Can't make promises." Jenna gestured to the driveway. "Let's go adventuring."

"Let's do it." Gracie waited for Jenna to catch up, then fell in beside her, their boots sloshing through the mud in unison as their laughter danced off the raindrops.

Laughter that Jenna hadn't felt in her heart for a very long time, and she hadn't realized it until right now.

Her daughter stopped suddenly. "Mom. It's the dog."

Jenna shined her light and saw a shaggy brown dog standing in the road up ahead.

"Oh..." Gracie's voice broke. "She's so skinny and muddy. We have to help her."

Jenna could see the dog's ribs through the fur plastered to her sides. She was a small dog, no more than fifteen pounds at most. Lost. Homeless. Jenna immediately went down on her knees in the mud. "Hey, baby. My name's Jenna."

Gracie knelt beside her. "I'm Gracie." Her voice was as soft as Jenna's, so sweet and kind that Jenna's heart turned over.

The dog stared at them, then turned and ran a few yards down the driveway.

"She's not coming," Gracie said.

"She will. Give me a sec." Jenna shrugged off her backpack and pulled out some of the deli turkey she'd been bringing to the house for a late-night dinner of sandwiches. She took out a couple pieces and tore them into little bits.

"She's coming closer," Gracie whispered.

Jenna smiled. "Of course she is." She loved dogs so much, but she hadn't had one since she was a kid. She'd known a scared puppy a long time ago, and she knew how to win them over.

She finished getting the turkey ready, then put the rest back in her pack.

Then she sat cross-legged in the mud, making a lap, and put a piece of turkey in her hand. "Hey, sweetie. Hungry?"

Gracie went still beside her as they watched the dog dance around, circling, getting closer and closer as fear warred with hunger. Finally, the little dog darted in, snatched the turkey, and darted away.

"We'll never catch her," Gracie sighed.

"We don't need to." Jenna put another piece of turkey in her palm and held it. "I can tell you're very brave," she whispered. "You know that we're here to help you. I know you do."

As she continued to talk, the dog moved closer and closer. This time, when she took the turkey, she didn't run away. She sat down in front of her and looked at her hopefully.

Jenna smiled as Gracie sucked in her breath. "I still have more," she said, holding out another piece.

The dog moved closer and took the snack.

"Yay! You're so brave." The dog suddenly crept forward onto her lap, put her paws on her shoulders, and started licking her face.

Jenna laughed, wrapping her arms around the dog. She was so skinny, shivering. Clearly homeless. "You're safe now," she whispered. "I promise you. It's going to be okay."

"Oh, Mom." Gracie leaned in, pressing a kiss to the trembling dog's head. "We've got you," she told the puppy. "My mom takes care of everyone. You're safe now."

Jenna smiled at her daughter's perception of who she was. She wished she had time to take care of everyone. But she could start with this dog, at least for now. "Shall we take her with us?"

Gracie's face lit up. "Of course, yes! We can't leave her out here!"

"I agree." Jenna gazed down into the dog's dark brown gaze, and her heart completely melted. She wanted to hug the dog to her and bury her face in the fur forever, but she knew that there was someone else in her life who might need to do that even more. She looked at Gracie. "Do you want to carry her?"

"Oh, *yes*!" Gracie held out her arms. "Come on, baby. I've got you."

As Jenna put the little shivering dog into her daughter's arms, she felt her whole body settle. The dog felt right. They needed this little girl in their lives tonight. And clearly, the dog needed them. A serendipitous finding.

Gracie hugged the puppy. "I think we should call her Simba. She needs a big, powerful name to remind her that she's strong."

Jenna smiled. "It's perfect. I love it." She pressed a kiss to Simba's nose. "Let's go get you warm, little one."

Ten minutes later, they were hiking again.

But this time, they were both smiling, and there was a lightness in both their hearts.

Because Jenna was wearing both backpacks, Gracie had zipped Simba up in her jacket and was cradling the dog in her arms, and the mud and the rain didn't matter anymore.

CHAPTER THREE

By the time the trio rounded the last bend of the driveway and the cabin came into sight, Jenna was pretty sure that crashing the truck had been one of her best moves ever.

Hiking in the rainy, muddy darkness had been exhilarating with Gracie and Simba. There had always been something about the outdoors that had made Jenna happy, but she hadn't done it in a long time. And Simba...it had been a long time since she'd received doggy kisses.

She'd forgotten how much she missed having a dog.

Gracie was also happier than Jenna had seen her in a long time. Laughing about the mud. Snuggling her face into Simba's wet fur. It was as if all the dark times had never happened.

They were laughing about a Gram escapade, when Gracie pointed to the cabin. "Lights are on!"

Jenna frowned as she looked at the cabin. "Gram must have sent someone ahead to start up the generator." But she hadn't said anything to Jenna about it. A surprise, maybe?

"That's so awesome. I'm first in the shower!" Still hugging Simba, Gracie hurried ahead, and Jenna broke into a run.

"Gracie! Wait!" She caught up to her daughter before she reached the steps.

"What?"

Jenna drew her back. "Gram hasn't been here in five years," she said, keeping her voice low. "Someone may be squatting here."

Gracie's eyes widened, and her lips formed a surprised "O." "You mean, like a murderer?" she whispered.

"Hopefully not." She drew Gracie back into the woods. "But I want to check it out before you go charging in there. Wait here."

"You want me to stay in the dark woods alone while you go into the house?" Gracie shook her head. "No way. I'm coming with you."

"But if there's a squatter—"

"What if there *is* a squatter and he was out hunting, and then he finds me waiting in the darkness, and he drags me away and chops me up into little pieces while you're in the house? What then? You'll feel so guilty and tormented for the rest of your life, knowing that you made the wrong choice."

Jenna stared at her daughter. "Really?"

Gracie grinned. "Yeah. That was good, right? You can't leave me now, can you?"

"No." Jenna sighed. "Okay, stay behind me, in case someone tries to shoot when I open the door."

"You'd take a bullet for me?" Gracie asked as she followed Jenna up the path toward the house.

"Of course I would, but let's hope I never have to prove it, okay? Now be quiet, so we can sneak up."

Gracie wrinkled her nose. "You're so dramatic."

"Me? You're the one who just made up the story about being chopped up."

"Because you started the whole murderer thing. So, it's on you, mummy dearest."

"We're not British. And be quiet." Despite her efforts, the front porch creaked under their feet, but overall, they were decently stealthy. Jenna smiled when she felt Gracie's hand on her lower back. If this was what it took to bring them together, then she'd welcome the murder drama any time.

She grinned to herself as she reached the front door and tested it. "Locked," she whispered. That was a good sign. If someone had broken in, the lock would probably be busted. But it was fun to pretend it was an adventure. "I'll unlock it, but stand to the side in case shots are fired."

Gracie rolled her eyes, but stepped back as Jenna slid her key in the lock. She winked at her daughter as she turned the lock, then pushed the door open. She stayed back, but no shots came flying out the open door. "Safe so far," she whispered.

"Seriously, Mom. This is ridiculous." Gracie pushed past her and ran into the house, then stopped so fast that Jenna plowed right into her back. "Mom," she whispered. "There's a man."

Fear shot through Jenna, and she grabbed her daughter and yanked her back behind her. "Run."

"What? No. He's asleep. He's hot. I want to see him again—"

"Gracie!" Dear God. Really? Jenna shoved Gracie out the door, but when no one flew at her with a butcher knife, she paused to inspect the cabin.

She found him on her first pass.

Asleep on the couch, with a baby sprawled across his chest. A little blue blanket was tucked around the baby, but the man wasn't using a blanket for himself. He had one hand palmed on the baby's back, and the other was by his side, a bottle of formula in his fingers, tipped over and dripping on the couch.

It was as if the two of them had passed out right in the middle of a feeding.

Jenna smiled, her heart turning over at the intimate moment. He was clearly very fit, with corded muscles even when he was relaxed in sleep. His arm was bandaged where he had it wrapped protectively around the baby, and he had stitches on his temple. He was wearing jeans, and his boots were still on. He was shirtless, and she could see another bandage on his side. That one had bloodstains seeping through it. What had happened to him?

Concern flickered through her as her gaze went back to the baby again. Were they in trouble?

"Mom," Gracie whispered, over her shoulder. "Isn't he hot?"

"Shh." The answer was obviously yes. He was a veritable specimen of manliness and tenderness. But this was literally not the time to notice that. So, instead of joining her daughter in a drool-fest, Jenna quickly inspected the cabin.

He'd turned the coffee table into a changing station. There were boxes of diapers and formula, bottles of water, and assorted grocery bags of food that weren't even unpacked yet. A pair of muddy jeans were tossed over a chair, still dripping on the floor.

She frowned as she looked around again, then froze when she saw a gun sitting on the mantle.

Gracie sucked in her breath. "Mom. He likes guns, just like you. I think you should marry him and get me a hot dad and a cute little brother."

"Oh, for heaven's sake." She bit her lip to keep from laughing at her daughter's drama, trying to stay focused. "Be quiet so we don't wake him up before I figure out what I'm going to do."

"Besides marry him?"

"Yes, besides that." Truthfully, the gun didn't really rattle either of them. Danny had been a private detective, and he'd carried a gun, so she knew that good people carried guns. Heck, she carried a gun most days as well. But it was still startling to see it. A man with a gun usually meant the stakes were high. An injured man with a baby meant that they needed help.

"That's so hot he has a gun."

"Gracie! Seriously, a gun isn't hot." Her daughter's obsession with the shirtless slumberer forced Jenna to make the decision to leave. "You know what? We're going to quietly slip out of here and go to a hotel."

"How are we going to do that? Hike back to the car and do what? Sit in it? Beg it to airlift us out of there? We don't have anywhere to go—"

At that moment, the man shot upright on the couch.

Jenna froze. He stared at them, confusion etched on his chiseled features.

Her fear fled the moment she saw his face. There was kindness in his vibrant blue eyes. Exhaustion. Confusion. And fear. He was definitely in trouble.

Then he suddenly leapt to his feet and lunged for the mantle, where the gun was.

"Mom! He's going for the gun!"

He moved so fast they didn't have time to run. All Jenna could do was shove Gracie behind her, fear clamped in her throat—

And then he stumbled and lost his balance. Both of his arms locked around the baby, and he twisted to take the hit with his shoulder, cradling the baby safely against his chest as he fell. He landed hard, and then tried to get to his knees, but he was swaying, unable to keep his balance.

Something was really, really wrong with him.

"Mom, is he sick? Hurt? A crazed murderer?"

"I don't know." Instinct took over, and Jenna rushed

across the room, kneeling in front of him as he fought to keep his balance. His muscles were visibly trembling, and his eyes were bloodshot. "Hey," she said gently. "My name's Jenna. Let me help you."

He stared at her, then shook his head. "No. Can't." His eyes were glazed, and there was sweat beading on his forehead. Was he sick?

"My name is Jenna," she said again. "You need help. I'm here to help you. And the baby."

He stared at her, then slowly sank to the floor. He rolled onto his back, holding the baby on his chest. The baby was watching Jenna with sleepy eyes, barely awake. "My name's Caleb," he said. "The baby is Zach."

Jenna smiled at the little boy. "Hi, Zach."

Zach stared at her.

The man touched her arm, drawing her attention to him. "People are after Zach," he said, his voice raw and rough, sending shivers of heat down her spine. "I need to stay hidden to keep him safe until I figure out what's going on."

Well, that woke up her mama bear protective instincts in a hurry. "The baby is in danger?"

He nodded. "I'm supposed to keep him safe. My job. My nephew." Sweat was beading on his lip, and she could feel the effort it was taking for him to speak and stay coherent.

"Holy crap, Mom," Gracie said from right behind her, startling her. "We need to call the cops."

"No cops. It's not safe." The man shook his head and tried to get up, but he almost fell again. "No cops. I'll leave."

Still hugging Simba, Gracie gave Jenna an impatient look as they watched Caleb stumble to his feet, staggering back to the changing station. Clutching the sleepy baby against his chest, he started packing things up, but he had to keep stopping to brace his free hand on the table.

Jenna was pretty sure he had only minutes left before he passed out.

"Mom," Jenna whispered urgently. "You're going to let them go out in this weather? It's a *baby*."

Jenna cocked an eyebrow at the dog in her daughter's arms. "Do you really need to ask me that?"

Gracie grinned. "No. It's like I told Simba. You take care of people."

"And dogs, apparently." Jenna stood up, walked over to the mantle, and picked up Caleb's gun. Danny had trained her how to use guns, and she often carried one when she was going on a run for the detective business that she'd inherited from him. "Caleb."

He looked over at her, then went still when he saw the gun in her hand.

"Do you have more weapons?" she asked.

He didn't answer.

"With two kids in this cabin, I need to know where all the weapons are." She indicated the gun in her hand. "And let's just move right past the worry that I'm going to use them all against you. If I wanted to shoot you, I already would have by now."

"Yeah, you totally underestimated my mom when you left the gun unattended," Gracie said. "Is it because she's a woman?"

"And a mom," Jenna said. "People definitely underestimate moms, which is silly, because we're about as fierce as they get."

Their witty mother-daughter banter seemed to break through Caleb's tension, and he finally relaxed slightly. "In the black duffel." He nodded at the corner. "On the bookshelf."

Jenna walked over to the bag that he'd set on the top shelf of the bookcase. She pulled it down, and the weight of it told her that he was serious about his hardware. She unzipped it, then let out her breath. He had three guns, several knives, zip ties, and plenty of ammunition.

She looked over at him. "Are we in danger here? Are the people hunting Zach going to find you here?"

He shook his head without hesitation. "I'm very good. There's no way they followed me. We're safe." He closed his eyes and braced his hand on the table, swearing under his breath.

This man wasn't a danger to her, at least not in the physical state he was in. "Did they do that to you? Injure you?"

Caleb didn't open his eyes for a long moment. "Yes," he said finally. "But I'm fine. I just need to regroup."

As he said it, Jenna saw his legs start to buckle. Gracie yelped at the same moment Jenna sprinted across the room. She snatched Zach out of his arms a split second before Caleb collapsed to the floor, unconscious.

Zach looked at her, then immediately started bawling.

"So, we're keeping them, huh?" Gracie looked delighted.

"For now." Jenna began bouncing Zach on her hip. Caleb was immobile on the floor, well and truly unconscious.

Gracie came over to stand beside her, staring down at Caleb. "You think he's dead?"

"God, I hope not." What would she do with Zach if he was? She couldn't just keep the baby...but put the baby in danger? No chance. "He better wake up, because I don't know what to do with Zach."

Gracie grinned. "You don't know how to take care of a baby?"

"You know that's not what I meant." Jenna said, her mind already making a plan. "You take Zach. Change his diaper, feed him. I'm going to hide the weapons and go through his belongings and see what I can find."

Gracie hugged Simba more tightly. "I have to take care of the dog."

"Simba can stand on her own. Put her down." Zach was crying now, clearly very annoyed at being deprived of Caleb.

Her daughter jutted out her chin. "I don't want to. I'm not a baby person. I don't even like to babysit the neighbors."

"Gracie. Really?"

"Fine." She wrinkled her nose and set Simba on the couch. "But I don't know how to change a diaper or feed a baby."

"Well, you're going to learn." Jenna put Zach in Gracie's arms, adjusting her daughter's arms so the baby was secure. Zach was no more delighted with Gracie than he had been with Jenna, and Jenna couldn't help but laugh at Gracie's disgruntled expression when Zach started screaming. She patted her daughter's shoulder. "You can handle him."

"I don't want to handle him."

"Tuck him against your chest and sing to him."

"Sing?" Gracie brightened. "Will that work?"

"With your voice? Absolutely."

Gracie tucked the screaming baby against her chest. "Are you going to report him to the cops?" She sang the question, which made Jenna smile, especially when Zach paused in his screeches to listen.

Gracie and her music were a special combo.

"That's what I need to find out." If Gracie weren't with her, Jenna would have more flexibility, but there was no way she was going to endanger her daughter.

She needed to get all the right answers, or Caleb was going to wake up with the zip ties around his wrists and the police on the way.

CHAPTER FOUR

By four in the morning, Jenna was the only one in the cabin who was awake.

Gracie was asleep in the bedroom with Simba, both of them well-fed, bathed, and dry.

Zach was cuddled up next to Caleb.

And the man in question was sleeping. Restless. Injured, but alive. Battered, but recovering.

His sleep almost reminded her of a vampire's: deep, healing, and restorative.

Periodically, he would wake up and take a rapid inventory of his surroundings. Each time, he'd finish with her, his blue eyes studying hers with a thousand questions.

But he wouldn't ask them.

He'd simply nod and go back to sleep.

Each time he woke up, she could tell he was more alert, more recovered, and more curious about her.

But each time, just when she thought he was going to launch into his questions, he'd close his eyes again.

She had a feeling he was taking advantage of the fact that she was sitting there, wide awake, with a gun. She was actually watching him, but he was clearly using her vigilance as a first line of defense if someone arrived to cause harm to him or Zach.

She kind of liked that he was relying on her to keep him and Zach safe. It made her feel a little badass. It made her feel like she was doing something that mattered, which wasn't something that her job gave her much of.

Despite her threat that she'd whispered to Gracie, she hadn't zip-tied his wrists or ankles. She had, however, hidden all his weapons, except the one she had decided to keep for herself.

She'd left him on the couch, and she was sitting in one of the armchairs, her knees pulled to her chest. She had changed into dry clothes, but she was still fully dressed and wearing her boots, with her new gun dangling loosely from her fingers...just in case.

Just in case, *what*, she wasn't sure. If she really thought he was dangerous, he would be tied up. But with her baby girl in the building, Jenna wasn't comfortable enough to sleep.

Sleep came rarely these days, so it wasn't much of a hardship to stay awake. At least she had eye candy this time, right?

Resting her chin on her knees, she watched Caleb's chest rise and fall.

She'd found so little and so much in his gear. Plenty of supplies. A medical kit that included several rounds of antibiotics that didn't have a patient's name on them, suturing supplies, an EpiPen, and other assorted medical gear that required a doctor's approval, but also didn't have any names on them. Medical supplies for any event that might happen to a man who couldn't risk going to a hospital.

Black market medicines?

He had a lot of cash, but no credit cards. No ID. No phone. His watch was electronic, but it was cracked and wasn't working. Nothing. Literally nothing. He was like a ghost.

She'd changed his bandages once, but the injuries looked all right. The wound on his side was the worst. It looked like a stab wound, but he'd already started the packet of antibiotics, so she figured the odds of him dying from an infection were low.

Which meant she was going to have to decide what to do with him when he was no longer conveniently asleep.

What do I do? Her husband had been a rescuer of people. That was why he'd opened his own private investigation business. He'd specialized in missing persons, and she'd taken over after he'd died. Not because she loved it, but because she had a baby girl to support and bills to pay.

Did this guy need rescuing? Or was he dangerous? Clearly, he was someone to be taken seriously.

Danny would know. He'd always had a good sense about people. Who to trust. Who to help. Who to walk away from. Who to have an affair with that his beloved wife wouldn't suspect...

Oops. Her brain didn't have permission to go there.

Danny's work had been gritty, but he'd always had the most glorious sparkle in his eye, ready to laugh, always keeping the moment light for everyone around him.

He would be having fun right now. Somehow, someway, he'd find the lightness in this insane experience they were having. The crazy things he'd involved her with over the years, and yet somehow, it had always been fun.

Until everything had fallen apart, but she'd decided two years ago to focus on the good memories, not the bad ones.

But as she recalled the fun times, she became aware that Gracie was right. Things hadn't been fun in a long time, until she and Gracie had had fun hiking up to the cabin with a stray dog and two backpacks of their belongings and food.

Danny might not be with them anymore, but there was no reason she needed to lose the fun that he'd brought into their lives. Even when things had gone south between her and Danny, his joy for life had still lit up Gracie. He was that kind of guy. Fun. Charming. Compelling. Even if what was underneath wasn't always a woman's dream.

Jenna sighed and let her gaze travel over Caleb's face. His cheekbones were chiseled. Whiskers thick on his jaw. Not a beard, but the effect of days without shaving. Like a man on the run.

He was handsome, the kind of striking man that would make a woman's belly get all quivery. Raw, untamed testosterone that should put her on alert...

Except for that baby, who changed everything.

The only time Zach had stopped crying was when he was snuggled up with Caleb. The baby trusted Caleb, which made her tempted to trust Caleb as well. Babies were like dogs. If someone was a bad person, they knew. The fact that Caleb had such a relationship with that baby meant something.

Simba had sniffed Caleb while he was sleeping, wagged her tail, and then licked Caleb's hand. Again, telling Jenna to trust him.

She listened to the rain hammering on the roof. Day one of their vacation wasn't turning out like she'd expected.

Her gaze went to Caleb's chiseled jaw. Not at all—

His eyes opened suddenly, and she realized instantly that they were clear, focused, and alert.

He was ready to come back to life.

She tightened her fingers around the gun, but smiled. "Good morning, Caleb. I'm Jenna."

Her voice was what Caleb had been dreaming of, but it was even more soothing and kind than what had been floating around in his mind.

Caleb became instantly aware of Zach asleep on his chest, so he didn't move. But he quickly, instinctively took in every detail about the cabin and Jenna. His mind was clear for the first time, crystal clear, and he greedily took advantage of it as he scanned the cabin again, this time able to really process what he was seeing.

Jenna had been through his gear. All of it had been touched. His weapons bag was missing. And she was holding his gun as if it were an extension of her own hand.

His gaze settled on her face, searching for truths. Could he trust her? She was familiar and comfortable around weapons, but he didn't feel any threat from her. "Do you mean us harm?"

If she did, he doubted she would tell him, but somehow, he was certain that he would be able to tell if she was lying to him.

And when her eyes widened, he knew he and Zach were safe. "Only if you decide to hurt me or my daughter," she said. "Other than that, I'll refrain from shooting you."

He smiled, relaxing into the cushions. He liked the sound of her voice. It was light and warm. Easy. Real. She wasn't trying to hide anything from him, and that felt peaceful. "Then I'm good, because I'd protect you before I'd hurt you."

When he'd collapsed, she could have done anything, including killing him and taking Zach. She hadn't. Instead, she'd gotten him to the couch, and apparently taken care of Zach's needs as well.

He'd felt her warmth even through his exhaustion. Her vigil had enabled him to succumb to his exhaustion and fatigue, to crash and sleep deeply until he had refilled his well sufficiently.

For that, he was deeply grateful to her.

Jenna smiled, a smile that seemed to light him up from the inside out. He swore under his breath, surprised by his reaction to her. She was like a spark of life. "Well, great," she said. "I believe you."

He smiled. "I believe you, too."

"Well, aren't we a trusting little couple then. Each of us with kids to protect, guns galore, and yet we're sitting here, ready to be besties." She sounded amused by it, and also not quite ready to believe it.

He shifted, and then grimaced when pain shot through his side.

"Yeah, you're pretty banged up. It looks like a knife wound on your side," she said. "An unusual injury for a man with a baby."

He adjusted Zach so the baby wasn't pressed into his injured side. "It happened before Zach."

"Did it?" Her hand was loose around the gun, relaxed, but he suspected she could raise that gun into a shooting position in a heartbeat. "I'd like to put this gun away for good, but I have a few questions first."

In the dim light of morning, her face looked almost surreal, like an angel with the faint gold streaks of dawn settling across her gorgeous brown skin. Her hair was in tight braids that were pure artistry, tied at the nape of her neck with a brightly colored scarf. Her eyes were dark, full of emotion, but also deeply shielded.

She had secrets. Like him. Or maybe not quite like him. Who knew what his secrets were?

"I'd prefer no gun, so ask away," he said, rubbing his hand over Zach's head.

"Who are you? Why don't you have identification? Or a phone? Or anything?" She grinned. "We'll start with that one."

Caleb let out his breath. He could lie to her, but what was the point? She was clearly competent and unflappable, so maybe she'd hear something in his story that he hadn't seen, a clue that would help him.

She raised her brows at his hesitation. "That bad, huh?"

"I woke up twenty hours ago in the middle of a house that appeared to have been blown up." He could still smell the acrid scent of incineration. He could feel the heat all around him again. "I'm assuming that I was inside the building at the time, but I don't remember what happened."

Her eyes widened. "Really?"

"Yeah." He paused to rub Zach's back. "When I woke up, Zach's dad was leaning over me. He called me Caleb, told me I had to protect Zach and raise him as my son if he didn't come back, and then said he had to go get Zach's mom, because they'd taken her." He filled Jenna in on the rest of the conversation, hoping that retelling it would spark his attention to a detail he'd missed or a memory he couldn't call up... but there was nothing.

When he finished, she was staring at him with an open mouth. "He *called* you Caleb?" she asked. "You mean, that's not your name?"

Caleb smiled at her question. Already, he knew enough about Jenna that it didn't surprise him that she'd picked up on the way he'd phrased it, and that she'd realized that something was off about it. "I don't know what my name is. I don't remember anything before I woke up after the explosion. I don't even know if it was an explosion. It just looked like it."

She held up her hand. "Wait a sec. You have no idea who you are?"

"That's correct." He gestured to Zach. "I don't remember him, but clearly, he knows me, and his dad trusted me with him, so I'm guessing I was close to them. But I have no idea about anything."

"Total amnesia?"

"I guess." As he said it, he felt a weird sense of loss. At best guess, he was around thirty years old, which meant he had three decades of people, experiences, and life that were simply gone to him.

She sat back. "Well, holy crap."

He laughed softly. "Right?"

"And this guy told you that someone was after Zach?"

"Yeah." He stroked the baby's head. "I appear to be very competent with weapons and babies, but I don't know more than that." He felt surprisingly peaceful right now. The couch was comfortable. Zach was sweet. And he liked Jenna's vibe. Maybe it was that she was a mom. Or a woman. Or the kindness in her eyes.

He didn't know exactly. But he liked it.

"And you're certain no one followed you here?"

He nodded. "Of that, I'm sure. I know what I'm doing." He met her gaze. "How I know, I have no idea. But I'm definitely good."

She smiled. "Typical male insecurity. The ego is so fragile," she teased.

He liked her smile. He liked the tone of her voice. He liked her gentle ribbing. "I can claim anything," he said. "There's no proof to say I'm wrong."

"Try singing," Gracie said from the doorway. "Maybe you're a singer."

Caleb looked over at Gracie with a grin. He'd heard her approach, and he'd known she was listening. He was surprised by the level of vigilance that seemed to consume his every moment. He was constantly assessing every sound, every shadow, every moment for threats.

What a fucking way to live. Maybe he was glad he didn't know who he was.

Gracie was standing in the doorway, their cute little dog by her left ankle.

"What song do you want me to sing?" he asked.

She studied him. "Sing country music. That's my favorite. A Garth Brooks song."

Music floated through Caleb's mind immediately, and he started to sing. The notes and lyrics came out easily, coming from somewhere deep inside him that remembered music. His voice was deep, and he immediately felt aligned with the song. Music mattered to him. He could feel it wrapping around his soul. As he sang, Gracie joined in with him, her voice beautiful and bright as she sang with him.

They finished the song together, and they grinned at each other, sharing a moment, while Jenna clapped her hands. "That was incredible."

"You're a fantastic singer, Gracie," he said, meaning it.

She beamed at him. "Thank you. You're pretty good, too. My dream is to become a country music star. I write songs too. Want to hear them?"

"Sure." As he spoke, he felt Zach stir beside him. He looked down at the baby, who was staring up at him with big brown eyes. Something inside his heart turned over for the little fella, and then Zach's face wrinkled up and he started to bawl.

Caleb laughed. "I think he needs to be changed." He started to sit up, then grimaced as pain shot through him. He froze, trying to catch his breath, stunned by the level of pain assaulting him. Not just his side, but his leg as well.

Jenna caught his gaze, and she frowned at him as she stood up. "I'll take him." She walked over to a built-in bookshelf by the fireplace, and set the gun on the top shelf, shoving it behind the books, so that any of them would need to climb on a chair to retrieve it.

That move sent an enormous message into the cabin. She

was declaring that she trusted him with her, with Gracie, with their little family.

Resolution flooded Caleb. With that move, their place in his circle of protection was secured forever.

Now he had three to protect.

And it felt good.

CHAPTER FIVE

"Come on, Zach." As Jenna's fingers brushed Caleb's when she took the baby, something shot through him. Something electric. Something intense. Something he wanted more of. They met gazes, and he saw Jenna's cheeks flush before she picked up Zach and turned away.

Caleb swore as he leaned back against the couch and closed his eyes, trying to release the pain. There was something there with Jenna. He didn't know what it was, but he knew that he wanted to pursue it.

But how could he? He didn't know what baggage he brought with him. For all he knew, he could be married—

The thought exploded through his mind like the knife that had sliced open his side. He immediately raised his left hand to look at it.

No ring.

No indent from a ring.

No tan line from a ring.

His finger had definitely never worn a ring.

He saw Jenna looking at him. "Are you married?" she asked, her voice edged with shock she couldn't quite hide.

He held up his hand. "I may not remember who I am, but I know I'd never be the type not to wear a ring if I were married." He had absolutely no doubt about that whatsoever.

Loyalty. Honor. Integrity. They were the cornerstone of his being.

Gracie grinned. "My mom's not married either. She hasn't even been on a date in years. She probably doesn't even remember how to kiss anymore."

Horror flashed across Jenna's face, and Caleb burst out laughing. "Thanks for the intel, Gracie. But I doubt she forgot how to kiss. It's not one of those things that you forget how to do."

Jenna's eyes met his, and he could see the mirth bubbling up in them. "I practice on my pillow every night," she said. "Just in case I decide to sweep some lucky guy off his feet."

He loved her sass. "Haven't found a worthy one yet?"

"Nope. I have high standards."

"As every woman should have," he agreed. "Remember that, Gracie. Don't settle for shit—" He paused. "Jerks."

"You can swear around me," Gracie said. "My dad used to say swearing was a sign of genius. You were going to say shitheads?"

Caleb shot a glance at Jenna. She was bent over the changing table with baby powder in her hand, but her lips were pressed together as she tried to hold in laughter.

He relaxed, curious now about Gracie's dad, her use of the past tense, and the fact that his affinity for swearing apparently didn't bother either Gracie or Jenna. Caleb assumed that the dad had passed away, leaving the two of them behind.

"I was going to say something of that sort," he acknowledged, trying to keep his voice light, even while his heart was going out to what the two of them must have gone through. "Pick nice guys with high integrity," he said. "Hold out if you have to."

Gracie rolled her eyes. "I'm not an idiot. I'd never date a stupid jerk."

Jenna's smile widened. "No dating for at least ten years anyway."

"Mom! I'll be twenty-three!"

"I can do the math."

Gracie rolled her eyes. "You're so annoying."

"I'm hilarious. Don't forget that. You love that about me," Jenna said.

Caleb smiled at Gracie as she wrinkled her nose. He could feel the affection between the mother and daughter, and he loved it. It felt like the energy he liked being around. He nodded at the dog. "Who do you have there?"

Gracie's face brightened. "Her name is Simba. We found her last night."

He liked dogs. He was sure of it. "Can I say hi?"

"Of course."

Caleb held out his hand. "Hey, Simba."

The dog immediately left Gracie's side, ran across the floor, and leapt up onto his chest. Caleb grunted with pain, gently catching the dog as her toenails hit his injury. As he did, he felt her ribs beneath her fur. He knew immediately all he needed to know about Jenna and Gracie: they'd found a dog in need and saved her.

Good people. Good hearts.

Simba sat down on his chest and gazed at him, her big brown eyes wide with trust. He smiled and scratched her chest. "I think we're both lucky Jenna and Gracie found us. Don't you think?"

Simba's tail thumped, and he smiled over at Gracie. "She agrees. We both owe you."

"Of course you do." Gracie curled up in the nearest armchair, her eyes wide as she pulled her pajama-clad knees to her chest, mimicking the position that her mom had been in earlier.

They were so much alike.

The teenager patted the chair for Simba. "Come here, Simba." As the little dog bounded off Caleb and onto Gracie's lap, Gracie studied Caleb. "Who do you think you might be?"

He shifted, trying to find a comfortable position. He'd seen painkillers in the medical kit that Zach's dad had given him, but he had no interest in taking them. He'd rather be in grueling pain than have his mind fogged by drugs. Plus, the pain wasn't that bad. He didn't have any desire to focus on it, so he didn't. "I don't know," he said. "I'm good with a gun. I know how to disappear."

"So, trained in the military most likely," Gracie said with surprising astuteness. "Do you have any tattoos?"

He grinned, amused by her question. "Listen, Gracie, I really appreciate your help, but it looks like I'm involved in something dangerous. The less you know, the better." He glanced at Jenna. "You, too."

She snorted as she fastened the diaper around Zach. "My husband was a private detective who collected people who needed help. He trained me, and I took over the business. Gracie learned how to flip a one-hundred-and-fifty-pound guy when she was eight, and took a gun safety class when she was nine. We're competent, skilled, and more interested in knowing what we're dealing with than being surprised by it."

Gracie grinned, her eyes radiant as she looked at her mom with almost hero worship.

Caleb raised his brows. "Damn."

"That's right," Gracie said. "So tell us." Her eyes lit up. "No! Hire my mom! We saw your cash. Hire her, and then she can stop taking the jobs that make her travel, and she can be around again."

Jenna's jaw tightened. "Baby, I'm sorry about the travel. I didn't know it upset you so much—"

"I told you a million times, you just didn't listen."

Caleb saw the way Jenna's shoulders slumped, and he knew that everything wasn't as easy as it had looked between the two of them. "Family can be tricky," he said. "But when it's all based in love, it's always a blessing."

They both looked at him. "Do you have a family?" Gracie asked.

Caleb paused, waiting for an answer that didn't come. "I don't know."

"That must be so frustrating," Gracie said. "I can't imagine if I lost my memory." Horror flashed across her face. "Then I'd never know Dad! I wouldn't remember him at all!" Sudden tears filled her eyes, and Simba climbed onto her lap and licked her cheek.

Caleb swore under his breath, immediately realizing that he'd been correct in his assessment that Gracie's dad had passed away. "I'm so sorry, Gracie. I didn't mean to upset you."

"Hey, baby, it's okay." Jenna quickly scooped up the freshly changed Zach, and handed the baby and a bottle of formula to Caleb before sitting down next to her daughter and putting her arm around Gracie and Simba. "You do remember him. You'll always remember him."

"Will I?" The teenager stared at Jenna, her eyes stricken with absolute anguish. "Caleb doesn't remember his family, if he has one. What if something happened to me, and I lost my memory, too? Dad would be gone forever."

"He wouldn't be gone." Jenna pulled out her phone, scrolled through it, and then held out a video. "Dad's always with us."

Gracie grabbed the phone, stood up, and hurried back to the bedroom, leaving Simba with Jenna. As she left, Caleb could hear a man's voice saying, "Hey, Gracie. It's Saturday morning, and you're probably still in bed, but I wanted to say hi from the Grand Canyon..." And then the door shut behind her.

Jenna paused for a moment to hug Simba to her chest, burying her face in the dog's fur as she struggled to regroup.

Caleb had an urge to comfort her, to offer her the support that she was trying to get from the dog. "Jenna—"

"I'm fine." She lifted her head with stubborn swiftness. "I need to go to her." Jenna cradled the dog against her chest and stood up. "Sorry about that. It's been two years since he died, but it's been a hard time."

"No apologies needed." He could see the weary lines around Jenna's eyes and mouth now, and he understood more. As hard as it had been on Gracie to lose her dad, he knew that it couldn't have been easy for Jenna either.

He had no idea if he had family, but he was sitting in the middle of one right now, one that was still struggling to get out of the darkness that had taken over their lives. "Take the bag of money. I don't need it."

Jenna shook her head as she headed toward the bedroom. "It's your money. You have no idea if you'll need it or not. You need to keep that baby safe. We're fine."

Caleb frowned. He could tell he had no chance of handing any money to them. There was almost two hundred grand in the bag. More than enough for anything he'd need. Zach's dad had given him enough to disappear with the baby for a very long time. "I heard Gracie's suggestion."

Jenna paused with her hand on the knob. "What suggestion?" she asked wearily.

"That I hire you to figure out who I am. Could you do that?"

She nodded slowly. "Danny found missing persons, and

that's what he taught me. You're kind of a missing person, so yes, I could do that."

He wasn't sure he wanted to get her involved, but there was no doubt that she could go places and investigate things that he couldn't do, because he had to stay hidden. Plus, it was a way to give them money that might set them free.

But he had to be honest. "I don't want to endanger you. I don't know what you'd turn up."

She dropped her hand from the doorknob, chewing her lower lip. "I don't take jobs that might get me shot at," she said. "I made that promise to myself after Danny died. I'm all Gracie has...plus my Gram, but she's not me. It's not the same."

He nodded quickly. "I agree."

For a long moment, they studied each other.

"I don't know if I want to hire you," he said honestly. "I don't want to get you involved."

Amusement flickered in her eyes. "Because I'm a woman, so you need to protect me?"

Busted. "Yes," he said honestly. "I guess I'm old school."

She laughed softly. "Caleb, you won't last a minute around us if you treat us like lace doilies."

He chuckled, then sucked in his breath when pain shot through him.

Concern furrowed her brow. "Are you okay?"

He managed to grin. "Jenna, you won't last a minute around me if you treat me like a lace doily."

She laughed then, a beautiful, rich laugh that seemed to fill the room with glorious warmth. "Okay, then. Point taken. No lace doilies in this cabin. I'm going to go take care of my daughter, and when I come out, I want breakfast made, the baby fed, a list of everything you remember about who you are and every clue you have. Then we'll talk. Got it?"

He raised his brows. "You plan to be in there a while, then?"

"Until I smell the bacon cooking. I saw you had some, so don't deny it." She winked at him. "Just kidding. If you move that wrecked body off the couch, I'll shoot you, injuries and all."

Then, before he could protest, she opened the door and slipped inside.

Before the door closed, Caleb caught a glimpse of Gracie curled up on the bed, watching the phone, tears glistening on her cheeks. His heart turned over as the door shut.

He looked down at Zach, who was still chugging away at the bottle. If Zach's dad didn't return, Zach would forget his dad, exactly like Gracie was worried about.

Resolution flooded Caleb. He needed to find out who he was, so that he could go and help and make sure Zach's little family got back together.

The sound of female laughter drifted through the closed door, and Caleb smiled. He would also find a way to make sure Gracie and Jenna were taken care of as well. Before they'd arrived, he'd been at the end of what he could do. He'd been running on sheer willpower, but as they all saw, that had finally run out as well.

He'd felt absolutely alone, gruelingly alone.

Until they'd showed up, injected some laughter, warmth, and help into his life.

He looked down at Zach. "We're not lace doilies, kid, but even absolute badasses need help sometimes."

But the instant he suspected that Jenna's help was putting her in danger, he was pulling the plug on it all, and he was going to disappear from their lives.

He just hoped it wasn't for a few days.

He wasn't ready to leave yet...for more than a few reasons.

CHAPTER SIX

"Mom?"

Jenna leaned her head against Gracie's, trying to breathe through the emotions clogging her chest. They were lying on the bed with Simba curled between them, and Gracie had been playing videos of Danny for almost a half hour.

Jenna knew her daughter needed to do it, but it was almost more than she could take. Since Danny had died, she'd been living life at top speed, cramming it full of work, mom stuff, and everything she could find.

Sitting here, reliving a life that was no longer hers was almost more than she could take. The longer Gracie had watched the videos, however, the happier she'd become, so Jenna was willing to suck it up for as long as Gracie wanted to. "Yes, babe?"

"Are you going to get married again?"

"No." Jenna didn't have to hesitate. She'd made that decision long ago.

Gracie put the phone face down on her chest, and rolled onto her side to look at Jenna. Her dark brown eyes were wide as she looked at her mom. "Why not?"

Um...how much did she tell a thirteen-year-old? "Because I want to focus on you."

"What if I want another dad?"

Jenna was too stunned to answer right away. Gracie had never, ever mentioned anything about her getting married again. She'd thought Gracie wanted to keep their tight little family and not change anything about it.

"I mean, if he was like Caleb, it would be cool." Gracie's face lit up. "He's a great singer. And he carries a gun, like Dad did."

Jenna let out her breath. "We don't know Caleb," she said gently.

"Dad always said that he could tell the important things about a person within the first five minutes." She shrugged. "He always said I had the same gift. And I think that Caleb's a good person. Don't you?"

Jenna pressed her lips together, but had to nod her agreement. "I do." Simba licked her face, as if knowing how hard it was for her to keep herself relaxed and focused. Jenna scratched Simba, her tension easing as she felt the soft fur under her fingers.

"So, maybe Caleb, then," Gracie said.

Ah...the black-and-white worldview of a thirteen-year-old. "He's in trouble, Gracie. Dangerous trouble."

"So?"

Oh, how she loved her daughter's fearlessness. "I don't want to endanger you."

Gracie rolled her eyes. "Dad never ran away from danger, especially not when someone else needed help. You're so uptight now. It's so annoying."

Jenna bit her lip. Danny's death had made her realize how fragile life was. On the day they buried him, she'd made a commitment that she would always be safe, so that Gracie would always have her. She'd earn money. She'd take the jobs that didn't pose a risk. She'd keep herself alive for her kid.

But the jobs that didn't have a risk didn't pay as much, which meant she was working long hours. Not seeing her precious baby.

"Never mind. Forget it." Gracie held the phone out. "Take it. I'm going back to bed. It's like six in the morning."

Jenna took the phone. "Gracie—"

"Take the job Caleb offered," Gracie said as she curled herself into a ball. "Help Caleb. I like him. He makes you smile. Dad would want you to help him." She closed her eyes. "Good night."

Jenna leaned over and kissed her daughter on the forehead. "Want me to wake you for breakfast?"

"No," Gracie mumbled. "I want to sleep."

"All right. We're going to take the ATV down to the truck to get our stuff in a little bit."

"Okay. 'Night."

"Good morning," Jenna teased as she slid off the bed. She smiled as Simba put her chin on Gracie's chest, her heart warming for the little dog who was giving them both the love and peace they needed. She patted Simba and was rewarded with a thump from her tail that made her smile. She trailed her fingers over Simba's neck. There was no indent from a collar, and the dog was so thin. Did she have someone looking for her?

She hoped not.

She felt like Simba was sent to heal the pain in both their hearts, just like another dog so long ago.

"See you guys when you wake up." She brushed her fingers over her daughter's cheek, put her phone in her pocket, and then headed for the door, where Caleb and Zach awaited.

She paused at the door and looked back at her sleeping daughter.

All she wanted was to help her daughter. Gracie had been so close with Danny, and a light had gone out of her daughter's eyes the day Danny had died, a light that had remained out ever since.

Until they'd walked into the cabin last night and met Caleb.

He had lit that spark in Gracie's eyes again. Fragile. Delicate. Precious.

Jenna sighed. She would do anything for her daughter.

Including agree to help a stranger find out who was trying to kill him?

That didn't feel like a good plan.

But neither did walking away from a man who was rebuilding a part of her daughter's spirit...a man trying to protect a baby.

She opened the door and saw Caleb on the couch, talking to Zach. Her heart turned over when he looked over at her and smiled, a warm, dimpled smile.

Who was she kidding? Caleb also lit a spark inside her that had been dead for a very long time.

Did she want that spark burning again? She wasn't sure she did. But she also wasn't sure she didn't.

~

CALEB FELT the weight in Jenna's spirit the moment she walked out of the bedroom.

She didn't make eye contact with him. Instead, she glanced vaguely in his direction. "My groceries are still in the truck, but I can whip up a quick breakfast with your stuff before I take the ATV down to get them." She opened the cabinet and began pulling out plates, moving with stiff, practiced efficiency.

He could feel how tightly she was strung, how much she was holding back.

Zach was sleeping again, so he edged the baby off his chest and stood up, grimacing at the stiffness of his body. He was much more badly hurt than he'd realized immediately after the explosion, when adrenaline had been coursing through him. But at the same time, he could feel that he was healing already from his near-comatose state of yesterday. His side wasn't quite as painful. He limped over to her. "Jenna."

She didn't look at him. "Scrambled eggs okay?" She pulled the eggs out of the fridge. "I can see you got the generator going, which is great. I wasn't sure if it would still be working."

"Jenna." He put his hand on her wrist. "Stop."

She went still, staring down at his hand. "I can't believe how good that feels," she whispered.

"How good what feels?"

"Your hand on my arm." She took a breath and closed her eyes. "I didn't realize how long it had been since I've been touched by a man. I didn't realize that I missed it, until right now."

Caleb lightly squeezed her wrist. "I'm sorry for what you and Gracie have been through. I truly am."

"Thank you." She took a deep breath and looked up at him. She hadn't pulled away from his touch, and he didn't remove his hand, leaving the physical connection between them intact. "Gracie lights up for you."

He was surprised at how good that felt. "She's a good kid."

"I know." Jenna turned toward him, sliding her arm away from his touch. "Can I—" She paused and held up her hand over his chest, sort of waving it.

He wasn't sure what she was asking, but he nodded. "Of course."

"Okay." She set her hand on his chest, right over his heart. Her touch was so gentle, so kind, so *something*, that it sent waves of emotion rushing through him.

He wondered how long it had been since he'd been touched like that, because he felt like he was freefalling into a crevasse of wildflowers just from her touch.

Silently, he put his hand over hers, holding her hand to his chest.

They met gazes, and sudden desire rushed through him. "I want to kiss you," he said.

The corner of her mouth curved up. "It's absolutely terrifying how much I would like you to do that," she admitted. "I haven't had even the slightest interest in anything romantic since Danny died. Not even a faint, distant longing. But right now..." She let out her breath with a puff of her cheeks. "It's pretty intense, and I don't even know you."

"I don't even know me, so no surprise there." He slid his gaze toward the bedroom door, but there was no sound from there. He was pretty sure Gracie was asleep. "I'm guessing I'm a good guy, though. I feel like I am."

She smiled then. "A good guy, yes, with a dark and checkered past littered with violent bad guys."

He blinked at her words, then dropped his hand from hers. "You're right." *Shit.* Who the hell was he? He clearly wasn't just a guy who knew how to change diapers and enjoyed hanging out with a single mom and her teenager.

What was he doing, thinking about kissing Jenna? Inserting what was clearly a whole lot of shit into their lives? He turned away, then stopped when she grabbed his wrist.

"Caleb."

He looked over his shoulder at her, and his breath caught when he saw the look of longing on her face. "I'm a liability, Jenna. We both know it. I don't know what I've spent my life doing, but it's not good." Well, maybe it was good. He'd like to think it was. "Definitely not safe." That was certain.

"But the man you are right now is safe. Good. Kind." She tugged his wrist. "It's been a very long time for me, Caleb. I need to know."

He closed his eyes against the urge to sweep her up in his arms. "Need to know what?"

"Whether it's real. Whether that part of me is really still alive. And whether I want it to be. It's only been you, Caleb. For whatever reason, it's just you."

He opened his eyes and looked at her.

"One kiss," she whispered.

He wanted that kiss as much as she did. Was he a jerk to want it? To want to lose himself in this oasis that he'd stumbled into? Maybe.

Hurt flickered in Jenna's eyes. "Never mind. Forget it. I was stupid to try to force you to kiss me—" She let go of his wrist.

"No." He caught her hand as she started to pull away, and gently tugged her toward him.

She came willingly, nervousness etched on her face.

He smiled as he slid his hands along her jaw, cradling her face. "I'm as nervous as you are," he whispered. "I have no idea if I know how to kiss."

The corners of her mouth quirked. "I'm pretty sure you know how to kiss."

"Well, let's see." He leaned in and brushed his lips lightly over hers. Electricity shot through him, stunning him. "How was that?"

She laughed then. "Not much of a kiss," she teased.

"Hmm... Let me see if I can do better." He angled his head, leaned in, and took her mouth with his. Her lips were soft and warm, responding to his kiss instantly. Heat rushed through him, intense, unexpected, and amazing.

He'd planned for only a quick kiss, but there was no chance of that when her arms went around his neck and she leaned into him.

Pain shot through his side when he locked one arm around her waist and pulled her against his body, but he didn't care. The sensations rushing though him from the kiss were so intense, so glorious, so addicting that he'd suffer through pain ten times worse for the chance to kiss Jenna longer.

She was trembling against him, but her hands were tight around him, holding him as if she were afraid he'd disappear on her. She tasted amazing, like sunshine and wildflowers—

He stopped suddenly and pulled back.

She blinked. "What?"

"I just thought that you tasted amazing, like sunshine and wildflowers. It's the second time I've compared you to wildflowers in the last couple minutes."

A slow smile spread over her face. "That's incredibly sweet."

"It's the truth." He loved that look on her face, pure awe that he could think something that nice about her. He made a mental note to say more of that. "Wildflowers," he said again. "Why would I think of wildflowers to describe a moment so exquisite? It's pretty specific."

Understanding dawned on her face. "You have a past with wildflowers. A positive association."

He nodded, excitement coursing through him. "We can do it, Jenna. We can figure out who I am. Even if I can't remember, we can put the pieces together."

She took a breath. "We probably can."

He felt her hesitation, and he took her hands, clasping them in his. "I'll make a promise to you."

She chewed her lower lip, not trying to hide her reluctance. "What promise?"

"I'll hire you to help me find out who I am. But I'm on my

own for this mess that I'm in the middle of. And the number one priority is keeping you safe and off the radar of whoever is after me. You help only as long as it is zero risk. *Zero risk.* I promise."

Jenna met his gaze. "I can't imagine what it's like to lose who you are."

He nodded. "It's like living with a black hole all around me."

She looked down at their joined hands, then looked back up at him. "What if...what if you don't like what you find?"

He frowned. "I've thought of that."

"I mean, you're so kind and nice and gentle..." She shrugged. "Knife wounds? Explosions? A baby whose mom was kidnapped? You don't seem to fit that."

He sighed. "I know." He glanced back at the sleeping baby. "Honestly," he said quietly, "if it weren't for Zach, I might just want to let it go. Start over." He raised their joined hands. "With this."

"Caleb—"

He didn't let her finish her protest. "But Zach has parents out there, and I owe it to him to reunite him with them if I can. And to keep him safe if I can't. And to keep him safe, I need to know who is coming for him and why."

Jenna followed his gaze to the baby. "He seems like he's your son," she said. "You two are so close."

"I know." He already couldn't imagine being without Zach, but he'd do whatever he had to do. "I call myself Uncle Caleb with him. I figure I have to be that close to his family for him to be so bonded with me."

"He's lucky to have you."

Caleb heard the genuineness in Jenna's tone, and it made him smile. If Zach's dad trusted him with his son, then that was another statement that he was the decent guy he felt like he was, despite the evidence to the contrary. "What do you say, Jenna? Team up and see what magic we can accomplish, while staying safe?"

At that moment, the bedroom door creaked. They both looked over, and Caleb saw that the door was open a crack, and he saw a brown eye peeking out at them.

Jenna smiled and turned back to him. "Gracie wants me to help you."

He appreciated that, but it wasn't entirely up to Gracie. He needed Jenna to be in on it as well. "And what do you want?"

She met his gaze, and he felt like he could lose himself in the rich, darkness of her eyes. Her gaze went to his mouth, and then back to his eyes. "Are you officially offering to hire me?"

He grinned then. "Yeah."

She took a breath. "I need a five-thousand-dollar retainer, daily expenses, and five hundred dollars a day since I'll be doing this full time."

Relief rushed through him. "Done." He held out his hand.

"All right then." She shook his hand. "We'll start over breakfast, with wildflowers."

"Perfect."

"I'm actually hungry for breakfast," Gracie announced as she flung open the bedroom door, Simba in her arms. "I'll eat now. I did a unit on plants for science last month. I can help with the wildflowers."

She walked over to the kitchen table with a notebook and a pen. She sat down, put Simba on the chair beside hers, then patted another chair. "Sit here, Caleb. I have questions for you."

He grinned as he pulled out the seat next to her, easing down onto the hard wood. "You're helping me?"

"I used to assist my dad and mom, before my dad died

and my mom stopped letting me help. I know what I'm doing."

Caleb glanced at Jenna. She was leaning against the kitchen counter, her arms folded over her chest, while she studied her daughter.

"It's okay with you?" he asked Jenna.

For a moment, he thought she was going to refuse. Then her gaze went to Gracie, and she sighed. "Gracie, you can help on one condition."

Gracie's face lit up. "What condition?"

"If Caleb and I decide it's too dangerous, then you agree to drop everything instantly, and leave, if that's what we need to do."

Gracie's jaw jutted out. "I don't want to leave."

"We don't need to yet. I'm just saying, if it's dangerous."

Gracie looked like she was going to argue, so Caleb spoke up. "Explosions." He pointed to his side. "Stab wound. You want one of those?"

She giggled. "No."

"So?"

"All right." She was still grinning, clearly not overly concerned about the boogeyman coming to get her. "I agree." She opened her paper. "First question. What kind of wildflowers did my mom's kiss taste like?"

Oh, *hell*. He looked at Jenna, but there was laughter dancing in her eyes. "Yes," she said. "What kind?"

"Violet and pink," he said, as the images flashed in his mind. "Tall stalks, waving in the wind."

Gracie grinned. "Would you recognize them?"

He could see flowers clearly in his mind. "I think so."

"All right. We'll go into town later and download some pictures to bring back to you, because you obviously have to hide out here." Gracie beamed at him and Jenna. "This is so fun."

Caleb leaned back in his seat, watching Jenna as she turned away and began to make breakfast. She was smiling, humming under her breath, letting her daughter take the lead on the questions. He loved the sound of her music. He loved watching her. And he loved sitting at the table with Gracie while she took notes on flowers.

He knew they couldn't stay like this forever, but he sure as hell was going to appreciate every moment while he had it.

CHAPTER SEVEN

"Caleb's so cool," Gracie said an hour later, her arms wrapped around Jenna's waist as they headed down to the road on the ATV.

"He's a good guy," Jenna agreed. He *was* a good man. She could feel it in every fiber of her being, which meant she was finding it impossible to reconcile the violence, the danger, and the drama with the man who was currently stretched out on the couch, making up songs about wildflowers to entertain a baby. Simba and Zach were both nestled happily on his chest, safe and loved.

"Let's keep him."

Jenna laughed as she rounded the last bend of the long driveway. "He's not a dog. We can't just decide we want him and keep him. He has a life he has to get back to."

"He doesn't have to get back to anything. You and dad always told me that we don't owe anyone anything, and we can live whatever life we want."

Jenna tightened her grip on the handles as the ATV bounced over a rut. "Yes, but there are limits—"

"Limits are in your own mind. That's what Dad used to say. And you used to say it, too."

Jenna bit her lip against the urge to tell her daughter that she didn't have the same optimistic view of life that she had once had, before everything had fallen apart. "That's a good point," she said instead. "But we can't control Caleb, and he might have to make choices that we don't like."

"He won't."

Jenna stopped the ATV and twisted around to face her daughter. She was so happy that Gracie loved Caleb and had her spirit back, but it also concerned her. "Gracie," she said, keeping her voice as gentle as she could. "Sometimes, people come into our lives, and they stay. Other times, they are only meant to pass through."

Gracie nodded. "Like Dad."

"Yes, like Dad. But also maybe Caleb." She didn't want to take away Gracie's joy, but she had to do what she could to protect her from heartbreak. "It's okay to love Caleb, but it's important to always remember that he is a gift that isn't meant to stay with us."

Gracie's jaw jutted out. "Maybe he'll stay. You don't know."

She let out her breath. "That's true. I can't predict the future. But it's important to understand that he might not be able to stay, even if he wants to. He has no idea what his life is, and we don't either. We have to be prepared to let him go if he needs or wants to go. I need you to understand that."

Gracie's eyes narrowed. "Mom—"

"We have to leave in a week. You need to go back to school. I have work. And—"

"No!" Gracie folded her arms over her chest. "We don't have to go back! You own the company! I don't want to go back and live with Gram while you're always gone. If I stayed here, I could stay with Caleb. I could hide with them!"

Oh, God. "Gracie."

"Mom."

She took a breath, trying a new tactic. Honesty. Maybe it was time. "I like Caleb, too. He makes me feel alive again. I'd love to have more time with him, too."

Gracie watched her, listening.

"But the truth is that his life is a big mystery right now. No one knows what it is, but there are signs that it's not a life he can just walk away from. Right now, our little cabin is an oasis, but the real world is still out there. It's going to come for us, and none of us know what will happen when it does." She put her hand over Gracie's. "It's been a long time for both of us since we had someone that makes us feel good. So, let's enjoy every minute, and remember that whatever happens, we had this time."

She chose not to add that they barely knew Caleb, and he could turn out to be a terrible person. Mostly because there was no point in saying that, but also because she honestly didn't believe it was possible. He was a good man. But a forever guy in their lives?

She was old enough to know that the odds of that were pretty much zero, for a million reasons. But he might very well be their healing guy, who made them both whole again.

And maybe they could do that for him.

Gracie sighed. "You're very depressing."

"Realistic."

"Realistic sucks."

"I know. Are we good?"

"I guess. I'm mad at you, though."

Jenna sighed. "That's fine." Not really, but that was life as a mom of a teenager, she supposed. She started the ATV back up and hit the gas. Gracie didn't say anything more, and the rest of the ride was in silence.

Until they emerged from the wooded driveway to the

main road and saw blue flashing police lights. There was a sheriff's car, two state police cars, and a black pickup truck.

Fear shot through her. Had Caleb been tracked there?

Gracie's arms tightened around her. "Do you think they're after Caleb?"

A state trooper looked over and waved them over.

Crap. "Don't tell them about Caleb," Jenna muttered as she drove up behind the pickup truck. "Stay on the ATV. I'll go talk to them."

Fear hammered through her as she parked the ATV and took her helmet off. What if Caleb was an escaped murderer, and the cops had tracked him here? No. He wasn't a murderer. What if the people hunting Zach had tracked him here? Her fear intensified at the thought, but she managed a smile as she walked up. "Hello, what's going on?"

The cop pointed at her truck, which was in the ditch. "Is this yours?"

"Yes. I slid off the road last night trying to avoid a stray dog." She pointed to Gracie and the ATV. "We came out to get our groceries. Last night was stormy, so we hiked to the cabin with what we could carry."

There was a man in a cowboy hat standing nearby. He was tall, broad-shouldered, and carried himself with an aura of confidence and lawlessness. He wasn't a cop. Who was he? He looked vaguely familiar, but her panicked brain might have been hallucinating.

He met her gaze and inclined his head. "Good to see you again, Jenna. I was going to drive up to the cabin to make sure you were all right. When I saw the Washington plates, I figured it was you."

She blinked at the voice. She recognized it. "Brody?" Brody Hart and eight siblings owned a massive ranch in the area. They were reclusive billionaires who had given her grandma a standing offer if she ever wanted to sell the cabin.

They were famous celebrities, but they had always been nice when she'd run into them. They were good people, and she relaxed slightly.

He nodded. "Everything okay up there?"

"Oh, yes," she said quickly. "The generator works, and the cabin is in good shape." She pointed at Gracie, who waved. "Mother-daughter vacation."

The police officer cleared his throat. "Have you run into anyone else?"

She looked over at him. "Like who?"

"There's another truck off the road a few miles north," Brody said. "Apparently, it was a stolen vehicle. We thought maybe he'd run you off the road."

So, that was how Caleb had gotten to the cabin. "No, a little fifteen-pound stray ran us off the road." She paused. "Has anyone reported her missing? She's brown and shaggy. Really thin."

"Nope. Haven't heard anything. Did you see anyone else while you were hiking in, or driving in the area?"

She let out her breath. No one was looking for Simba. Why did that make her so happy? It wasn't like they could keep the dog forever. Gram was too old to take on a dog, she was always traveling, and Gracie had school.

"Ma'am? Did you see anyone else?"

Shoot. She needed to focus. "Sorry, I was thinking about the dog." She shrugged. "I haven't seen anyone. We own a lot of property, so we never do." Were they going to do a manhunt for Caleb? She needed to warn him.

"Do you have identification, ma'am?" The officer asked.

Jenna felt her pockets. "No, I didn't bring anything with me. We were just coming down to get our things—"

"I can follow you back to the cabin," the trooper said.

Panic hit her hard, but Brody interrupted. "I can vouch for her. I've known Jenna and her grandmother for years." He waved at Gracie. "Your daughter is so big now. I remember when she was a toddler."

Gracie waved back. "Hi, Brody!"

What a clever girl. Clearly, Gracie was listening hard from her spot on the ATV. "Who stole the truck?" Jenna asked.

The trooper shrugged. "We don't know, but keep an eye out. He could be on foot."

Yeah, he sure could be. "All right," she said. "I'm not worried, though. I have a private investigator's license, and I carry."

"She does," Gracie yelled. "My mom's a badass!"

Jenna had to bite her lip to keep from grinning. "I do try to get her not to swear," she said, "but you have to pick your battles with teenagers."

The sheriff nodded. "That you do. I have three girls myself. I'm never sure if I'm going to survive the day."

Jenna laughed, hoping that she didn't sound awkward and forced. "That's so true." She gestured to her truck. "Would it be all right if I got my groceries? The sun is starting to come up, and I have some perishables in there."

The cop nodded. "Sure, that's fine. Call if you see anything or anyone suspicious, though. Don't try to handle it yourself."

Jenna nodded. "I won't." She punched the remote and unlocked her car. "Come help, Gracie!"

"You bet!" With enthusiasm far surpassing last night's, Gracie pulled off her helmet, leapt off the ATV, and ran over. "I'm so hungry," she announced. "I can't believe you made us leave all our groceries in the truck. There's no food in the house!"

Jenna cleared her throat. "All right. Enough with the drama. Let's load up." She opened the door and handed a bag to Gracie.

As Gracie trotted off, Brody walked down the incline and peered into the truck. "You won't fit all that on the ATV."

"I know. We'll have to make several trips. It's fine. It's a nice day, and activity is good." She pulled out another bag, but Brody took them from her.

"I'll load the stuff into my truck and drive it up," he said. "Then you'll only need one trip."

Alarm shot through her. "Oh, no, that's fine. Really. It's good mother-daughter bonding."

He flashed her a grin. "It's no problem. I'll get a tow truck over here later today as well. Even my truck won't be able pull that out, or I'd do it right now."

"The tow truck would be great," she said, as she took the bags back from him. "But we're good on the groceries—" She paused when she saw the police officer watching her with a frown.

Crap. Was it suspicious not to want Brody to come back to the house? That she'd rather drive back and forth all morning taking a few bags at a time, rather than have Brody do it all for her?

"You're sure everything's all right at the house?" the police officer asked. "You want me to come check it out?"

So, yes, apparently it was suspicious. She managed a smile. "We're good. Really."

His gaze went to Brody, and then back to her.

Brody picked up another few bags. "It'll take you all morning," he said. "I really don't mind. Your grandma would have my head if I didn't help."

Jenna managed a stifled laugh, aware of the cop still watching her. "That's true. She would. Fine, I accept your offer. That's incredibly generous of you."

As she spoke, Gracie shot her a "What the hell are you doing, Mom?" look.

"I'll follow you up," the police officer said. "I want to look around just to be sure."

Oh, man. Gracie's eyes widened, and they looked at each other in horror. *Shit. Shit. Shit.*

There was nowhere for Caleb to hide. He was badly injured, and he had a baby.

"Fine," she said, "but no sirens. If you wake the baby, I might have to go mama bear on you both." She leveled a hard look at both of them. "And I mean it. Any slamming of car doors, and you're both banned for life."

Gracie's mouth dropped open, and both men looked startled.

"Baby?" The sheriff said. "You left a baby alone at the cabin?"

Seriously with that question? "Of course not." She hoisted a bag and set it in Brody's arms. "My husband is with him."

Gracie's face lit up.

"Your husband?" Brody looked startled. "I'm sorry. I thought he passed away—"

"Danny did. Yes," she said. "I'm remarried."

"Oh, congrats," Brody said. "I'm happy for you."

The sheriff was frowning. "Why isn't he down here with the groceries?"

"Oh..." Gracie grinned. "My mom isn't going to like that question."

Jenna had to fight not to laugh. "You think I should be with the baby while the man drives the ATV? Is that what you're saying?"

The sheriff blanched. "No, I wasn't. I mean—"

Brody laughed out loud at that one. "You better stop talking now. You're just going to get yourself in deeper. She's a woman with a gun and kids. Don't mess with her."

Jenna grinned. "That's right." She liked Brody. He was a

good guy. The sheriff, she wasn't so sure about. "All right, let's back up, and then we'll lead the way."

Gracie gave Jenna a worried look, and Jenna managed a smile. They could talk plans on the way up. She only hoped it would be enough.

CHAPTER EIGHT

BOUNCING ZACH on his knee while Simba napped in the sunlight coming through the kitchen window, Caleb sat at the table, filling out the list that Jenna had left him.

She'd asked him all sorts of things, like his favorite singer, what he would do for fun, where he would go for vacation, what he would wear in the morning if he could wear whatever he wanted.

She'd explained that she was trying to follow up on the wildflower incident, putting together pieces of his subconscious to get a sense of where he was from, the life he might have led, the influences that guided him.

So far, they'd discovered that he liked jeans, sweatshirts, animals, and sunsets. He knew how to read clouds for approaching storms. He wasn't a computer genius. And he wanted to go to a fancy dude ranch for vacation.

He was surprised by how much she'd drawn out of him, and there was still more coming.

Once Jenna felt she had enough info, she was going to put together a snapshot of him from those answers. Then she and

Gracie would head into town and use the Wi-Fi at the library to do some research.

He was impressed with Jenna. She was very smart, quick-thinking, and innovative. He had no doubt she was great at her job. She was also beautiful, funny, engaging, and he hadn't been able to stop thinking about that kiss.

He wanted more.

Him, a man who carried with him violence, a baby, and an unknown present and past wanted to get up close and personal with a single mom. What did he have to offer? He had no idea.

He probably shouldn't be thinking of Jenna. Of Gracie. But they felt right to him, and that was the simple truth.

"Dada dada dada dada." Zach was chatting happily, gibberish nonsense delivered with a smile.

Caleb smiled as he handed the baby a horse-shaped potholder to play with. "Look at that outside, Zach. It's pretty gorgeous here, isn't it? I'm pretty sure I'm not a city guy, because that view feels good." There was a clearing behind the house, and trails that led off. Trails for hiking. Or riding a horse. He'd like to take Gracie and Jenna riding—

He froze at the idea. Riding horses? He wanted to take them riding on trails?

Yes. His heart pounding with anticipation, he wrote it down, and then went on to describe the ride he'd like to take them on. Sunny day. Galloping across an open plain. It would be a blue-sky day. The sun on his face. Wind whipping. The freedom of riding. He could feel the horse's hooves pounding beneath him, the breathing of the animal as they galloped.

Laughter. Freedom. Power. Independence.

He could almost see the horse. The pricked ears...he flipped the paper over and started to sketch the scene. His pen moved quickly, instinctively, creating life in the animal.

The rippling of the horse's muscles. The details on the saddle. The rider. No, riders. There were more than just one.

He drew a second horse and rider. Excitement pulsed through him as the image took shape. Both riders were men, wearing cowboy hats, and jeans. One had cowboy boots. Another had sneakers. And then more. He drew another one, this rider smaller, younger, more like a teenager, also wearing a cowboy hat, his arms raised to the sky, his face etched with joy.

Caleb bent over the table, sketching furiously, lost in the world he was creating as he drew another horse and rider. And another. And another. Until there were nine. All male. Ranging in age from teenager to early twenties.

It wasn't until he finished the ninth one, drawing in the cheekbones until they were just right that his hand finally stilled, and the pen fell out of his grasp, clattering to the table.

He stared at the drawing, stunned as he inspected it.

Did he know the men and boys in the drawing? He looked closely, and saw that one of them was him, the face he saw in the mirror earlier in the morning. The others...he didn't know them. But he *felt* them. Some of them looked like him. Same jawbone. Similar facial features. Were they all drawings of himself or were they people related to him?

Emotion suddenly overtook Caleb, and he bent his head, swallowing the sudden grief. Were these men important to him? Family? Friends? Brothers? Or strangers. He had no idea. Whoever the people on that page were, they were lost to him. Everything was lost to him, except for what he had in this moment, Zach, Gracie, and Jenna. And of course, Simba.

The four of them were his entire world right now. His anchors. His sanity. And none of them were his. They were just a fleeting presence in his life that he couldn't hold onto, because they weren't his.

Would he ever remember? Would he ever regain his past? He traced his finger over the faces of the riders in his drawing. And if he did regain his past, would he lose his present?

Zach moved, bumping his injured side, jerking Caleb's focus back to the present. To the violence that he'd awoken to, violence that held no appeal to him whatsoever. He didn't dream of guns. He dreamed of trail rides with Gracie, Jenna, and Zach—

The roar of a truck engine caught his attention. Swearing, he shot to his feet, then stumbled, nearly falling when his leg gave out. Hugging Zach to his chest, he limped over to the front window and slipped the curtain to the side in time to see Jenna stop the ATV in front of the cabin.

Behind her was a massive black pickup truck and a sheriff's car. *Holy shit.*

Gracie vaulted off the ATV and sprinted toward the front door, while Jenna walked over to the other vehicles, waving her arms to make them stop.

He unlocked the front door and opened it just in time for Gracie to bolt inside. He shut the door behind her as she whirled to face him. "You're my dad," she said quickly, panting hard. "You married Mom. Zach is your baby and hers. You work construction back in Washington. You fell off scaffolding at a job site and got badly hurt. Your name is Ted Schofield, and you're napping with Zach in the bedroom right now, so they have to be quiet."

He didn't move. "I'm not hiding—"

"Yes, you are." Gracie shoved at him. "Brody is our neighbor, and he brought our groceries and stuff up in the truck. The sheriff is searching for the guy who stole the pickup truck and left it in the ditch. He wants to make sure we aren't being held hostage. No one is looking for Caleb. It's just bad luck that they were there when we went down to get the groceries."

He swore.

"Mom said this was the plan," Gracie almost shouted at him. "Listen to my mom! Don't be a stubborn male!"

He almost laughed at that. "I wouldn't dare."

"Go! And don't get your gun. This is not a shooting situation. Get in the bedroom. Now! Do you want to endanger all of us by having them realize you're worthy of reporting? I don't think you do!"

She was right. Now wasn't the time to play hero. He had to play the injured, non-threatening husband and dad. "All right, but you better eat your vegetables if I'm your dad."

She grinned. "Deal. Now go!"

"All right, but if anything goes sideways, call me Dad. If you call me Dad, I'll know that something is wrong. Okay?"

She nodded. "Got it."

He heard men's voices outside, and he swore. Every instinct in his body was shouting at him to go on alert. To get his gun. To be ready to fight, escape, whatever it took.

But his instincts had gotten him blown up and stabbed, so yeah, fuck those instincts.

He grabbed the bottle of formula he'd prepared earlier, then limped past Gracie into the bedroom. She pulled the door shut behind him as he heard the front door open.

Swearing under his breath, he limped over to the window and edged the shade aside to look out. Armed men weren't encircling the house. No traps were being set. It was simply the same woods he'd been looking out on earlier.

He heard the front door open, and the low rumble of men's voices. Tension shot through him, and his fingers tightened on the curtain. The instinct to engage was so strong he could barely stop himself.

Then Zach tugged at his arm, and he looked down into the innocent little face. The sweet little baby he needed to keep safe.

The men out there weren't looking for him. They weren't the enemy that he had to worry about. He might not know who he was or what his past was, but he knew enough to trust what he knew. And he knew that he could trust Jenna. If Jenna said this wasn't a shooting situation, then it wasn't.

She was tough. Experienced. Capable.

And his only tether to life right now.

He took one final look out the window, saw nothing but nature, and then let the curtain drop closed. His heart pounding, he limped across the room as he heard footsteps outside his room.

He couldn't make himself get trapped under the covers, so he stretched out on top, still wearing his jeans and boots. He tucked the baby in the crook of his arm, gave him the bottle, and then leaned his head back in the pillows.

As he did so, he felt himself relax, sinking into the mattress. It was the first time he'd been in a bed since the burned-out house. He was surprised how good it felt, how normalizing it was. His tension began to ease, replaced by a calm alertness as he listened to the activity in the living room.

He couldn't hear the words of the men, but he listened to their tone, their intonations, and to Jenna's voice as well. She sounded completely relaxed, and the men did as well. Footfalls were easy and relaxed, and he could hear Gracie's laugh.

He looked down at Zach, whose eyelids were getting heavy. "I think it's okay, kid. I think we're good."

Not that he'd relax yet, but he was feeling okay about it. Why? Because he trusted the woman in the living room who had decided to trust him.

Trust.

It felt good.

He heard the doorknob turn, and he closed his eyes. Trusting.

The door squeaked as it opened, and he could feel the

presence of others in the doorway. He kept his breath even and deep, and again, his eyes closed.

"Don't wake him up," Jenna whispered. "He needs his sleep."

Caleb almost grinned at the possessiveness in her voice. She was staking her claim on him, and he loved that so much.

The door closed, and he opened his eyes, just to double check. No one was in the room with him. They'd checked on him and believed Jenna's story.

He took a deep breath as he heard the men say good-bye. The two vehicles started up outside, and then they drove off.

He'd just let himself relax, when the door flew open and Gracie raced in, and flung herself on the bed next to him, jarring his injuries. "That was awesome," she announced. "They had no idea!"

He hid the pain. "Yeah, you guys did good."

Zach awoke with a start, but Gracie picked him up and started playing with him before he could start screaming.

Caleb grinned as Jenna walked in behind her daughter. "Good plan."

She smiled. "Thanks. Good job faking sleep." She looked thoughtful. "It couldn't have been easy to just lie there."

"It wasn't." He met her gaze. "But I trusted you."

Emotion flickered across her face, deep emotion that was raw and rough. But she simply nodded in acknowledgment. "How about you get off your lazy bum and come help me with the groceries and fill me in on that gorgeous picture you drew of cowboys?"

The picture. Right. "I don't know who they are."

"Yet," she said. "You don't know who they are, *yet*."

～

BRODY HART PULLED his truck over a mile down the road from Jenna's cabin. He leaned back in his seat, stunned by what had just happened. He was pretty damn certain that Caleb Stockton was in that cabin. The missing brother that his Stockton in-laws had been trying to track down for ten years.

He'd recognized the Stockton brothers in the drawing on the kitchen table, barely able to hide his surprise. And then, even in the shadowy light of that bedroom, he'd seen enough of Ted Schofield to recognize the facial structure so common to the Stocktons.

Why was Caleb using a different name? Did Jenna know he was actually Caleb Stockton, or was he lying to her? Did he have an entire new life and identity?

And what should Brody do about it? Tell the Stocktons? Go back there and out Caleb? Or trust that there was a reason Caleb was hiding in a cabin in eastern Oregon under a different name, and find a way to help him?

Brody had plenty of experience with the need to hide, to escape a life and danger. Hell, his entire family of Harts had been runaways as kids, living under a bridge, hiding from assorted levels of shittiness in their lives.

But he knew the Stocktons very well. They were his family now. They were good people. Great people. If Caleb was in trouble, they would help. Hell, they were still broken without Caleb in their lives. They bled every day for the brother that had gone missing ten years ago.

They would want to know.

If he told the Stocktons, there would be no stopping their descent onto that cabin. A family reunion to beat all family reunions.

But Caleb had stayed off the radar for ten years. He had to have a reason. What if Brody broke through that reason and put Caleb or the others in danger? What if the best thing to do was leave Caleb alone in whatever life he'd clearly chosen to follow. Obviously, he was alive and well, right? So, doing okay.

Or not. Who the hell knew what was going on in that cabin? What if Jenna was in danger? He might not know her well, but neighbors were neighbors, and he had a duty to make sure she was safe.

Then again, Caleb was a Stockton. Any woman and child would be safe with a Stockton.

Right?

Shit.

Brody leaned back in his seat and braced his hands on his steering wheel, his mind racing as he tried to figure out what to do.

CHAPTER NINE

CALEB LEANED back on the couch, moving gingerly, mesmerized by the way the morning sunlight created auburn highlights in Jenna's dark brown hair. Her braids were tight, flawless works of art, and the sun made them look like they were on fire.

On the floor in front of the fireplace, Gracie was playing with Zach, chatting with him effortlessly. The teenager was a natural with Zach, and the baby had fallen for her quickly, giggling as she flipped her hair around to make him laugh.

Simba was stretched out beside the kids, her brown eyes watching intently, her tail thumping every time Gracie patted her. Simba was a good dog. He could tell. Sweet, trusting, and healing.

If Jenna didn't keep her, he would.

Jenna was muttering under her breath, drawing his attention back to her. Her brow was furrowed as she meticulously went over each of his answers, making a chart to track the themes.

Some of her braids had fallen forward over her shoulder, and without even thinking about it, he reached up and moved them back over her shoulder, his fingers lingering on the ends of the braids.

The moment he touched her hair, she looked over at him.

She didn't pull back. But she did give him a small smile, drawing a smile from him.

There was so much to this incredible woman. Caleb wanted more time with her. Private time without kids around, where he could delve into her secrets, unpeel the layers, and find out every secret she had.

She was so warm. So smart. But also guarded.

He supposed he should feel guarded, but with her and Gracie, he didn't want to be. He simply wanted to breathe in all that they were. Their laughter. Their camaraderie. The little temporary family they'd created.

"What are you thinking about?" Jenna asked.

"You. Gracie. Zach. Simba. Being here with you. I like it." He didn't bother to hold back. What was the point? He had no idea how long this would last before the illusion was shattered.

She smiled. "You mean that."

"I do." He let his hand slide over her shoulder and down her back. She glanced toward the kids, then leaned into him slightly. "I know this is temporary. A blip in our lives. But it feels like a gift. An oasis."

Tears glistened in her eyes, surprising him. "It does," she agreed. "I haven't felt this at peace for a long time." She looked over at Gracie. "And she's happy, too. That hasn't happened since before Danny died."

He wanted to ask what had happened with Danny, but he didn't broach the subject. There was no way he would make them relive that tragedy. If one of them wanted to talk about it, he'd listen. But force them to immerse themselves in those memories? Never.

He frowned at that thought. Was that why he lost his memory? Because he didn't want to remember his life?

Jenna raised her brows. "What's that look for?"

He kept his voice low. "What if I don't remember because I don't want to?" He gestured at her paper. "What if we're working so hard to figure out who I am, and I forgot for a reason?"

Jenna looked down at the pen in her hand, then set it on the coffee table. She scooted back on the couch, then turned sideways to face him, pulling her knees to her chest. "Do you want to stop?"

Her toes were almost to his thigh. Instinctively, he edged over slightly, so that his leg was against her feet.

She didn't move away.

They exchanged silent, knowing glances, acknowledging the heat burning between them in that one spot of physical connection.

"In a vacuum, yeah. I'd want to stop looking into my past. I'd want to simply stay right here." He glanced over at Gracie and Zach. "What else could I want than this?"

Jenna's eyes darkened with emotion. "You don't even know me. Or Gracie. How could you possibly know that this is what you want?"

He shrugged. "I feel it. I trust my gut. Don't you feel something?"

She swallowed, then shrugged. "Maybe."

"Maybe?" He grinned, leaning into her. "You're a little liar," he whispered, his voice rough and low. "It's intense as hell. Unexplainable. But it's real."

She mimicked his stance, leaning forward toward him, until their lips were inches apart. He had a feeling she hadn't realized she was doing it, but instinct was drawing her to him as strongly as it was doing to him. "Caleb—" She paused.

"Tell me," he urged, keeping his voice low and quiet, for her ears only. "Caleb, what?"

Her brown eyes flickered to his. "I don't even know how to experience this," she whispered. "I'm not ready for it. And Gracie... God. This will break her heart when it ends. She's already claimed both of you."

He traced his fingers over her jaw. "Why does it have to end?"

Jenna made a strangling sound. "You sound just like her! How could it not end? Literally nothing about this makes sense—"

Caleb put his finger on her lips, and she stopped talking. "Not everything good ends in loss."

She stared at him, then sudden tears flared in her eyes and spilled down her cheeks.

Caleb swore under his breath. "I'm sorry. I didn't mean to upset you." Shit. He was such an idiot.

Jenna shook her head as she wiped the back of her hand over her cheeks. "No, it's fine. It's not you. It's me." She managed a smile. "Maybe Gracie's right. Maybe I'm not as all right as I think I am."

"You're just fine," he said, meaning it.

"Am I?" She shook her head. "I look at you, and I just want to fall into you. The way you are with Zach and Gracie and me..." She swallowed. "I didn't realize how much I missed that, until you broke into our cabin."

He grinned. "I didn't break into it. I'm much too skilled to break into anything."

"See?" she whispered. She took his hands and held them up. "What have these done? What do they still need to do? We don't know."

He flipped his hands around so that he could wrap her hands up in his. "I don't know, but I'm clearly very good with my hands." He intentionally left the innuendo in his tone, and he grinned when her eyes widened and amusement flickered in her eyes.

"Is that so?"

"It is. I can whip up a baby bottle and change a diaper in no time."

"And?"

"And—" He glanced in the direction of Gracie and found her staring at them, clearly listening intently. "And I can make breakfast," he added lamely.

Jenna glanced at Gracie, then started laughing. "I love you, Gracie."

"Keep going," Gracie said. "This is better than Netflix."

They both laughed, and Caleb let go of Jenna's hands. "Sorry, kid. That's as far as this goes today."

She wrinkled her nose at them. "My mom's stubborn and annoying, Caleb. It's not going to be easy to budge her. Don't give up, though, okay?" The hope in her voice made something turn over in his gut.

He realized Jenna was right. Gracie was all-in on him and Jenna making it real, and making it forever. He let out his breath. He had to do better. He might talk about how he wanted this, but he and Jenna both knew the truth of what they were facing.

Gracie clearly didn't, or at least, she was refusing to acknowledge it.

He turned to face her. "Gracie, you need to remember that we don't know what my secrets are. Regardless of how I feel about you, I might have to disappear in the middle of the night without saying good-bye." He hated to say it, but he needed to.

Her eyes widened. "You can't do that."

"The moment my presence puts you in danger, I have to leave. Instantly."

"You have to say good-bye. You can't leave without telling

me." The panic in her eyes got to him, hitting him right in his gut.

He glanced at Jenna and saw the concern on her face.

He swore under his breath. "I promise I will find you if I can."

"No." She stood up, gripping Zach. "That's not enough. You have to promise you'll say good-bye. You can't just leave. You can't!"

Shit. How had this gotten so intense so fast? He couldn't make a promise that he might not be able to keep, but he could feel the depth of her terror. He suspected that her dad's death must have been sudden, and she hadn't been around for that last moment, making her terrified of sudden loss.

He leaned forward, bracing his arms on his knees. "Gracie—"

"Don't you dare give me a speech that sometimes people's job is to pass through our lives and not stay. I'm so over that!"

Jenna tried next. "Gracie—"

Gracie held up her hands in protest. "No, Mom. Don't start. Forget it. *Forget it!*" She turned and ran into the bedroom and slammed the door, taking Zach and Simba with her.

Caleb bowed his head, clasping his hands between his knees. "Do I leave now? Is that best?" The thought of leaving sank in his gut like a stone, but there was no way that he would hurt them.

Jenna didn't answer, so he looked over at her, expecting her to look upset, but she didn't. She was staring at the bedroom door with a look of stunned shock on her face.

"Jenna?"

She dragged her gaze off the door and looked at him. "Since Danny died, she has been locked behind a wall. So closed off. I was so worried about her. But you've opened her up." She looked over at him. "You're making her feel again, and that's beautiful."

He frowned. "I don't want to hurt her."

"It's too late for that," she said. "Will it make it worse by staying longer? Or better, because she can keep healing?" She looked at Caleb helplessly. "I don't know."

He let out his breath. "Maybe I should leave—"

"And go where? With a baby? The minute you step outside this cabin, you endanger both of you." She shook her head. "I can't let that happen just because we might be scared of falling too hard. No. *No.*" She stood up. "I'm going to talk to Gracie, but don't leave—"

There was a sudden knock at the door.

They both froze. "Did you hear a car?" Jenna whispered.

"No." Caleb stood up, flexing his hands. "Someone walked in." He walked over to the bookshelf, stood on a chair, and grabbed his gun from the top. "They meant to surprise us."

Jenna paled. "Go into the bedroom with Gracie. Keep her safe."

"I'm not letting you deal with whoever's at that door—"

She held out her hand for the gun. "If it's nothing, I don't want you involved. If it's something, I can handle myself."

Swearing under his breath, Caleb handed her the gun. "Where are the rest of my weapons?"

The knock sounded again. "Jenna? It's Brody. I need the keys to your truck for the tow."

Jenna immediately relaxed. "It's Brody."

"We didn't hear his truck. He didn't drive up."

"He's fine." Jenna handed him the gun. "I'll take care of him. Go in the bedroom."

"Not this time." Caleb knew something was off. For Brody to come back, without his truck... It was wrong. "Answer the door. I'll stay beside it."

Jenna frowned. "Brody isn't dangerous—"

"What if he's not alone?"

Jenna stared at him, then silently walked to the door. She waited until Caleb positioned himself next to the door, his gun up and ready. She leaned on the door. "Brody? Is everything all right?"

"Yeah, fine. Sorry to bother you. Just wanted to grab the keys."

She looked at Caleb, who shook his head. "He's fine," she whispered. "Don't shoot him."

Caleb shrugged his inability to promise anything, and Jenna sighed as she picked up the keys from the table by the door. "Okay." Giving Caleb a hard look, she pulled the door open.

Caleb watched her body language and facial expression carefully to see if there was anything amiss, but Jenna stayed relaxed as she smiled at Brody. "Thanks for taking care of the car." Then she looked past him. "Where's your truck?"

"I walked in. It's a nice day for a hike."

"It is," she agreed as she held up her hand with the keys. "Here you go—"

"Can I come in for a sec?"

Jenna glanced at Caleb, then back at Brody. "I don't think that's a good idea right now. The baby's napping and—"

"I need to speak with your husband."

Caleb swore at the tone in Brody's voice. Their visitor wasn't going away. Slowly, he lowered his gun and hid it behind his back, then he stepped away from the wall and stood beside Jenna. "What do you want?"

Brody's gaze settled on his face, and he drew his shoulders back. "Son of a bitch."

Caleb's fingers tightened on his gun, but Jenna put her hand on his hip, stilling him. "What's going on, Brody?" she asked.

Brody leveled a hard look at Caleb. "Jenna's under my

protection, but I'm going to assume you're a good guy because your brothers are the best fucking men I've ever met. But you're going to tell me right now whether you mean her harm. Don't lie, because I'll know it, and then I'll have to shoot you, and I don't want to do that."

Caleb felt like he'd been gut punched. "My brothers?" he echoed. "You know *my brothers?*"

CHAPTER TEN

CALEB WAS SO stunned that he barely noticed that Jenna caught his arm.

Brody nodded. "My sister married Maddox, so they're my family now. Which means you're my family, which I don't yet know whether I'm happy about."

"Maddox?" Caleb felt like the world was spinning, and he grabbed Jenna's hand, using her to ground him. "I have a brother named Maddox?"

Brody's fierce scowl faded into confusion. "You don't know?"

"I—" Son of a bitch. He gripped her hand more tightly. "How many brothers? How big is my family?"

Brody narrowed his eyes. "Nine of you total. Plus a sister."

Holy shit. "Do they know I'm here?"

Brody frowned. "No. I didn't tell them. I wanted to find out what was going on." He paused. "I don't know why you've been off the grid for ten years, but I wanted to hear your reason before I told them anything."

Caleb's mind was whirling as he held up a hand to pause Brody. "Off the grid? What do you mean?"

Brody's gaze went back and forth between Jenna and Caleb. "Ten years ago," he said slowly, speaking carefully, "you left home. No one has heard from you since. They've hired private detectives to look for you, including my brother, who's one of the best. Not a single thread of your existence was ever found. Until today, when I saw that sketch on the kitchen table."

Jesus. What had he been doing for ten years? "Why did I leave?"

Brody shook his head slowly. "I don't know. I don't think any of them know specifically." He paused. "But your family is complicated."

"Hell." Caleb was so stunned. "You didn't tell anyone I was here?"

"No one."

"No one knows?"

Brody raised his brows. "No one but us."

Hell. He let go of Jenna's hand and limped over to the couch. He buried his face in his hands, fighting off the emotion surging over him. Family? Brothers? People who had been searching for him for a decade?

The couch moved as Jenna sat beside him. He took her hand and crushed it between his. "What the hell, Jenna? Who am I?"

She shook her head. "I don't know."

Brody wandered in and shut the door before walking across the room and sitting down in one of the armchairs. He braced his forearms on his quads. "What's going on, Caleb? You don't know who you are?" He looked at Jenna. "And you? You know this?"

She nodded. "We found him. Injured and no memory of what happened before yesterday."

Brody frowned at him, and Caleb could see his skepticism. Of course he'd be skeptical. Who woke up in the aftermath of an explosion with no memory of his life before that moment?

He wanted to ask more questions about his family. His brothers. The life he'd left. But he must have had a reason for leaving them behind, and until he knew what it was, he wasn't going to bring them back into his world.

"I'm in danger," he said. "I'm protecting a baby for a man who gave him to me right after I woke up from an explosion. He said they're hunting us. Until I find out what's going on, find Zach's dad, and ensure their safety, I can't bring anyone else into it. Including my family." He looked at Brody. "And you."

Brody raised his brows. "Me? I'm very skilled. You don't need to worry about me."

"No." Caleb stood up. "I'm not widening the net of the people I put in danger. This is getting too big." He looked at Jenna. "I'm going to take off—"

"No!" The bedroom door was flung open, and Gracie raced into the room, cradling Zach against her chest. "Brody is rich and connected. He has resources. He can help!"

Caleb ground his jaw. "I don't know who to trust, sweetheart—"

"I do," Gracie said. "My mom and I do. Brody is awesome. His family is badass. They can help." She held up Zach. "They'll help keep him safe."

Caleb swore under his breath. "Gracie—"

"She's right," Jenna said. "I trust Brody and the Harts. They're capable and smart. I've even heard of his brother Dylan, who is a fantastic PI. Danny admired him."

Caleb looked back and forth at them. "I don't want to be responsible for harm coming to any of you."

"All of the Harts and Stocktons have been through tough, dangerous shit. A lot of it, actually," Brody said. "We're born to get dirty protecting those we love. And since you're a

Stockton, you're already in my circle of protection. That's what family is."

"Gracie and I are already involved," Jenna added. "It's too late for that."

Caleb limped to the window in the kitchen. He braced his hands on the counter and looked out at the woods. He remembered how he'd wanted to take Gracie, Jenna, and Zach on a trail ride. He couldn't do that until he fixed this. Until he answered questions.

"Your brothers are very capable," Brody said. "I recommend we bring them in on it, as well."

Caleb closed his eyes against the almost insurmountable need to say yes, to connect with *family*. People who knew him. "I left them for a reason," he said. "What if that reason still exists?"

"And what if it doesn't?" Jenna's voice was quiet. "I lost Danny, Caleb. And my parents. They were gone before we were ready. If you still have family who is wonderful and loves you... God. I'd give anything for a chance to bring back my parents...and Danny." Her voice broke, and he looked over at her.

Gracie was sitting on the couch next to Jenna now, cradling Zach to her chest while Simba leaned against her. His family, for what it was. He understood what Brody meant about a circle of protection, because the four of them were in his.

How could he best protect them? By keeping them close and ending the threat. Jenna was right. He'd already involved them. His trail led right to them, and if someone found him, they'd find Jenna and Gracie, even if he left them behind now.

He could do it on his own, but he was smart enough to know that having an army behind him was a hell of a lot better. But he didn't know the Harts. He didn't know the Stocktons.

He let out his breath. "Jenna, would you trust the Harts with Gracie's life? Because if we open the door and let them and the Stocktons in, that's what we're doing."

She didn't hesitate. "Yes."

He nodded, then looked over at Brody. "How can you be so sure I'm the missing Stockton?" There could be no mistake. Not even one.

Brody pulled out his phone, scrolled through a few pictures, and then held out his phone. "This is your oldest brother, Chase."

Caleb walked over and took the phone, then he swore, stunned. The man in the photograph was wearing a cowboy hat and a blue collared shirt. He looked rough and ready. A stranger...who could have been his twin brother. "He looks like me."

Brody nodded. "The Stockton blue eyes and facial structure."

Gracie held out her hand, and he gave her the phone. Jenna and Gracie looked at it, and they both gasped. "He looks so much like you," Jenna said.

"Scroll to the right," Brody said. "There are more."

Caleb sank down onto the couch beside Jenna, leaning over her shoulder as Gracie flipped through the pictures. "It's the men I sketched." So many of them. He didn't recognize any of them. Total strangers...who looked like him. Two of them were clearly mixed race and had brown eyes instead of the Stockton blue eyes, but they still had that same facial structure.

Brody nodded. "Yeah. That's how I knew it was you."

Caleb looked at Jenna. He trusted her. She was his anchor. His lifeline. "What do you think?"

She nodded. "Do it." Again, she didn't hesitate.

He took a breath. "Will you come with me?"

Her eyes widened. "What?"

"They're in Wyoming," Brody said. "We can take my jet and be there in a few hours."

"A private jet to Wyoming?" Gracie said. "That's awesome."

"I can't leave you here," Caleb said. "If anyone tracks me here and finds you guys..." He shrugged. "If you won't come, I'm staying here."

"Mom! Let's go! A private jet!"

Jenna met his gaze, and he could see her indecision.

He took her hand and leaned in. "I know we don't know each other well," he said. "I don't even know who I am, but I know that I can swear that I'll protect you both and keep you safe." He nodded at Zach and Gracie. "They're my number one priority. The minute I feel like any of you are in danger, we'll shift tactics. Get out. Go underground if we need to."

Brody leaned in. "We're experts in this area, and so are the Stocktons. Whoever is after you will never be able to get through us."

Jenna bit her lip. "What if you're the threat?" she asked. "Caleb, what if you're the danger?"

Caleb was well aware that was a possibility. "If I get my memory back, that won't change how I feel about you."

She looked at her daughter, and he understood her concern. They were getting in deeper and deeper. He needed to offer her more.

"If I do anything to endanger the three of you, Brody will stop me." He looked at the man. "Do I have that promise? Based on what you've said about my brothers, they might think before shooting me. I need you to promise that you won't hesitate."

"Oh, Caleb, don't say that," Jenna said.

He took her hand and looked at Brody, waiting.

The cowboy swore under his breath, but he nodded. "If you become a danger, I'll stop you."

"Whatever it takes."

Brody nodded. "Whatever it takes."

"Brody! You can't shoot him," Jenna protested.

Brody looked over at her. "I'll do whatever I can to avoid it, but if it comes down to it, I've made the man a promise that I intend to keep. It sets him free."

Gracie was leaning against her mom, watching the exchange with wide eyes. "You're not dangerous," she said. "You'd never hurt us."

Caleb smiled. "I agree with you, but I don't know what I don't know."

"I do. I know it." Gracie's face was solemn. "You can trust me, even if you can't trust yourself."

He let out his breath, glad that he had Brody at his back. He'd die a thousand times before he'd let any harm come to his little trio. And having two families at his back to help him figure out what was going on would make this end so much faster. "Jenna, I want their help. I want this to end. I want to do it my way, not sit around waiting for someone to track us down and catch us unaware."

She sighed, and he saw the moment that she gave in. "I have to admit, I don't love it when bad guys surprise me."

"Right?" He grinned. "I'm pretty sure I don't either."

"So, it's decided then?" Brody asked.

Caleb and Jenna met gazes, and then together, they nodded. "Let's do it."

"Yay!" Gracie shrieked with joy. "I'll go pack!" She handed Zach to Caleb and then took off for the bedroom, Simba bounding after her with delight. Then she paused at the door and swung to face them. "We're taking Simba, right? We're not leaving her?"

Jenna let out a breath. Caleb expected her to tell Gracie

that they couldn't take the dog, but she didn't even hesitate. The little dog had won her heart completely, and she knew they'd find a way to fit her into their lives. "There's no way we're leaving her behind."

"Awesome. Come on, Simba." Gracie bolted into the room and immediately started throwing stuff into her suitcase, leaving the three adults looking at each other.

Caleb was sure it was the right thing to do to keep Jenna, Gracie, and Zach safe, but going to meet his family? His brothers? *Damn.* He looked at Brody. "Don't tell them I'm coming. I don't know why I left, so I want to go in quietly. Under the radar. Start with one of them."

Brody nodded. "I agree. We'll start with Chase." He pulled out his phone. "I'll have the jet readied. How long do you need to pack?"

Caleb looked at Jenna, and she shrugged. "A half hour? We've barely unpacked."

"Perfect. We'll be airborne by early afternoon. I'm going to call Dylan in on it. He's an excellent shot and a great investigator. We'll start work on the plane."

Caleb glanced at Jenna, and she nodded that it was all right to call in Dylan. "Okay."

"I'll bring my truck up," Brody said. "I'll be back in a few." He headed out the door, leaving Jenna and Caleb on the couch.

Neither of them moved as the door closed behind Brody.

Jenna smiled. "So, you're a Stockton, huh?"

He shrugged. "Apparently." He held out his hand. "You ready?"

She put her hand in his, and she smiled when he closed his fingers around hers. "When Danny was alive, we had a lot of adventures, but nothing since. I guess it's time for another one."

There was a sparkle in her eye that made him smile. Jenna

wasn't afraid. He could see it in her body language. He smiled. "You're not really worried, are you?"

She shook her head. "Honestly, it's the most alive I've felt in a long time. And I can see Gracie feels the same." She shrugged. "The Ward girls aren't meant for a boring life, and that's what we were doing."

He raised his brows. "What if I turn out to be boring?"

"Then we'll leave you behind while we go cliff diving, of course."

He laughed softly and leaned in, brushing his lips over hers. He'd meant it to be quick, but the minute their lips touched, heat exploded between them, and the kiss became electric in an instant. His hand went to her hip, and she gripped the front of his shirt, heat skyrocketing between them—

"Mom! Is my shampoo in the shower?"

At the sound of Gracie's voice, they both pulled back. "Yeah," she called out. "I'll pack our toiletries."

"Okay, great!"

The connection between him and Jenna was electric, but Caleb knew this wasn't the time or place. Maybe there never would be the right one. But maybe there would.

They were going to find out soon.

He took a breath. "Ready to go meet my family?"

She nodded. "Are you nervous?"

"To meet the family that I abandoned a decade ago? Hell, yeah."

Hell, yeah.

But he was damn glad that she was going with him.

CHAPTER ELEVEN

Jenna had never imagined she'd one day get to take a ride in a billionaire's private jet.

And yet, here she was.

Even if she *had* taken the time to imagine what it would be like, she would have vastly underestimated the sheer opulence and luxury that was even possible to attain. The plane was literally breathtaking. Every detail had been meticulously planned.

There were enough seats for about fifteen, with each one still having plenty of room. She looked down at Zach, who was snuggled against her chest, chatting happily as he played with a stretchy toy horse that the Harts had managed to procure even on no notice. Zach had initially resisted going to anyone but Caleb, but she'd won him over. "Because I'm stubborn like that," she whispered to him.

It had been a long time since she'd held a baby. She'd once thought she'd have three kids, but she'd forgotten about those plans after Danny had died. But Zach made her remember them.

She wiggled his nose. "You're a very good baby."

His dark brown eyes looked up at her, and he tried to grab her necklace.

"No, sorry, Zach. No jewelry for you," she said as she gently extracted the necklace Danny had given her on their first anniversary from Zach's hands.

Danny. She hadn't allowed herself to think much about him for a long time, but with all that had happened in the last twenty-four hours, he seemed to be around all the time. Looking out for her and Gracie?

Maybe. Maybe he was telling her it was time for them to finally heal, and proving it by sending them on a billionaire's private jet for a surprise family reunion of people she didn't even know.

Or maybe she was just trying to find a way to justify the craziness of what she was doing right now.

"Mom!" Gracie poked her head around. "Brody's going to take me to the cockpit! Can I go?"

"Of course. Have fun." Jenna smiled as she watched her daughter practically bound up to the front of the plane. God, to see her eyes sparkle again was worth anything, including throwing in her lot with a gun-toting amnesiac and his estranged family.

Caleb sat down beside her with a tray that held two gorgeous grilled sandwiches, a pair of salads, and two bottles of water. "We missed lunch, so the chef whipped something up." He grinned. "I love that. Our private chef whipped us up a lovely lunch."

She laughed. "Who else would make us lunch?"

"Right?" He stretched out his long legs and held his arms out for Zach. "I'll take him while you eat, and then we can switch."

"Okay." She was surprised that she felt a little wave of regret as she handed Zach off to Caleb. "Thanks." The scent of fresh bread drifted up to her. "It smells amazing."

"I know." He tucked Zach into the crook of his arm and absently jingled a set of plastic keys for him. "How are you doing?"

She was surprised he'd asked. He was the one with the issues. "Fine. Thanks."

"No." He stayed her arm as she reached for her sandwich. "How *are* you?"

Electricity shot along her forearm from his touch, and she couldn't help but suck in her breath. "Does that happen to you, too?"

He frowned. "Does what happen?"

She looked up at him. "When I touch you?" She brushed her fingers over his forearm, and she heard his sharp intake of breath.

"You, too?" he asked. "I thought it was just me, and I was trying to play it cool."

She laughed. "We're too old to have any chance at being cool. At least that's what Gracie would say."

"She's probably right." Caleb took her hand and wrapped his fingers around it. "Talk to me, Jenna. I want to make sure you're doing okay. And Gracie."

She looked down at their hands. "I don't know what I'm doing," she admitted. "I feel like I'm flying by the seat of my pants and making it up as I go."

"And is that bad?"

She looked up at him, and a slow smile spread across her face. "It actually feels really good."

He grinned. "I'm glad to hear that."

"It helps that you gave me a gun, and they let me bring it on board."

His eyes darkened. "Is it weird that I think it's hot that you carry a gun?"

"Probably. You might be some weird sex pervert."

"Maybe. Would that be a turn off?"

"Absolutely not. I love perverts, as long as they're really attractive and great kissers."

"And I qualify on both fronts?"

"You pass. I'm not giving out grades this early in the semester."

He laughed then, a gorgeous deep laugh that seemed to reach inside her and call out answering laughter. "You're all right, Jenna Ward. You're all right."

"I'm awesome. Don't ever forget it." She gave him a hostile glare, which had them both laughing by the time she reached for her sandwich. "Go away. I'm eating."

As she knew he would, he settled more deeply into the seat beside her. "What did you think of Dylan?"

They'd spent the first hour in deep consult with Brody and Dylan. "He was impressive."

Caleb raised his brows. "But?"

She smiled. "He's good. I could see why Danny thought highly of him."

"But?"

She laughed then. "How could you hear that in my voice? I was very careful."

He shrugged. "Apparently, I'm great at reading the tone of women that I'm incredibly attracted to."

Her cheeks got hot. "Shut up."

"Can't. We need to talk." He looked around, then lowered his voice. "Look, Dylan is good. But he's personally invested. He's a Stockton fan as well."

She nodded. "I noticed that."

"They all want this great reunion with me and the Stocktons." He looked troubled. "I don't know why I left, but I had to have a reason. I need you to be on the alert. Be my set of eyes and ears to figure out what I don't remember." He met her gaze. "You're the only one I trust, Jenna. I need you."

Her heart tightened. "I'll do my job. I'm good at it."

"Not just your job." He caught her wrist again and leaned in. "I need you to be you. Be my friend."

Her breath caught. "Just your friend?"

"I didn't say 'just.' Not by a long shot." His blue eyes searched hers. "I know I have no right to make a move on you romantically when I have no idea who the hell I am or what I'm bringing with me, but..." He shrugged. "What do you think?"

She swallowed, and took her time before she answered. She knew she should tell him to back off, but she couldn't. Danny had taught her that life's gifts were fleeting. She could choose to hold off living life until everything was safe, which would be never. Or she could live to the fullest in whatever moment she had.

It wasn't until she and Gracie had run their truck off the road that she'd realized how completely they both had stopped really living.

She didn't want to be like that anymore. She wanted to find her way back to living, and she wanted the same for her daughter. So instead of telling Caleb that they needed to shake hands and part ways as business partners, she said, "I think that you and I both know that there's something between us, and that you could get shot at any moment. So, take it one moment at a time, and don't look further ahead than that?"

His eyes lit up. "All right. And Gracie?"

She bit her lip. "We keep it cool in front of her. I mean, she's smart enough to figure some of it out, and I can't protect her from the heartbreak, but you...and us...we're giving her life back in her soul. So, I guess we just try to be aware with her and protect her as best we can?"

He nodded. "Deal."

At that moment, she heard the engines shift, and she met Caleb's gaze. "We're descending."

He nodded. "To meet my family."

"You ready?"

He took her hand. "Hell, no, but I'm ready to eat."

She'd totally forgotten about the food. "Never put yourself at physical and emotional risk on an empty stomach, right?" She tried to sound chipper, but she was nervous. About him. About them. About Gracie. About meeting the family he'd abandoned.

And about what secrets from his past were coming for them.

And her heart.

She was really, really worried about her heart.

CHAPTER TWELVE

CHASE STOCKTON LEANED back against his kitchen chair, laughing as he watched his boys quiz each other on the names and ages of every horse in their barn. It wasn't an easy endeavor, as they were always bringing in new rescues and rehoming the ones who were ready to go.

But for the two boys, it was joy. Their whole world was his ranch, and the horses, which made Chase so happy.

Horses had saved him and his brothers as kids, and he loved knowing that his boys would have horses from the start.

Mira, the woman who had saved his heart and his soul, smiled at him, her eyes dancing. "You look happy," she said.

"I am." He took a breath. "Last night, I decided to stop looking for Caleb. I'm going to tell Dylan to stop looking for him."

Mira's eyes widened. "What?"

He nodded. "I've been waiting for Caleb for so long. I feel like I've held myself in pause, like I can't truly live until he's back. But seeing Frank and Abby getting married this weekend, embracing life even in their seventies, it made me realize that I need to live, too." He leaned forward. "Not having Caleb back is breaking me, Mira. I let it weigh on me every minute of every day, wondering if he's alive, or dead, or in trouble. Since I can't find him, I can't help him if he needs it. I feel completely helpless, and it's killing me."

She scooted her chair around so she was next to him, sliding her hand under the table to hold his. "It's not killing you," she said softly. "You're present with us every day. You pour love into your sons, your siblings, and their families. You're the anchor who has brought everyone together, and you still are."

He smiled, gripping her hand. "I am," he agreed, "but there's always this weight in my chest that never goes away." He looked at her. "I feel like if I keep holding onto him, I'm going to break, but..." He couldn't finish the rest, but Mira did, because she understood him even better than he knew himself.

"But you're terrified that if you give up hope, then that part of you will die forever," she finished.

He nodded, watching as his boys descended into hilarity after cracking themselves up. He was so glad they were growing up with a good home, solid family, and all the support and love they could ever need.

Not like him and his brothers.

"Here's the thing, sweetheart," Mira said, drawing his attention back to her. "Every one of your brothers is waiting for Caleb as well. Quintin and Emma won't even get married until he comes back."

"I know. That's what made me decide to stop looking for Caleb. I think we're all holding off living, and I need to be the example that it's time we lived."

"You won't convince them," Mira said gently. "They aren't waiting for Caleb because you are. They're waiting for him because he's their family, too. If you told Dylan to stop looking for him, then they'd tell Dylan to keep going. No one's giving up, Chase, including you."

Relief settled deep inside him, relief that he didn't have to follow through on the choice that he'd made last night. But also, that same weight. "So, how do I move forward?"

She smiled. "By loving with all your heart, just as you've been doing."

"Uncle Quintin's here," Alexander shouted. "Can we be excused?"

"Yeah, sure, go see him." As the boys scrambled down from their seats and raced to the front door, Chase turned to his wife. "I fear that it's my fault Caleb left."

Mira's face softened. "Sweetheart, you did the best you could to protect all your brothers from your dad. You sacrificed everything to try to keep them safe. There's nothing more you could have done."

"What if there was? What if my dad pushed Caleb so far that he'll never come back? What if—" Guilt was thick and rough. "There were nights I went to Ol' Skip's ranch with some of my younger brothers, and I left Caleb at home because he didn't want to go. But I always wondered if something happened to him one of those nights."

"If something did, it's your dad's fault. He's the bad guy. Not you."

Chase looked over at her. "When Caleb was fourteen, he changed. He'd been a pretty happy kid. Gentle even. The gentlest of all of us. Somehow, he'd kept his kindness in a way the rest of us didn't. It felt like the darkness of our lives simply didn't touch him." He smiled, remembering. "He would bring home any injured animals he found, hide them in his room, and take care of them until he could set them free. He never kept them. He always believed that every living creature should be free."

Mira cocked her head. "You never told me that before."

Chase rubbed his thumb over his palm. "It was painful for me to think about, so I didn't. But even now, I can see him, all radiant and happy, cradling a baby bird in his hands. The kid was a nurturer, Mira."

She raised her brows. "Like you and all your brothers?" she teased. "Because you all are the biggest bunch of softies I've ever met."

Chase shook his head. "No. Not like us. He didn't have a violent side. When things got ugly with my dad, he would simply wander off into the woods or the fields and just lose himself in nature. He seemed unaffected by it."

Mira cocked his head. "He sounds lovely."

"He was... But then one day, Caleb changed, almost overnight. He got hard. He got quiet. He got angry. He shut down. And he never came back to who he'd once been. I've replayed that day a thousand times in my mind, and I don't know what happened to him, but something did. And it was probably my dad."

Mira squeezed his hand as Chase heard the shouts from outside, the laughter as his boys raced out the front door to see their uncle, his fiancée, and their new cousin, who, like most of the kids in the Stockton clan, wasn't biologically related to the Stockton men. Because that's what they did. The Stocktons collected kids in need, loved them, and became their parents.

"Chase," Mira said softly. "You all suffered at the hands of your father, but every one of you has come back and rejoined the family. At the end of the day, brotherhood won out. Even Jaimi came back, and she didn't even know she had brothers until a few years ago!" She leaned into his shoulder. "Right?"

He managed a smile. "This is true."

"And that's because you, as the big brother, created a safe space for your brothers, and created a bond that held onto everyone. It's taken time for them to return, but they all did.

Caleb will be back. Keep your heart open for him, and he'll return."

Chase bowed his head against the sudden rush of emotion. "Hell, Mira. I hope so. Even if he doesn't come back, if I can at least know he's all right, that will be enough."

She laughed softly. "You won't be okay until he comes back. Just admit it."

He finally chuckled. "You're right. That's what I want. That's what we all want. But how long do I hold onto hope?"

"Forever. You never let it go."

"Forever feels like a long time."

"It is. That's why they call it forever. But in a good way. Hope lasts forever, Chase, and that's the most powerful gift we can give ourselves. Right?"

He looked up at her, his emotions thick in his throat. "Have I told you lately that I love you?"

"Not for at least three minutes, so you're due."

He laughed softly and slid his hand along her jaw. "I love you, Mira. And I'll love you forever."

"See? Forever is good."

"It is in this case, yeah." He leaned in and kissed her, his entire body easing into peace as he tasted her lips. Even after all this time, she still saved him with every single kiss. "I'm the luckiest man in the world."

She smiled. "And I'm the luckiest woman. That makes us quite a pair, huh?"

He finally laughed, lightness working its way back into his heart. "That we are."

There were more shouts from outside, and Mira's eyes danced. "Shall we go say hi, then?"

"Yeah." He took a breath, just as his phone rang. "I'll be right there." As Mira headed off to meet their guests, Chase pulled out his phone to check the screen, as he always did. If it was family, he took the call, no matter what. It was Brody, so he answered it. "What's up?"

"Meet me by the north gate in fifteen minutes. I need to show you something."

Chase frowned as Quintin, Emma, and the others came in the front door. "Quintin just arrived with his family. Can you come here?" He hadn't even realized Brody was in town, but that wasn't unusual for the Harts. The Stocktons had several businesses going with the Harts, so there were usually a few of the Harts around.

"No. This is private."

Brody's tone made Chase sit up. "What's going on? What's wrong?" Brody knew that Chase kept nothing from his family and his brothers, and Brody was the same with his brothers and sisters. So, to tell Chase that it was private set alarm bells ringing.

"I need you to trust me," Brody said. "Meet me there in fifteen minutes. It matters that we keep this off the radar."

Chase swore as he met Quintin's gaze. His brother immediately narrowed his eyes, said something to Emma, and walked over. "What's going on?"

"It's Brody. He wants me to meet him in fifteen minutes."

"Really with that?" Brody sounded resigned. "Do you have any idea what the word 'private' means? Don't tell anyone."

Chase gestured to Quintin, and the two of them exited the room and went into Chase's study. He nodded at Mira, who was watching him, and then he closed the door. He put the phone on speaker. "It's too late now. Quintin knows. What's going on?"

"Hell, Chase. We don't have time for this shit. Meet me at the north gate alone in fifteen minutes. Don't tell anyone you're coming. Got it?"

Chase and Quintin looked at each other. "I'm bringing Quintin."

There was a long silence, and finally Brody spoke. "I get it, Chase, but I think that's a bad idea."

Chase exchanged glances with this brother. "What the hell is going on, Brody?"

"I can't tell you." He swore. "Fine, bring Quintin, but don't tell anyone, don't let anyone follow you, and get over there now." He hung up before Chase could ask any more questions.

Chase fisted the phone in his hand as the study door opened and Mira slipped inside. "What's going on? I know that expression you have on your face. Something's wrong."

He didn't hesitate to bring her in, because Mira was his world, and he never kept anything from her. When he finished, she was frowning. "Well, why are you guys sitting here? Go find out what's going on! Brody is family, and I'm sure he has a valid reason for his request. So get over there!"

Chase grinned. "All right." He looked over at Quintin. "You coming?"

"Hell, yeah. Let me just tell Emma what's going on."

"Sounds good. Meet you in the driveway." Chase grabbed his cowboy hat and keys, kissed his wife and kids, and then headed out the door to meet Brody at the north gate.

CHAPTER THIRTEEN

Nothing looked familiar. Plains. Endless blue sky. Miles of old, barbed wire. Horses grazing, galloping along with the truck as they drove past.

Cowboy country.

This was his world? It didn't look familiar, and Caleb was too tense to decide whether it felt good or not.

He leaned forward, resting his forearms on his thighs as Jenna drove the extra Hart pickup truck down the winding dirt road, following Brody.

Brody had suggested they drive together, but Caleb and Jenna both refused. They needed their own wheels and their own space. Gracie, Zach, and Simba were in the backseat where he could protect them, and they'd already decided that when they arrived, Jenna would stay in the truck, behind the wheel, ready to drive away if the situation wasn't right.

The Harts kept six vehicles at the airport, so it was easy for Jenna and Caleb to get their own.

Jenna pointed. "That must be Chase's truck."

Tension shot through Caleb as he jerked his gaze off the horses and looked ahead. Parked by a gated part of the fence was a massive black pickup truck. He let out his breath. Was his brother in there? And what would happen when he met him? "I wish I knew why I left," he said. "I wish I knew whether I need to go out there prepared to shoot him."

"Don't shoot your own brother," Gracie ordered him. "That's ridiculous."

He managed a tense grin. "I was sort of kidding."

She hit him on the head with Zach's stuffed monkey. "Don't be an idiot, Caleb."

"I'll try, but I can't promise anything. Stop here."

Jenna eased the truck to a halt as Brody pulled up next to the other truck. As Brody and Dylan got out of the Hart truck, the doors to the other vehicle opened. "There are two people in that truck."

His heart began to hammer, and he double-checked that his gun was secure by his hip.

"Holy cow, this is so exciting!" Gracie leaned over the console between them. "I wonder what they're like!"

Caleb's knee was bouncing restlessly as two men in cowboy hats got out of the truck. They were both tall and athletic, but the one on the driver's side was taller. Caleb was too far away to see their faces clearly, but that was fine. It meant they couldn't see him either.

"Do you recognize them?" Jenna asked.

He shook his head. "They look like complete strangers." They walked over to Brody and Dylan and the four men huddled up, talking. He knew Brody wasn't telling Chase about him, because Caleb had told Brody that he wanted to see the expression on Chase's face when he first saw Caleb.

That reaction would tell him whether or not he could trust Chase.

The phone that Brody had loaned to them rang, and Jenna answered it with the steering wheel button. "We're here."

"It's clear," Brody said.

"Who's there?" Caleb asked.

"Chase is the tall one. Quintin is the shorter one. I told Quintin not to come, but these Stocktons are a pain in the ass and do what they want. That's it, though. No one else. It's time."

"Give me a sec."

"Whatever you need." Brody's voice was softer. Understanding.

Jenna hung up the phone and looked over at him. "What do you want to do?"

"Drive closer. I want to be able to see their faces the moment they realize it's me." He looked back at Gracie. "Is there room for me back there? I don't want them to see me through the windshield as we approach."

Gracie's face lit up. "Yeah, sure!" She scooted to the side, and Caleb unstrapped himself, then climbed into the back. By the time he got himself settled between Simba and Zach, both Jenna and Gracie were laughing.

"That was so awkward," Gracie said.

"You're definitely too big to be climbing over seats," Jenna agreed.

"I'm injured. Give me a break." He pulled Simba onto his lap and set his hand on Zach's little foot as the baby gurgled happily. "I think this is the happiest baby I've ever met."

"How would you know?" Jenna asked, still laughing over his relocation efforts.

"Maybe it's the only baby you've ever met," Gracie said with a giggle.

He laughed then, relaxing into their good humor. He liked that the mother-daughter duo could keep a sense of humor even when things got tense. "Could be," he agreed. "Or maybe I work at a day care, and I'm with babies all day."

Gracie and Jenna looked at each other, then burst out

laughing. "That would definitely explain the guns, the explosion, and the stab wound," Jenna agreed.

"For sure," Gracie said. "I've never forgiven my mom for not putting me in a day care like that. Think how badass I'd be, right?"

"You're doing pretty good from what I can see," Caleb said, meaning it. He smiled when he saw Gracie flush with pride.

"Okay, we're here." Jenna pulled the truck up beside the men.

The Stocktons looked toward the truck, frowning at Jenna in the driver's seat.

Caleb knew he was hidden behind the tinted rear windows, so he took his time studying them. Chase and Quintin both looked like the men he'd drawn. Chase had the blue eyes. Quintin was mixed race, with dark brown eyes, but his facial structure was clearly Stockton. Both men were wearing jeans, boots, and cowboy hats. They looked like men of the earth. Strong. Capable. But with no airs. Just solid.

They were both studying Jenna, clearly trying to figure out who she was.

"Just do it, Caleb," Gracie said. "Sometimes you just gotta go for it."

"I have my gun ready," Jenna added. "Just in case you left them because they put a hit out on you or something."

He looked over at her. "You think they put a hit on me?"

She burst out laughing. "No, I don't. Brody would know them better than that, and if they had, he wouldn't have brought you here."

Caleb realized the depth to which he'd trusted Jenna, putting not only his own life but also Zach's in her hands. For a moment, tension shot through him. What was he doing, out here on these Wyoming plains with four men he didn't know? With two kids in the backseat?

Then Jenna looked back at him and smiled with understanding. The moment she did, the doubt left him. He knew he was right to trust her, not just her intentions, but her judgment. "All right. I'm getting out."

He leaned over Gracie and opened her door, so that he was getting out on the far side of the truck. As he did so, Brody had Chase and Quintin turn around, so their backs were to him, as they'd planned.

Gingerly, trying to avoid the stabbing pains in his side and leg, Caleb climbed out past Gracie. The moment his boots thudded down in the dirt, calmness settled over him. He could feel the power of the earth beneath him, steadying him, supporting him. "I don't think I'm a city guy," he said to Jenna and Gracie. "I like how the air smells out here."

They both smiled. "Go meet your brothers," Jenna said.

"Right." It was time. He took one last look at the truck of people who mattered to him, gave Gracie a nod, then shut the door.

He took a breath, then started to limp around the back of the truck toward the men waiting for him.

CHAPTER FOURTEEN

CHASE TENSED when he heard the truck door shut.

He didn't like having his back to a vehicle he didn't know. "It's a good thing I trust you," he muttered to Brody.

"I'm a trustworthy guy. You're a smart man." Brody was standing off to Chase's left, and Chase could see his face.

He watched Brody's eyes, tracking whoever was walking toward them. He could hear the footsteps in the dirt, slightly off, as if their visitor was injured.

Beside him, Quintin stood utterly still, his shoulders back, his head cocked as he listened as well. He met Chase's gaze, and Chase was suddenly very glad that his brother had come with him.

He didn't know what Brody was up to, but it was weird as hell, and out of character for him.

"All right," Brody said. "One at a time. Chase first. Turn around."

Chase glanced at Quintin one more time, then turned to see a tall, muscular man standing in front of him. It took his brain a split second to process who it was, then recognition flooded him. *"Caleb?"* A disbelieving whisper ripped from his throat, and then his legs gave out and he dropped to his knees in shock. He suddenly couldn't breathe. His chest was tight. His throat hurt. His vision blurred. "Is that really you?"

At Caleb's nod, Chase bowed his head, pressing his hands to his eyes, so overwhelmed he couldn't even stand up to go to him, as tears flooded him. He looked up, unable to believe what he was seeing. But it was his brother, standing there, looking at him, alive. There. On the ranch.

"Caleb?" Quintin whirled around, then let out a whoop. "Caleb!" He lunged for their brother to hug him, but Caleb held up his hands and stepped back, out of range.

Alarm shot through Chase the minute he saw Caleb react that way. He recalled his conversation with Mira, how Caleb had once been so gentle and full of love, and then turned hard and cold.

Caleb was still hard. Still cold. *Fuck.* Pain stabbed through Chase's chest, almost devastating in its intensity as he rose to his feet. "Caleb," he said, as softly as he could. "What's wrong?"

He knew there had to be a million things that were wrong, that it was probably the stupidest, most understated question he could ask, but that was the one that came out.

∼

CALEB DIDN'T RECOGNIZE THEM.

The emotion pouring off his brothers was so palpable that he could almost touch it with his hands, but Caleb felt nothing for these men.

He wanted to. God, he wanted to, but there was nothing inside him that answered to these men.

He looked at the men he'd sketched yesterday. Chase was down on his knees. Quintin had retreated back beside Chase after Caleb had instinctively warned him off by stepping back. The two men were practically gaping at him with stunned, heart-wrenching expressions on their faces.

He believed they were his brothers. Their emotions were too raw and authentic.

But he felt nothing for them.

Frustration poured through him. He wanted to remember them. He wanted to feel the connection they felt. Why would he have left this?

Instinctively, he looked back at Jenna. She was his foundation right now, the only connection he actually felt.

Silently, she opened the door and got out of the truck. She walked over to him. "I believe them," she said softly.

He nodded. "I do, too."

"Caleb." Chase's voice was low and rough, drawing his attention back as Jenna came to stand beside Caleb. "How can I help?"

Caleb knew then he had good family. He'd ditched them a decade ago, left them stranded with no word, and their first instinct was to help him. His kind of people. Or were they? Felt like it.

Jenna lightly touched his hand, and he turned his hand to hold onto hers, needing the grounding of contact with her. "Tell them," she said. "Tell them all you know."

Chase frowned. "Tell us what?"

Trust these strangers? With his life and Zach's? And Jenna and Gracie?

He searched their faces for any sign that he was wrong to believe they could be trusted, but he saw nothing but truth and honor. Jenna squeezed his hand, telling him that she also trusted them.

All right.

He took a breath. "I don't remember." His voice caught as he said it, surprising him with his own emotions.

Jenna squeezed his hand again, grounding him as Chase frowned. "Don't remember what?"

"You. Him." He gestured to Quintin. "This place." He swung his hand to encompass the ranch. "My name."

Chase blinked. "Your name? What do you mean?"

Caleb met his gaze. "Brody found me. Told me I was Caleb Stockton. Said you were my brothers. But I don't remember anything before the day before yesterday. Every single thing is gone."

∽

CHASE STARED at his brother in shock, stunned by the revelations. The most important thing in the entire world to the Stocktons was each other. Their family. Their identity as siblings who stood by each other unconditionally. The love that bound them together, no matter what.

And Caleb had lost all of that? Every last bit?

It was *devastating*.

For the first time in a long time, Chase wanted to cry. He wanted to give up. They'd fought through so much together, and now, to have lost the most important thing, their connection, was almost too much. He had his brother back...and yet he didn't.

The man standing before him knew him only as a *stranger*.

It was agonizing. Crushing.

But Chase didn't give in to the desolation threatening to take him.

Because, as Mira had said earlier, he was the oldest brother, the one who always held everyone together.

So instead of reeling in the anguish of the loss, Chase raised his chin, forcing confidence into his voice. "It'll be all right, Caleb. We'll figure it out."

Caleb met his gaze. "Why did I leave?"

Chase frowned. "Leave the ranch?"

Caleb nodded. "Yeah. The ranch, you." He gestured to Quintin. "You. The others. Why did I leave? You seem like good people. Why would I leave?"

Chase let out his breath. He might not know what had happened when Caleb was fourteen that had changed him, but he knew exactly what their childhood and their dad had been like, which had driven all the brothers away.

Suddenly, he realized that Caleb losing his past might be a gift. If Caleb didn't remember the hell they'd grown up in, maybe he could be the brother who truly became free.

If Caleb regained his memory and reconnected with his brothers, he would also remember the nightmares that still haunted them all.

Suddenly, Chase didn't know what he wanted for his brother anymore.

"Chase? Why did I leave?"

Chase looked at Quintin. He could tell from the expression on Quintin's face that he was thinking the same thing. Could Caleb become truly free to be the good, kind, gentle person that he'd been meant to be, before life had ripped that peace from him?

Quintin shrugged his shoulders once, clearly unsure what to tell Caleb.

Chase didn't know either.

Hell.

CHAPTER FIFTEEN

JENNA SAW the tension in Chase's face the minute Caleb asked him why he left.

Chase knew the answer. Maybe not every detail, but he knew enough.

She was sure of it.

But from the glance he exchanged with Quintin, she knew the men didn't want to tell Caleb.

The obvious intensity of emotion between the brothers was staggering, so the loss of connection from Caleb's side made her want to cry. She lifted her chin, refusing to succumb. Danny's death had taught her to rein her emotions in tightly, and she fought to hold onto them now, to keep the even keel that had kept her going.

The three men were reeling in emotion right now, which was a little funny, since men were supposed to be the emotionally strong ones. As the woman, it was apparently her job to keep everyone on track and rising above the emotions that were obscuring critical issues.

"Clearly, there is a lot about Caleb's relationship with you guys that needs to be sorted out," she said. "But we have a pressing situation that has to be managed, or you won't have the time to figure everything personal out."

All three Stockton brothers looked over at her, as if she'd poked a hot rod into their bubble of emotions.

It struck her as so funny that she almost started laughing. But, being the consummate professional she was, she kept her expression neutral. "Someone is hunting Caleb and the baby that his friend gave him. We need to figure out who it is and stop them before they kill both Zach and Caleb."

The expressions of raw protectiveness that came over Chase's and Quintin were literally the sweetest thing Jenna had ever seen. It reminded her of when she'd had Danny, and how he'd been her protector.

Before everything had fallen apart, of course.

She'd forgotten what it was like to have someone else be the strong one. She was suddenly so grateful that Caleb had come home. That he had the chance to reconnect with people who cared so much.

Chase looked sharply at Caleb. "What's going on?"

As Caleb started to fill Chase and Quintin in on what little he knew, Jenna turned and headed back toward the truck. She opened the back door to check on Zach, who was sucking on a bottle that Gracie had made for him.

Simba climbed over Zach and gave Jenna a tail-wagging welcome, which made her heart warm. She smiled at her daughter as she snuggled Simba. "You're doing great with Zach."

"Thanks." Gracie grinned, then nodded toward the Stocktons. "They're really his brothers, don't you think?"

"I do." She leaned in and wiped some milk off Zach's chin. "They really seem to love him."

"That's what I thought." Gracie was chewing her lip, a sign that Jenna recognized as an indication that her daughter was trying to get up the courage to say something.

"What's up?"

"Why would he leave them? Without saying good-bye?"

Ah... Jenna glanced over at the cowboys. They were standing closer now, in deep discussion. "I don't know. I'm guessing he had a good reason."

"Well, he's not dead, so what other reason is good enough to justify leaving them? And without saying good-bye?"

Jenna sighed. "I don't know, baby."

"You told me not to trust Caleb. I didn't believe you. But he already said he'd leave without saying good-bye if he had to, right? And he already did it once in real life."

Jenna leaned across Zach and took her daughter's hand. "Baby, Daddy would have said good-bye if he could have. He didn't know what was going to happen when he went on that case."

"But he didn't say good-bye. He just walked out the door, talking on the phone. He didn't say good-bye, and then he didn't come back." Tears were bright in Gracie's eyes, making Jenna's throat tighten.

Because Danny hadn't said good-bye to her that day either. He hadn't said good-bye for a long time, but Gracie hadn't known that. They'd hidden from Gracie how tough things had become. She'd never told Gracie about the text messages she'd seen on his phone. The work they'd been putting in trying to rebuild a trust that she hadn't been able to get back.

"He loved you," she said instead. "With every fiber of his being." Which was why he'd stayed. Why he'd agreed to end the affair. Because of Gracie.

Tears filled Gracie's eyes. "I always believed you, but when I see how much Caleb's brothers love him, and then he left without saying good-bye...well, maybe Caleb didn't love them back. Maybe Dad didn't actually love me back." She stared at Jenna. "Maybe Dad didn't love you back either."

Oh, God. The words were too close to home, to a truth she'd had to face the day she found those text messages. "Gracie, I promise you with all my heart that Dad loved you more than anything. He truly did."

Gracie searched her face, but this time, for the first time, Jenna saw doubt in her eyes. She glanced at Caleb, who was still huddled up with his brothers. She'd thought Caleb was going to heal them, but instead, he'd broken the one whole piece that had remained of her daughter. "Maybe it's time to go."

Gracie's eyes widened. "Leave Caleb?"

"Yes."

They both looked over at him. "I don't want to," Gracie whispered, tightening her fingers around Jenna's.

"I know. Me either. But maybe it's time for us to take control." Or maybe she was simply being a wimp, afraid to trust again, especially a man who didn't even know his own secrets.

The only reason to believe in Caleb was if she trusted her gut. Caleb could produce nothing to show he was trustworthy, except who he was in that moment. Her gut told her to hang on tight to him, to give him every chance, but what if she was wrong?

"What if he used to be a bad guy, but now that he's forgotten, he can be the guy we see?" Gracie whispered, hope etched in her voice.

She and Gracie looked at each other, and she saw the angst in her daughter's eyes. Pain that her daughter had hidden from her for so long. The discussion was painful, but it was her daughter's truth, and she was finally sharing it. So, maybe Caleb was healing them, even if it was hard.

But what if they stayed, he remembered who he was, and then he became that guy again? The guy who had abandoned a family who loved him?

Dammit.

"He's coming back," Gracie whispered as Simba climbed back onto her lap. She wrapped her arms around the dog and rested her chin on Simba's soft head, the little dog giving her comfort.

Jenna stiffened as Caleb headed toward them, and the other men dispersed toward their trucks.

She and Gracie were finally rebuilding their relationship, and that was all she wanted. What was best for her daughter? For their relationship? Because it wasn't about herself. It could never be about her.

As Caleb approached, Jenna felt little fingers close around her thumb. She looked down and saw Zach gripping her tightly. She'd promised Caleb that if anything happened to him, that she'd take care of Zach. Make sure he was safe. If she left Caleb, then she broke that promise to Zach.

Crap.

"They're going to help." Caleb walked up and rested one arm on the doorframe. His tall frame was blocking the afternoon sun, as if he were physically shielding them. "We decided—" He cut himself off as he glanced at Gracie's face, and then Jenna's "What's wrong?"

Jenna met Gracie's worried gaze, then took a breath and looked at Caleb. Her breath caught at the concerned expression on his face. He was so handsome. So strong. So caring. Right now, he wasn't the man who would walk away from his family. She was sure of that. But this man wasn't who he really was. Who would he be when he remembered his past? She wouldn't take that chance again, not for herself, and not for her daughter. "That's great they'll help you."

He nodded slowly, watching her. "Chase has a house he just finished building on his property. He was going to use it for the Harts when they visit, but we can stay there."

"Together?"

He nodded slowly, frowning as he looked back and forth between them. "It's a five bedroom. Plenty of room for all. Great sightlines to know if anyone is coming. All security measures have been installed. It sounds great, but I'll need to check it out first. I'm pretty sure I'm an expert in security stuff, but we'll see."

Jenna looked over at Gracie, and she saw the longing and the worry on her daughter's face. Gracie wanted to go to that house. Desperately. Too desperately. She couldn't put her daughter through loss again, and she had already become so attached to Caleb. Of course, Jenna didn't know for sure that it *wouldn't* work with Caleb, and if it wasn't for Gracie, she'd be all-in on the adventure and the spark that Caleb lit inside her.

But Jenna was a mom first, and that meant she had to think of her daughter before herself. No matter what the cost. "They'll protect Zach if something happens to you?" She had to ask that first, to make sure the baby she already loved would be safe.

He frowned. "I didn't ask them that specifically, but yeah, I believe they would."

"Great." She looked at Gracie, and her throat ached at the tears shimmering in her daughter's eyes, because Gracie already knew what she was going to do, what she had to do. "Then Gracie and I will be on our way. You guys are all set, so we need to get back to our life." She stared at Zach's little fist, wrapped around her thumb. "If you can ride back with one of your brothers, we'll take the truck to the airport. Good luck with everything."

CHAPTER SIXTEEN

CALEB FELT like he'd just been kicked in the gut. He fought to control the sudden panic rising in him. "You're *leaving?*"

"Yeah." Jenna wouldn't look at him, and neither would Gracie. "We need to go."

"Why?"

"It's time." She scooted away from him and flagged down Brody as he was driving past.

The cowboy pulled over and rolled down his window. "What's up?"

"Gracie and I are going to leave. Can we take your truck to the airport and leave it there—"

Caleb interrupted before Jenna could finish. "Give us a sec, Brody."

The cowboy raised his brows. "You bet. We'll wait over here for you guys to sort it out." He caught Caleb's gaze, and gave him a hard look that was very clear in its message. *Don't let them go.*

Yeah, he heard that message loud and clear, because it was coming from his own gut.

As Brody drove away, Jenna turned back to him. "What?"

"Why do you suddenly need to leave? I thought we agreed it was safest for us to stay together." He didn't bother to bring up the fact he was paying her, because he already knew enough about Jenna that she'd never make a choice solely based on money.

She hesitated, then glanced back at Gracie.

Her daughter had tears shimmering in her eyes as she watched them.

Son of a bitch.

What the hell was going on? "Gracie? Do you mind if I steal your mom to chat with her for a sec?"

Silently, Gracie shook her head, her big brown eyes wide and vulnerable.

"Great. We'll be right over here." He took Jenna's hand, but she immediately pulled away.

Caleb ground his jaw and let her walk ahead of him. Up ahead, the two pick-up trucks idled, waiting for them. He liked that feeling of having those men there. Of having a team at his back.

He was a team player? Good to know.

Jenna stopped about fifty feet from the truck and turned to face him. She was facing the truck, probably so she could keep an eye on Gracie and Zach. "What is it?"

He took a breath, trying to find the words that would strip away the shield that she'd thrown up between them while he'd been talking to his brothers. "What changed?"

She blinked. "What?"

"When I got out of the truck, we were in this together. When I came back, you're on your way out. What changed?"

Emotion flickered in her eyes, but she raised her chin. "Caleb—"

"No." He cut her off, reading her body language. "I want the truth. Hell, Jenna, you're the only one I have right now who I trust. Tell me what's going on."

She stared at him, and then her shoulders sagged, and all the defiance left her body. She looked weary, exhausted, and vulnerable, which made him want to sweep her up in his arms and swear to protect her and take away her fears.

"Before Danny died," she said quietly. "Things weren't great between us. He'd been having an affair."

Shit. "I'm sorry."

"I was completely blindsided. I loved him with all my heart, and he'd always made me feel special." She shrugged with a dismissal he didn't quite believe. "We were trying to rebuild our relationship, but it wasn't working. Things were tense, but we were trying to hide it from Gracie."

"Does Gracie know?"

She shook her head quickly. "She has no idea. But she did notice he wasn't around as much, and when he was, he was distracted. They had always been so close, and she tried to get his attention, but he just wasn't there for her."

Caleb could hear the tightly controlled emotion in Jenna's voice. The anger. The hurt. The worry for her daughter. He felt the same way. "Gracie's an awesome kid."

A smile flickered across Jenna's face. "I know she is. He did, too. He was just...going through things."

Caleb thought that was a little generous. The bastard had been cheating on his wife and abandoning his family. "There's no excuse for what he did." He couldn't keep the tension out of his voice. "Family is everything, no matter what. It's all that matters."

Jenna met his gaze. "But you left yours."

Guilt shot through him. "I know. I could see the pain it caused my brothers." He spread his hands helplessly. "I don't know why I did it. I can't imagine a reason good enough for it."

Jenna bit her lip. "When Danny left the house for his last business trip, he was on his phone. Gracie shouted good-bye to him, but he didn't hear her. He just walked out the door without saying good-bye, without even acknowledging her. I knew that he didn't mean it that way, but it broke her little heart. And then he died and never came back."

Caleb swore under his breath, imagining that scenario. "Poor Gracie." And he also felt Jenna's pain, because Danny clearly hadn't said good-bye to her either. He'd abandoned them in life, and then in death.

Jenna nodded. "Gracie loves you, Caleb. She's already fallen for you. But when she saw the reaction of your brothers to you, how much they loved you, and then she realized that you'd abandoned them just like Danny had abandoned her... It scared her." She met his gaze. "It scared me, too. Gracie can't go through that again, and neither can I."

Caleb rubbed his jaw. What kind of bastard was he? "Jenna—"

She held up her hand. "I know that we barely know each other. I know that this might not lead to anything. But there's a bond there that already holds us together."

He nodded. "There is."

"So, if we stay, it gets tighter. And it will break her...and maybe me...if you become the man you once were and walk away again. From your family. From us. I get it if things simply don't work out, but if you were to walk away the way you apparently did to your brothers..."

"Without saying good-bye," he finished. Now he understood Gracie's fixation on him leaving without saying good-bye.

She met his gaze. "We were abandoned once. And that's what you did."

Was that really who he was? Was he the bastard that he'd called Danny? It sure seemed like it. Caleb let out his breath. "I can't defend what I did, because I have no idea why I did it. But from where I stand today, there's no reason good enough for what I did." He met her gaze. "I would never do that now. Not to you. Not to them."

"But what if you remember and become him again?"

He fought to choose the right words. "Remembering who I once was won't make me forget who I am now."

The corner of her mouth quirked up. "That's a good line right there."

"Right? I thought it was." Relief rushed through him at her little quip, making him realize how desperate he was to make her stay.

She was right. They didn't know each other well at all. But she was also right that they had a bond. Jenna and Gracie were already in his heart. Jenna's kindness. Her warmth. Her loyalty. Her strength. Her courage. And Gracie...the kid was a treasure. He knew he'd been meant to find them.

They were meant to be his. He was meant to be theirs. He just knew it, deep in his gut.

He was glad to know about Danny, to understand more of what drove them. It helped him clarify the man he needed to be for them. "Jenna." He held out his hand for her.

She stared at his hand for a long time. "I want to take your hand," she said softly. "But I can't."

He dropped his hand. "Losing my past and my identity has given me the chance to define who I am without any baggage."

She chewed her lower lip, watching him. Listening.

"I don't give a shit who I was. What I did before. I know who I am today, and that's a man that would never let down you and Gracie. I won't let that happen."

Hope flickered in her eyes. "You told Gracie that you couldn't promise that you'd say good-bye. That if things got dangerous and you had to leave, you would do it. You're still in danger, Caleb. No matter who you want to be, your past will find you. It's hunting you right now. It's just a matter of when, and what happens when it does."

She was right. No matter what he wanted to promise Gracie and Jenna, he would leave in an instant if that would keep them safe. But it didn't have to be the whole picture. "Hang on." He gestured to Brody, who put the truck in reverse and backed up until he reached them.

The cowboy lowered the window. "What's up?"

He addressed his question to Dylan, who was the high-tech private investigator. "Can you get me three untraceable phones? I want to give one to Gracie, one to Jenna, and one to myself, so that they can reach me at any time, no matter what, without endangering them. Can you get that for me?"

Dylan raised his brows. "I can have that for you by tomorrow morning."

"Great." Caleb looked at Jenna. "I might have to leave unexpectedly to keep you safe, but the good-bye won't have to happen. We'll be able to stay in touch."

She bit her lower lip, and he could see her wavering.

He turned toward her and took her hand. "Jenna," he said softly. "It hasn't changed that you're a target, even if we separate. I need you and Gracie to stay with me to keep you safe. If you want to stay as business only, I'll respect that. Whatever you need. But I can't let you and Gracie leave until it's safe."

She didn't pull away from him this time. "I can make the choice to keep it professional between us, but Gracie can't. If you try to keep a distance from her, it'll just hurt her."

Caleb was losing her. He could tell. Panic started to hit him. He needed more time with her. With them. "Jenna—"

Brody cleared his throat. "Can I jump in here?"

They both looked over at him. He was leaning across the seat toward them, one arm on the steering wheel. He grinned. "We grew up as homeless kids under a bridge," he said. "We were always in danger, but we survived because we stuck together and protected each other."

Caleb raised his brows. He hadn't heard that about them. "Really?"

"Yeah." He was focused on Jenna. "When the shit gets tough, you have to hold onto people you trust and let them help you."

"I don't want to hurt Gracie—"

"Caleb's a good guy. Gracie needs him, and so do you. I can see it in the way you guys look at him, and how he looks at you. We never know how long people are in our lives, but when we find good ones, it's our job to go all-in and hold onto that gift for as long as we have it. Living in fear is bullshit, Jenna. It's not going to get you anywhere good."

Jenna sighed. "That was an even better speech than Caleb's."

Brody grinned. "When I saw you drive up on that ATV, you were literally sparkling with energy. You were *alive*. Honestly, I've never seen you like that before. You really want to walk away from the chance to live again? Because if you run now, you'll always regret not trying." His eyes darkened. "Trust me. I know this."

"Here's the question," Dylan added, leaning on the door frame. "Do you trust Caleb? If you look past that noise and the bullshit, do you trust who he is on the most basic level?"

Jenna looked at Caleb, and silently nodded. "I do."

Dylan shrugged. "Then that's all you need to know." Then he grinned. "Plus, he's a Stockton. Being good people is in their DNA—"

"Mom?"

They all spun around to find Gracie standing behind them, holding Zach in her arms, Simba sitting by her ankle.

Jenna caught her breath, as they realized Gracie had been listening. "Gracie—"

"I'm not afraid. I want to stay."

Caleb turned to face Gracie and went down on his knees so that she was taller than he was. "Gracie, I don't know who is after me, and if staying with you puts you in danger, I'm going to draw that danger away from you by making them target me. I'm going to keep you safe, even if it means leaving."

She nodded, meeting his gaze. "I understand."

He put his hand over his heart. "But you're right here already. In my heart. And I will fight like hell to never leave, and to come back if I have to go. And to say good-bye if I can." It wasn't the promise he wanted to make, but his past was an unknown that couldn't be underestimated.

"I heard you ask Dylan for the phone." Gracie raised her chin. "I want that phone."

"I'll have it by morning," Dylan said.

Gracie nodded, then looked to her mom. "They need us, you know. Zach and Caleb need us. I want to help them. I know he might have to leave, and I'm okay with that. Can we stay?"

Caleb and the two Hart brothers all turned to look at Jenna.

She looked around at them, and then started laughing. "You guys all look like injured puppy dogs. I don't think I've ever seen three more pathetic expressions in my life."

Caleb grinned. "Did it work?"

She sighed. "Tall, dark, and handsome cowboys have no impact on my decision-making, but my favorite daughter does."

Gracie smiled. "I'm your only daughter."

"And that's a good thing, because if I had more than one, you'd still be my favorite, and wouldn't that be sad for the others?"

"It would," Gracie said with a grin. "So, we're staying?"

Jenna put her hands on her hips. "I'm doubling my fee."

Relief rushed through Caleb. *They were staying.* "Why?" Not that he cared why. He'd pay it. He was already planning to give her all the money in the bag, as soon as he figured out where his own money was.

"Because I'm going to leverage your guilt into more money to support myself and my adorable kid." She gave him an innocent smile. "I mean, the situation is dangerous, so I have to up my hazard fee. That's what I meant. I'd never try to use your personal attachment to my well-being to squeeze more money from your wallet."

"Perfect. Because I never do anything out of guilt."

Jenna raised her brows. "Or maybe you do. Who knows, right?"

He grinned. "Right."

Gracie looked up at her. "Is that a yes?"

Jenna smiled. "Yes, it's a yes."

"Yay!" Gracie broke into a huge grin, and hugged her mom, squishing Zach between them. When the baby started to howl in protest, she handed him off to Caleb, then hugged her mom again.

While Caleb tucked the baby against his chest, he met Brody's gaze. He saw the weight in them, and he knew that Brody was thinking the same thing he was: he couldn't let them down.

No matter what happened.

No matter who he turned out to be.

He couldn't let them down.

CHAPTER SEVENTEEN

JENNA LEANED against the door frame, watching her daughter sleep in the biggest bed, and nicest bedroom, that she'd ever been in.

It was seven in the evening, too early for bedtime, but Gracie had crashed as soon as they'd settled into Chase's extra house.

Zach was also asleep in a nursery that Chase and Quintin had put together in record time, assembling baby gear from the other Stocktons.

They'd agreed not to tell any of the other Stocktons that Caleb was back, due to the danger hunting him. Caleb had said he wanted to figure out more about the danger he was bringing before exposing anyone else. The more people who knew he was there, the more likely that the folks hunting him would hear about it.

But Jenna knew that wasn't the reason.

The reason Caleb had delayed meeting the rest of his family was because he wasn't ready.

She'd felt his tension the moment Chase and Quintin had met them at the house. There was awkwardness between the three men. Strangers who had once been brothers. Stilted conversation where there had, presumably, once been the natural flow between siblings.

"Jenna." His hands slid over her shoulders.

She knew she should push him away, but his touch felt too good. She closed her eyes, absorbing the warmth of his touch. "I like that," she whispered.

"Like what?"

"You touching me. It's been a long time."

She heard his low chuckle as he continued to rub her shoulders. "Gracie asleep?"

"Yep."

"Zach, too." He was quiet for a moment as he continued to rub her shoulders. "Thanks for staying. I need you guys with me."

She smiled. "That's what Gracie said. She'll be happy to know she was right."

"I mean it." He kept up with the massage, which was beginning to unwind the tension she'd been holding so long. "How are you doing?"

She smiled at his question. Danny had never asked her how she was doing. Or if he had, it hadn't been for many years. So maybe things hadn't been as all right as she'd thought. Or maybe her needs had changed. "I'm fine."

"Fine?" Caleb laughed softly. "That's not an answer."

"Of course it is. That's what women say when they don't mean it, and they don't want to discuss it. It's a pretty great answer actually."

He grasped her shoulders and turned her to face him. Her breath caught at how close he was. She could practically feel the heat from his body. She could see the flecks of gray in his blue eyes. She could catch the faint scent of the shampoo that he'd used so many hours ago when they were back at her grandmother's small cabin. "What can I do to help you actually feel fine?"

She smiled. "You're very focused, aren't you?"

"Maybe." Caleb slid his hand along her jawline. "Or maybe it's just with you." He met her gaze. "I'm drawn to you, Jenna. I can't stop myself, and I don't want to."

She swallowed, her heart starting to race. "We don't even know who you are, Caleb."

"I know." His gaze went to her mouth. "Chase and Quintin are coming by after they have dinner with their families. I think we'll learn a lot more about who I am. So, this might be our last moment without the past dancing with us."

"Dancing?"

"Yeah. I bet I can dance. Can you?"

She laughed as he slid his arm around her lower back and pulled her against him. "I haven't danced in a long time."

"I think I danced two days ago, but maybe I dreamed it." He began to sing softly, his voice melodic and beautiful. "Dance with me, pretty lady, for our last moment before the dark truth is revealed."

She laughed and surrendered to him, letting him sweep her away from Gracie's room and down the hall. He moved as well as he sang, his body rhythmic and agile. He was a wonderful leader, using his body and the lightest touch of his hands to guide her. His voice seemed to wrap around her, lightening her heart, making her forget the weight she always seemed to carry.

He danced her into Zach's room, where they both peeked in at the sleeping baby. "He looks so much better sleeping in an actual crib instead of on a couch," she said.

"Hey," Caleb said as he spun her back into the hallway. "That was my chest he was on. It's a great chest for sleeping. You should try it."

She laughed as they bumped into the doorway, and she fell

into him. "You did that on purpose, so I'd fall onto that manly chest of yours."

He winked at her. "Did I? Maybe I'm devious like that. I'm a mystery of the best kind."

"Are you?" She laughed out loud as he twirled her. "Maybe you're the worst kind."

He spun her so that she ended up against his chest, locked in his arms, her face inches from him. "I'm pretty sure I'm a great guy."

Her breath caught when she realized he wasn't going to let her go. "Just pretty sure?"

"Yeah. About eighty-two percent sure. That's good enough for a kiss, right? I mean, that's a B-minus."

"I kiss only A-plus guys."

"Well, awesome. Since you already kissed me, then you must know more than I do about my worthiness. So, yeah, I'm an A-plus kind of guy then, because I trust your judgment implicitly."

She giggled. "I think you're a dork."

"I might be." He grinned wickedly. "So, this dorky guy really wants to kiss this badass private detective single mom. Does he have a chance?"

She tried to look imposing. "No, not at all."

He immediately put on a crestfallen expression that made her laugh out loud. "Why not?" he asked.

"Because the badass single mom is afraid she forgot how to kiss and is consequently sort of terrified of kissing the dorky guy who is actually super hot."

A slow grin spread across his face. "I might not know how to kiss either. But we did okay last time, so let's try again. What do you say? No judging allowed."

She took a breath, well aware that both kids were asleep, and there was nothing to stop them if the kiss was as good as last time. "I'm not giving you my heart."

He nodded. "I can't make the same promise, but I'm okay with you being however you need to be." He slid his hands in her hair. "Jenna," he whispered, all traces of amusement gone. "You're my anchor."

Her throat tightened. "Kiss me before I run away."

A smile flashed across his face. "Yes, ma'am." He didn't give her the chance to run. He just bent his head and kissed her.

His kiss was tender, but electric. Need exploded through her, a desire that seemed to come alive of its own volition, calling for *him*. Not for *a* kiss. Not for *a* man. But for *his* kiss. For *his* touch. For *him*.

The kindness that was such a part of who he was filled the kiss with a magic that she'd never experienced before. Danny had been charming and funny. Dangerous. But never *kind*.

And she loved that about Caleb. She loved how he'd gone down to his knees when he was talking to Gracie. She loved how he was so gentle and adorable with Zach and Simba. And she appreciated his pain when he saw how his leaving had hurt his brothers.

She was falling hard for this man she barely knew, and that was making the kiss a thousand times more intense, more magical, more beautiful. With a deep sigh, she surrendered to her need for him. The moment she slid her arms around his neck and leaned into him, she felt an answering surrender from him.

His arms tightened around her, he deepened the kiss, and he leaned into her, drawing her into the muscled strength of his body.

He was quite a bit taller than she was, much broader, and so much stronger, making her feel tiny and safe in his arms. Safe to relax. Safe to trust. Safe to stop holding back.

The kiss quickly grew hotter and more intense. She palmed his chest, and felt the muscles tense under her touch.

As he kissed her, he slid his hands down her back and cupped her butt, making need coil within her.

She slipped her hand between the buttons on his shirt, and he sucked in his breath when her bare fingers touched his chest. She laughed between the kisses. "I feel like a teenager in her first make out session."

"That's pretty much what it is for me." With only a little grunt of pain, he swept her up in his arms, cradling her against his chest. "I literally don't remember kissing a single woman in my life. You're my first."

She laughed as he carried her into the master bedroom, giggling as he kicked the door shut behind them and locked it.

CHAPTER EIGHTEEN

JENNA FELT SO decadent and free.

They were so close to Gracie and Zach that they'd hear either one of them if the kids needed help, but with the locked door, they were also gloriously, dangerously alone. "We're not having sex with Gracie next door." Right? Wasn't that what good moms were supposed to do? Sacrifice themselves for the imagined good of their kids?

"Totally fine. I can't lose my virginity to a woman who doesn't love me." Keeping his voice low so they wouldn't be overheard, Caleb gently tossed her on the bed, then pretended to dive next to her. "But if you did love me, then we could have sex. I mean, I can try, but since you're my first, I have no idea if I'm any good."

She laughed as he pulled her shirt up and spread his palms across her belly. "I'd guess you're very good." She also kept her voice quiet, which made the moment feel even more decadent and glorious.

"Really? Why do you say that?" He pressed a kiss to her belly button, and then began to work his way across her stomach.

She released a shaking breath. "Because you're very sexy, really hot, and you kiss like the devil himself came down to this moment to sweep me away."

Caleb lifted his head to look at her, a wicked gleam in his eyes. "Damn. I like that. I accept. I'm the devil when it comes to the bedroom. Should we see what I can do?"

She burst out laughing as he buried his face in her stomach and growled. "No," she gasped between muffled giggles. "I think we should just be friends."

"Friends? Yep. I'm good with that." He rolled on top of her, his hips pinning her to the bed. "You're my only friend anyway. And my only lover. And my only business partner."

Heat coiled in her belly. "I'm not your lover."

"We can work on that." He then lowered himself on top of her and kissed her again. As hot as the kisses in the hall had been, it was nothing compared to the pure sensuality of this kiss. He was seduction, desire, tenderness, and mystery all wrapped in one set of decadent lips.

He slid his fingers around her wrist in a caress, not an imprisonment, drawing her into his web of magic with one kiss after another.

Kissing Caleb was so incredible. She'd never been kissed the way Caleb was kissing her. She'd never felt so special, so treasured, so safe, so ready to laugh with joy.

And she loved that he couldn't remember ever being with anyone else.

For Caleb, she was his first. There was no baggage in his past obscuring their moment. There were no shadows of other women. No fractures on his heart. Just her. She was all that he knew, all who he'd kissed, the only one who drove him.

She loved that. Loved that so much.

He could be the purity in their kiss that she couldn't

bring, because she still carried her own shadows, fears, and fractures.

Caleb paused and pulled back, his beautiful eyes searching hers. "What's going on in that beautiful mind of yours, Jenna?"

She smiled and brushed her fingers over his jaw. "I'm a little envious that you get to kiss me without any shadows from your past dancing around the edges of our kiss."

His smile faded. "I'm envious that you know who you are, but the truth is that this moment is what it is. We can't change it. I can't change the fact that I'm living in a brand-new world, and you can't change the past that has made you who you are. So all we can do is embrace it."

She nodded. "You're right." She managed a smile. "I'm not the best at accepting who I am."

"Let me help." He began to nibble her earlobe. "You went through hell with Danny, but somehow managed to raise a great kid, have a successful career, and have the courage to help a stray guy and his temporary baby when they needed it." He pulled back, meeting her gaze. "You're kind. You're quick with humor that lightens the moment when things get too heavy. You have the warmest smile, and your kid looks at you like you're her entire world. The light shines from you both, irreverent, irresistible, and incredibly beautiful."

Tears filled her eyes. "That's how you see me?"

"It is." He bent his head and kissed her, a kiss that seemed to fill the heart that she'd shut down so long ago.

"How can I feel this way about you?" she whispered. "It's so fast."

He pulled back. "Are you scared?"

She nodded.

"Me, too." He framed her face with his hands. "I don't know what's going to happen when Chase and Quintin get here. What I'm going to find out. But I'm pretty sure there's a lot I'm not going to like, given what we know about choices I've made." He rubbed his fingers over her cheeks. "A part of me wants to go back to your cabin with you all and just be there. Because you guys feel good." He smiled. "Especially you, Jenna. You feel good to me."

She nodded, biting her lip. "That's how it feels with you."

He gave her a half smile. "You might decide you hate me in a couple hours."

She could hear the tension in his voice, and she knew he was legitimately aware that ugly things could come out when they began to unravel his past. "As long as you're the man you are now, I'm okay with whatever happened before."

He met her gaze. "You don't know that."

She put her hands on his shoulders. "Kiss me, Caleb. This is our moment. The calm before the storm, if you will. Just kiss me, and let's breathe in this gift we have."

He searched her face, but they both knew there was nothing more they could say, no promises they could make, not until they had more information.

Silently, acknowledging the truth that held so much power, but silently agreeing to set it aside, Caleb kissed her again.

Jenna wrapped her arms around his neck and held him close, kissing him back with sudden desperation. She was scared of what was coming for them, for him. She'd already been through enough trauma and loss.

It made her wary, but it also made her realize that they owed it to themselves not to run away, but to embrace the gift they had in this moment, in each other, in the kindness, the romance, and the bond.

Caleb seemed to feel the same drive to embrace this chance they had, because the kiss suddenly became so much hotter and more intense. Visceral. Hands moving across each other's bodies. Lips moving. Suddenly, her shirt was off, on the floor next to his.

She couldn't help but giggle. "You're literally like a perfect male specimen." She lightly bumped her fist on his abs. "You have like a ten pack here."

He caught her hand. "Careful. I'm pretty sure I was stabbed recently."

Embarrassment flooded her cheeks as she glanced at the bandage on his side. "I'm so sorry. I totally forgot."

He laughed and rolled her onto her side. "I love the fact that my kisses were so astounding that it made you forget I'm hurt. I'm taking that as a win." Then he proceeded to show her exactly how okay he was with it.

Layer by layer, their clothes hit the floor, until there was nothing but skin between them. Jenna closed her eyes, basking in the feel of their bodies against each other. It felt so unbelievably good to be in his arms, having his hands moving across her body as if she were the greatest gift he'd ever experienced.

"Jenna." He moved over her and kissed her again, deep, powerful, claiming.

She almost whimpered as he worked his way down her body, kissing her ribs, her breasts, her belly, her thighs, and then—

She gasped and arched her back as his tongue worked sudden and delicious magic on the parts of her that had seen no action for years. Decades? Centuries? The way he was stoking desire in her made her feel like it had been a thousand years since she'd been so alive.

Her fingers curled into the pillows, and she had to bite her lip to keep quiet as ripples of need shuddered through her. Her hips moved and bucked, inviting him, teasing him.

When he wrapped his arms around her thighs, holding

her still, it felt so delicious and glorious, freeing her to push against him.

Her body quivered, teetering on the precipice, when he suddenly stopped. "I want to make love to you," he said.

"God, yes," she said, almost laughing. "Please? Should I beg? Would that be uncool?"

He laughed. "We'll both beg." He scooted to the edge of the bed. "I hope Chase planned ahead for possible shenanigans happening in this room, because there's no way I'm making love to you without a condom. I mean, I'm pretty sure I'm a virgin, but a man never really knows these things."

Her heart turned over as she watched him pull out the nightstand drawer. The heat between them was electric, and the need coiling in her was almost crazy. She was sure he was feeling the same thing, so the fact that he was going to put a dead stop on the activities if he couldn't keep her safe said all she needed to know about who he was.

He grinned and held up a box. "My brother gets a gold star."

She laughed, as a fresh surge of desire rushed through her. "He sure does." She took the box. "I'll do the honors. You're injured. I don't want to tax you." She lightly pushed him onto his back, and he went willingly, amusement and heat dancing in his eyes.

As Jenna opened the box and tore the wrapper, she couldn't help but smile. There was no way that Caleb would let her push him back unless he decided it was where he wanted to be. He was a wall of solid muscle, and she'd noticed the numerous scars decorating his skin. Some small. Some bigger. But enough to tell her that his body held many secrets that weren't pretty.

His eyes were dark and hooded as she unrolled the condom, watching her with unabashed desire. The moment she had it in place, he grabbed her and pulled her down for a tantalizing, decadent kiss. She straddled him, basking in the feel of their bodies against each other, hot, sweaty, and intimate.

He caught her hips and lifted her, and they locked gazes as she settled on him, a slow, languid entry that had both of them sucking in their breath to contain their reactions.

They couldn't be loud, but they could connect with whispers and muffled laughter. With secret words of tenderness and need. She loved the way he whispered her name as she settled deeper on him, as his fingers added to the symphony building between them. She gasped and leaned back, resting her hands on his corded thighs as an orgasm suddenly exploded through her.

Caleb grasped her hips, holding her steady as he bucked beneath her, relinquishing his control to coincide with hers. As the orgasms exploded through them, they held tightly to each other, riding out the glorious storm together.

As one, in this moment before everything changed.

Because it would.

Within an hour. Maybe two.

Would it all shatter and fall apart?

Or would the truth bring them closer together?

As Jenna collapsed beside him, closing her eyes as he pulled her into the curve of his body, she realized what she wanted. How she wanted this story to end.

And she also knew that she couldn't even think about it.

Not yet.

Maybe not ever.

Caleb kissed her forehead gently, his breath warm against her forehead. "Perfection," he whispered.

She smiled and snuggled her face into the curve of his neck. She knew they had to get up soon, but she wanted to hold onto this moment for every last second that she could. "How do you know? You have nothing to compare it to."

He ran his hand over her braids, playing with the ends. "Some things, a guy just knows. Why? Do you disagree?"

She spread her fingers over his chest, watching how his lighter skin seemed to be the perfect complement for her brown complexion. "It was perfect," she whispered. "I wish this moment could last forever."

His arms tightened around her, and he hugged her. "Me, too."

She closed her eyes. "How long do we have?"

"Maybe an hour until they get here."

An hour.

Not enough time.

Not nearly enough.

CHAPTER NINETEEN

CALEB LEANED on the kitchen island, shifting restlessly while Jenna put the last dish away.

Chase had left them with dinner supplies, and Caleb and Jenna had made sandwiches while they watched the clock ticking relentlessly.

He braced his palms on the counter, watching as Jenna shut the cabinet door. He loved watching her, and he grinned when she looked over her shoulder at him. "What's that smile for?" she asked.

"I liked making dinner with you," he said. "It felt good to do it together."

Her face softened. "It did, didn't it?" She tossed the dishtowel on the counter. "You're easy to get along with. It's easy to be with you."

He grinned. "I feel the same way about you." He paused. "Earlier, when we made love—"

Jenna held up her hand. "Caleb, let me talk."

Tension coiled through him at the edge in her voice. "What's up?"

She took a breath. "I think we need to put that on hold until this is sorted through."

His fingers tightened on the edge of the counter, but he kept his voice even. "Why?"

"Because it makes us focus on each other instead of the situation. This isn't a time to get romantic and fall in love. We have to stay aware and focused. We don't know what's coming and how dangerous it is." She met his gaze. "I can't afford to be soft right now, and you make me want to be soft."

He let out his breath. Fall in love? She'd said *fall in love*. Rightness pulsed through him, but he kept his focus on the discussion. "I'm always paying attention to our circumstances. I'm always aware."

She raised her brows. "You seemed entirely focused on me while we were in bed."

"I wish I had been, but no." He swore under his breath when her eyes narrowed. "It's not personal, Jenna. I just have this switch inside me that I can't turn off. I'm always scanning for danger. Always aware of every sound. Always paying attention to what weapons are within reach. Where my exit points are. Where someone's entry points could be."

She folded her arms across her chest and leaned against the counter. "I didn't sense that at all, and I was pretty close to you."

He nodded. "It's internal. It's like I have two personas. I can be gentle and chill on the outside, but inside..." He bumped his fist against his chest. "It's war. It's readiness. It's —" He took a breath. "I feel like I'm waiting to fight to the death at every moment."

She stared at him. "Really?"

He nodded. "Yeah."

"I had no idea." She gestured at him. "You look so relaxed right now."

He realized he was leaning back against the counter, his

hands resting loosely by his hips. "I am relaxed. And I'm not. At the same time. It's weird." He grimaced. "Fucked up, I guess."

Jenna studied him. "If you have a life where people are stabbing you, kidnapping children, and blowing up houses, it makes sense to be always vigilant."

"Yeah." He let out his breath. "I like being here. With you. With Zach. With Gracie. I love that dog, too. I fit here, but at the same time...I don't." He gestured to the window. "I belong out there, doing shit that winds up with people dead."

Her eyes widened. "You kill people?"

He ground his jaw. "When I look at that open window behind you and imagine someone coming through it, I'm ready to shoot them between the eyes to keep you safe. No hesitation. I'm ready." He hated saying the words. He hated knowing what he was capable of. What he'd apparently spent the last ten years doing.

Jenna let out her breath. "Wow. I didn't realize. I was taking you at face value for what you show me." She raised her brows. "Are we in danger from you, Caleb?"

"No." He didn't hesitate. "I don't give a shit who I am or what I might have done. I'd never hurt any of you, and I'll do whatever it takes to keep you safe." But that she had to ask, that a part of her wondered if he was lying, ate away at him.

"Which is why Zach's dad gave him to you," she said softly. "Because he knew you could and would keep him safe. No matter what."

No matter what. But what was it that he'd have to face? He didn't know. He paused. "Jenna."

"Yes?"

He met her gaze. "I feel like I'm treading close to the edge of bad shit. But when I'm with you, Gracie, and Zach, I feel..." He paused, trying to articulate what he wanted to say.

"You feel what?"

He rubbed his jaw. "I feel like I'm where I'm meant to be. When I touch you, even if it's just brushing your arm, everything inside me settles. I'm still aware and vigilant, but that edge inside me quiets." He met her gaze. "You bring out the part of me that feels right. Kindness. Peace. A sense of purpose that feels authentic."

Jenna pressed her lips together. "I'm glad I help you, Caleb. But what you just told me is a little unnerving." She pointed her index finger at his chest. "So much violence inside you, right?"

He nodded once. "Yeah. I don't know exactly what it is, but it's there."

Hesitation furrowed her brow. "And we don't know what could get unlocked at any moment. What if I trigger you?"

He swore, now wishing he hadn't told her. "I know that I'll keep you safe. I swear it."

She grimaced. "Caleb—"

Tires crunched outside, and they both tensed. His hand went instinctively to his hip, looking for the gun he wasn't wearing. His tension ratcheted tighter. He didn't like being without his gun.

At the same time, he didn't want it. Wearing a gun around the house when two kids were around felt insanely wrong. Again, the two sides to him. The dichotomy that was ripping him apart.

He had to remember that he wasn't just a guy living in domestic bliss. He was a man with a duty to protect a baby that was being *hunted*. He swore under his breath. He had to stop pretending he wasn't the guy who lived in a world he didn't like. He had to admit who he was, even if he didn't want to. "I'm going to get my gun."

Jenna raised her brows. "You don't think we're safe here?"

"I don't know. But if we're not safe, and my gun is locked

away in a cabinet while people steal Zach, I'm not going to feel great about it."

She pressed her lips together. "I agree. Go get it. Get mine, too."

"You don't need to—"

"I do. It's my kid upstairs, too. So get mine."

Caleb wanted to lean over for a quick kiss, but there was so much hanging unresolved between them...

Screw it. He wasn't letting who he was stand in their way.

So, he slid his fingers around her wrist and tugged her in. She gave him a look like he was an annoying puppy, then surrendered, letting him draw her against him and kiss her. She leaned into him ever so slightly and kissed him back. He didn't stop kissing her until she sighed and he felt her surrender to him, letting down her shields.

Only then did he pull back, searching her face. "You're an amazing woman, Jenna."

She smiled. "Thanks."

He nodded, forced himself to release her hand, and strode into the den, where they'd locked up all their weapons when they'd arrived. As he left, Jenna leaned over to move the curtain aside again, clearly checking to make sure it was Chase who got out of the truck.

He liked her attention to detail. She knew what she was doing. She was soft and tender, sweet, generous, and also a courageous, tough badass. She had it all, and he loved it.

Her.

He loved everything about her.

But he knew he couldn't go there yet.

Not yet.

He unlocked the cabinet and retrieved their guns, made sure they were loaded, and then headed back toward the front hall.

Jenna was standing in the entry, her hand on the knob. "It's Chase and a woman. You ready?"

He let out his breath. "Yeah." This was it. When he was going to find out why he'd chosen a life of violence and abandoned his family. Why he'd become a man he didn't like.

Jenna looked at him. "You don't want to know, do you?"

He shrugged. "People are in danger because of me. I have a responsibility to know."

She smiled and squeezed his hand. "Then let's do it."

At that moment, the doorbell rang.

He shook out his shoulders, checked through the window to make sure no one else was lurking, then opened the front door to let in the brother he didn't know.

CHAPTER TWENTY

CHASE DIDN'T COME INSIDE. His face was wary, but he had his arm around the woman beside him. "This is my wife, Mira. She wanted to come. I hope that's okay."

She didn't give Caleb a chance to decide. Her face simply lit up, and she held out her arms. "Welcome, Caleb."

Chase cleared his throat. "He's not a hugger—"

"Who cares?" Mira walked in, grabbed Caleb, and pulled him into a hug.

For a second, he hesitated, unsure of who this woman was, but then he saw Jenna smiling, and something inside him relaxed. He let out his breath and hugged her back. "Thanks. Good to meet you."

Mira pulled back, beaming at him. "I met Chase after you had already left town," she said. "That means, you and I have never met before, so there's no history that you've missed." She smiled. "So, we get to start new on both sides."

Somehow, her words made Caleb relax. No history that he couldn't recall. "Sounds good."

"Great." She smiled at Jenna. "Mira Stockton. The first woman to tame a Stockton man."

Jenna smiled and shook her hand. "Jenna Ward. Nice to meet you."

Having Mira there shifted the tone of the evening. She was light-hearted and fun, teasing her husband out of his tension.

By the time the four of them sat down in the living room, Caleb was feeling decently relaxed. At least enough to sit down and stay relatively still.

And the moment he thought that, he heard a truck outside and shot to his feet. "Are you expecting company?"

Chase nodded. "It's Brody and Dylan. They set up security when we built this place, and they're outside checking on everything. They'll be in shortly."

Caleb still had to go to the window and watch the men get out of the truck. He waited until they had both exited the vehicle, giving him the all-clear sign, and headed around the back of the house before he turned back to the living room.

All three of them were watching him with assorted expressions of concern.

He held up his hands. "Habit."

"A good one," Chase said. "It's cool."

Caleb nodded, then walked back across the room and sat down beside Jenna. He took her hand in his, pulling their joined hands toward him so he could play with her fingers. "Talk to me."

"Wait a second." Mira held up her hands. "You two men are so rigid with each other. This has to stop."

Chase shrugged. "He doesn't remember me. I get it. He can't afford to trust anyone. It's fine."

"It's not fine." Mira frowned at them both. "You guys have been through hell and back with each other—"

Caleb held up his hand to stop her. "Hell and back?"

Mira and Chase looked at each other, then Chase slowly nodded. "There's a reason why the nine of us are so tight. It was the only reason we survived our childhood. It was stand together or die."

Caleb tensed. "Literally?"

"Yeah."

Caleb began rubbing his thumb on Jenna's palm to ground himself. "Tell me."

Chase looked at Mira, then leaned forward, rested his hands on his thighs, and bowed his head. For a long moment, he didn't say anything, but then he finally looked up. "Caleb, the rest of us have spent our entire lives trying to deal with the darkness our childhood etched into our souls. It haunts us at every turn." He took Mira's hand and pressed his lips to her knuckle. "Without Mira, I never would have made it. Same with the others."

Caleb tightened his grip on Jenna's hand. "All right."

"No. What I'm trying to say..." Chase looked at Mira, then back at Caleb. "I love you with all my heart. Which is why I want to set you free." He took a breath. "You have the chance to live a life without the shadows of our past haunting you. You have the chance to be free." His voice became rough. "Take it, little brother. Take it and run as far and fast as you possibly can, and never look back."

Caleb blinked, startled. "You want me to abandon you again? I thought..." What was going on? He thought they were all close.

"No." Chase stood and paced across the room. He braced his hands on the kitchen counter and bowed his head. "I just... *Fuck*." He turned around to face them, and Caleb saw the torment in the face that looked so like his own. "I want you to remember us. Our family. What we meant to each other. But not at the cost of living in the hell that will never let us go."

Caleb's throat tightened. "Chase—"

"Stay on the ranch. We'll help keep you and the others

safe. We'll track down whoever is after you. But leave the past behind. Don't ask." Chase's voice broke. "Seeing you sitting there with Jenna...the look on your face when you glance at her. Jesus, Caleb. I haven't seen that kind of softness on your face since you were fourteen. I thought the Caleb who is kind, gentle, funny, and happy was gone forever. And now... you're back." He clasped his hands on his head. "I can't steal that from you," he said, his voice rough. "No matter how badly I want you to remember me. I'd never forgive myself if I turned you back into that guy that you became when you were fourteen...and never recovered from."

Caleb stared at his brother, emotions whirling through him. He could feel the love from Chase. It was almost staggering in its intensity. But the anguish was equally as strong. The need to bond warring with the need to protect him.

"Chase." Caleb released Jenna's hand and stood up.

His brother looked at him with desperate, lost eyes. "I never thought I'd see you again. I lost you when you were fourteen, and then again three years later when you left physically. And now..." He held out his hands, palms up. "I have to let you go again."

Caleb didn't know what to say.

But he walked across the room and reached for his brother.

Chase's eyes widened and he opened his arms, dragging Caleb into a hug. Caleb wrapped his arms around the man he didn't remember. Chase was bigger than he was, equally as muscled. The instant Caleb hugged him, he knew it was right. He felt the bond between them. He *knew* this man was his brother. He could feel it in the depths of his soul.

It took a long moment before either man was willing to let go, but when they did, Caleb could see the tears in his brother's eyes. "My brother," he said softly. "I feel it."

Chase nodded. "Yeah. It's real."

"I know." Suddenly, Caleb was ready. "I want to meet the others."

Chase raised his chin and nodded. "Now?"

"Yeah. Text them. Tell them I don't remember. Tell them to come."

Chase's eyes widened. "All right." He pulled out his phone, and Caleb leaned over his shoulder while Chase started to type.... He got as far as Caleb's name then stopped. "I don't know what to say. 'Caleb's back, but he doesn't remember any of us, and by the way, someone's hunting him and the kid he's protecting?'" Chase raised his brows. "It seems a little anticlimactic after all that time."

"I think Caleb should come to breakfast tomorrow. We'll gather who we can and then just surprise them." Mira was grinning. "That's the way to do it. It'll be fun."

Chase nodded. "I like that. We'll fill them in as they come. Sound good?"

Caleb glanced at Jenna, who nodded. "Yeah, that'll work. What time?"

"You'll need to be there by six. People can show up at any time around here. That's the only way to ensure you'll be there first," Chase said.

"All right. We'll be there." Caleb could see Chase's house from the front porch, so he knew where to go.

Chase grinned. "Awesome. I can't wait to see everyone's faces."

Caleb grimaced. "What if I left because I did something terrible to one of them?"

Chase shrugged. "Family matters. No one would care at this point."

Caleb wasn't so sure about that, but before he had time to discuss it, a knock sounded at the door, and both he and Jenna jumped. Caleb had his gun out and aimed at the door before he'd even had time to process it. Swearing, he gripped the gun as he waved Jenna back.

Jenna, who also had her gun out.

Grimly he stared at the guns. He didn't want this to be his life. He suddenly knew that with absolute truth.

Which meant he had to find out his past, unravel it, and leave it behind.

Chase held up his hands. "It's all right. It's Brody and Dylan. I told you they were here."

Caleb didn't lower his gun until Jenna inched over to the window and peered out. "It's Brody and Dylan," she confirmed. "They're alone."

Swearing, Caleb lowered his gun, ignoring the frown on his brother's face, while Jenna opened the door. The Harts came in cheerfully. "The security system looks great," Dylan said. "We added a few features, but it'll alert you if anything happens."

Caleb nodded. "These guys are good."

Dylan winked. "So am I. Check this out."

It took only a few minutes for Dylan to set up his computer on the coffee table. He showed Jenna and Caleb all the motion sensors, the cameras, the weight sensors in the ground, and the infrared ones. "Anything larger than a kid will set it off, so you might get some false alarms, but we figured that was better."

Caleb nodded, flexing his fingers. "Seems simple."

Dylan looked at him, then at his brother. "It's not simple. The fact you think it is means you've done this before."

High-tech surveillance was part of his life? Not surprising.

Dylan suddenly pointed at his wrist. "What's with the watch?"

Caleb looked down at it. "It was on my wrist when I woke up after the explosion. It's busted, though."

"I might be able to fix it. A digital watch could have info." He held out his hand. "May I?"

"Yeah, sure." He quickly unstrapped it and handed it over to Dylan, who turned it over in his hands, inspecting it. "What else?"

Brody answered. "We had one of our brothers install some security at Jenna's cabin."

Caleb put his hand on Jenna's back. "In case someone tracked me there."

Brody nodded. "It seemed likely. If they're good, they're going to find you."

Caleb shook his head. "I'm good at going missing. I was careful."

"For the moment, yeah." Dylan turned the computer around so he and Jenna could see the screen.

It was a grainy, black and white image of the cabin where they'd been sleeping less than fifteen hours ago. Caleb could see the breakfast plates they'd left on the rack to dry. It felt like so long ago that he'd been sitting there with Jenna and Gracie, and yet it had been only this morning.

"We'll be alerted the moment anyone enters the cabin or the surrounding area," Dylan said. "We have a hired security team waiting about a mile down the road. They'll be there as soon as someone shows up."

Caleb let out his breath. Seeing the place where Gracie, Jenna, and Zach had been staying last night set up as bait was grim. He was so glad they'd left. "That looks good."

Dylan nodded. "We were untraceable from the cabin to our plane. I think we can assume you're safe for the moment, because I think they'll need to follow you to the cabin before figuring out where you are now."

Caleb nodded, trying to relax. "So, we have time."

"Not much," Dylan said. "Your trail isn't going to be difficult to follow. We already tracked that truck that you ran off the road back to the store where you stole it. A mile down the road, the previous truck you stole was found. We kept following each stolen vehicle, and I already tracked it back to a small town in southern Oregon, just off the coast."

Caleb swore. "I thought I was good."

"You are good, but you were working on limited resources with a baby. It was impressive what you pulled off. But that made you vulnerable and trackable."

Shit.

Dylan typed on the computer then the image of a burned-out house appeared on the screen. It was flattened, with nothing but burning embers left. "House explosion two nights ago on the outskirts of town. Look familiar?"

Jenna gasped. "Is that where you woke up?"

Caleb was stunned by the decimation. "There's no way I was in that house when it went off. I'd be dead." In the moment, he'd been focused on survival. He hadn't looked around. But now? It was chilling.

"Is that the house?" Dylan repeated.

Caleb recognized the street, and the backyard that he'd walked through to escape. "Yeah, that's it."

Dylan nodded. "I agree. You weren't in that explosion." He looked at Caleb. "Either you arrived right after, or you set it yourself."

Caleb met Dylan's eyes, and suddenly felt sick. "What if I blew it up? What if there were people in it—" He stared at Dylan in sudden horror. "*Were* there people in it?"

"One. A woman. Thirty-five years old. She didn't survive."

Fear clamped through Caleb's gut. "What was her name?"

"Jessica Smith. She was married to a guy named Ben Smith, but no one saw the husband much. He wasn't very sociable and wasn't around very often. But there was one picture that I found on the neighbor's security camera." He turned the camera around.

Caleb didn't even have to look. He knew what he'd see.

But he looked anyway.

It was his face on the grainy camera. He was wearing a sweatshirt with a hood up and a baseball cap, but the light from the streetlight caught just enough of his face that it was clear it was him. "I was married?" The words stuck in his throat.

"I don't know if it was a real marriage or a sham," Dylan said. "I'm still trying to unravel it. But you were definitely using the name Ben Smith. You two moved in two years ago. She worked from home, and was quiet, but the neighbors said she was friendly."

Caleb felt like he was drowning. "Kids?" His voice was raw and hoarse. "Did we have kids? Were there kids in that house?"

Jenna put her hand in his, and he held tightly.

"No kids," Dylan said. "No pets. No one else died in the explosion."

Jesus. Had he been married? Had he killed her? Or had he arrived later? "I need to know what happened. Did I kill her?" *Jesus.*

"No." It was Jenna who answered. "You didn't kill her."

"But—"

She grabbed his shoulders and turned him toward her. "You're a good man, Caleb. We all know it. No matter what life you got dragged into, it would never change your heart. You'd never do that."

"He might if she was an enemy," Dylan said. "He might have had to."

Caleb knew Dylan was right.

"No." Jenna glared at Dylan. "He wouldn't have. I know his heart. He'd never do that."

"Not today, but who knows who he was?"

"I do." Chase finally spoke up. "I know who he was."

CHAPTER TWENTY-ONE

JENNA HAD BEEN FOOLED by her husband. She'd believed in him, and she'd paid the price. So had Gracie. She'd known him for years, and she'd trusted him when she shouldn't.

The man sitting beside her, clutching her hand so desperately, had been in her life for days.

Days.

All the evidence was pointing toward terrible things in his past, things that made him a worse man than Danny had ever been.

She should run.

She should take Gracie and leave all of this behind. Fast. Without looking back.

But she didn't move.

She couldn't make herself get up.

Instead, she looked at Chase and waited for him to speak. Why? Because she trusted Brody. Brody trusted Chase. And Chase...what did he have to say about his brother? It was obvious he loved Caleb. But that didn't mean that Caleb was the great guy she wanted him to be.

Chase looked at Caleb. "You were the nicest kid," he said quietly. "You saved animals. You used to steal abused horses and sneak them over to Ol' Skip's farm, where you'd take care of them. You're the reason that the Stockton Ranch focuses on rescuing horses now. You have the biggest damn heart of any of us."

Jenna felt her throat tighten. That was the Caleb she knew.

Chase smiled. "When the shit got bad at home with our dad, you would walk away. You'd head out into the fields, lie down in the sun, and literally smell flowers. You didn't care how dark the violence was. You simply rose above it and found peace in nature and in animals."

"A nurturer," Jenna said. It was how Caleb had been with them since they'd met him.

Chase nodded. "One day, when you were fourteen, you changed. You withdrew. You stopped rescuing horses. You stopped nature. You started using drugs." His voice broke slightly. "Every one of us stays away from alcohol and drugs. We saw what it did to our dad. But one day, you went down that road, and you never came back. And then you left."

Jenna pressed her lips together, and Caleb tensed beside her.

"I don't know what happened to you," Chase said. "But it was overnight that things changed. I don't think it was that time wore you down. I think something happened. But I don't know what. None of us do. But it didn't make you into a bad guy. It took you away from who you really are." He gestured at Caleb. "This is you, little brother. The kindness. The warmth. Loving on Jenna. That's you."

Still bracing his forearms on his knees, Caleb dropped his head and pressed their clasped hands to his forehead.

Chase leaned forward. "There's no way you would ever kill

an innocent person or anyone you love, or even someone you knew was a decent human being."

Caleb looked up. "But I'd kill a human for another reason? That's what you think?"

Chase let out his breath. "I killed Dad. He was beating up on our youngest brother, Travis. I think he would have killed Travis, I stepped in. I took his life to save Travis's, and the rest of us. You do what you have to do, sometimes."

"It makes you a hero, not a demon," Mira said, putting her arm around her husband. "Never lose sight of that."

Jenna felt her heart breaking for all the darkness surrounding the Stocktons. She couldn't imagine the weight that sat on Chase. On all of them. On Caleb, if he remembered.

Caleb stared at his brother, but he said nothing. Jenna could feel him trembling against her. She didn't know if it was stress, exhaustion, or his injuries, which he hid so well that she forgot about them half the time. No one in the room had any idea how badly he'd been hurt.

But she knew he was at the end of his coping. "I think that needs to be all for tonight," she said gently. "This is a lot for Caleb to process."

Caleb didn't resist, but Chase looked like he wanted to argue, until Mira touched his arm. "I think that makes sense," she said, meeting Jenna's gaze with understanding. "Come on, boys. Let's go."

Chase stood up reluctantly, as did the Harts.

Dylan put a sticky note on the table. "That's the app and the login info for the alarm at this house, and the set up at Jenna's cabin. You can manage it all from there. Text me when you log in, as I need to approve you."

Caleb took the sticky note. "Thanks." His voice was gruff.

Jenna looked up, as did Caleb. "Why don't we switch the

Stockton gathering to evening," she said. Getting there at six in the morning felt too early right now. "We could be there around four."

Chase nodded. "Sure. That sounds good." His eyes were full of all the things he wanted to say, but he let Mira guide him toward the front door. "We'll leave you guys to do your thing." He cleared his throat. "It's great to have you back, little brother. You have my number. Call if you need anything, even if it's just to talk."

Caleb nodded. "Thanks." He and Jenna escorted Chase and Mira to the door, but Mira paused with her hand on the doorframe.

"You have eight brothers and one sister," Mira told him. "We all just found out about her a few years ago. Between the ten of you, you have eight different mothers and the same dad, who was an abusive alcoholic and a terrible man. Everyone left town, trying to escape the nightmares of their childhood—"

Jenna's heart dropped as Caleb sucked in his breath.

"Stop, Mira." Chase put his hand on his wife's arm. "Look at Caleb's face. Just telling him makes the darkness come back. Let it be in the past, Caleb. Be the one who really made it. Just don't ask."

Mira slid her hand into Chase's. "Everyone has come back," she continued, "drawn by the bond of this amazing family. Everyone lives in town now, married with kids." She smiled. "The Stocktons are the most wonderful, most special family anyone could ever hope to have. I am grateful every single day that the Stocktons are in my life. Love them, Caleb. Love them with every single bit of your heart. Chase is right. Don't look for daggers to stab into your heart. Just let them lie where they are."

And with that, she kissed his cheek, hugged Jenna, and

then led her husband outside. The Harts followed behind them. Jenna shut the door behind them, then turned to Caleb, who was standing with his hands loose and aimless by his hips.

He was so tense she could feel it pouring off him. "Do you want to talk about it?" she asked.

For a long second, he didn't answer. He didn't even seem to hear her. He was staring at the door, as if he could burn through it with his gaze and unlock all the secrets that were hiding from him.

"Caleb?"

His gaze swiveled off the wood and he looked at her. "What if I killed that woman? What if she was my *wife* and I *killed* her?" His face was tortured, his voice raw.

She couldn't make herself go to him.

Was this man a killer? A murderer? Someone she should run from?

At her hesitation, pain flickered in his eyes. "I'll sleep downstairs," he said as he turned away. His limp came back as he started to walk away, and she saw he was on the edge of collapse. It made her realize how hard he'd been fighting to be strong, to not give away a single weakness.

"Caleb."

He didn't turn. He simply held up his hand as he kept walking. "Follow your instincts, Jenna. They're good. Trust them. If you think you need to stay away from me, you're probably right."

"The noise in my head is what's telling me to run, not my instincts," she said softly.

He stopped, but didn't turn to face her. "What does that mean?"

"My instincts trust you with every ounce of my soul," she whispered. "I believe in you, Caleb."

He turned to face her then, anguish etched on his face. "Is that the truth?"

"Yes." She walked up to him, her heart aching when she saw him tense. "If you were married to that woman, if you loved her, if you cared about her at all, if she was anything but evil, you didn't kill her. I know it. Chase knows it." She put her hand on his heart. "You know it."

CHAPTER TWENTY-TWO

When Jenna put her hand on his chest, need rushed through Caleb. For her touch. For her acceptance. To connect with her.

He put his hand over hers, fighting the almost unstoppable need to drag her into his arms and crush her willing body against his. "I know who I am right now, but I don't know what I did two days ago." He couldn't get the image of that house out of his mind. "What if I set that bomb?"

"You didn't—"

"And if I didn't, then what if my work caused it to happen? What if my life brought death to that woman? Either way, I'm responsible for her death." He felt gutted. Absolutely gutted. He'd let himself believe he was a good guy, the guy who deserved Jenna, Gracie, and Zach. A family. A second chance.

Jenna lifted her chin. "I can take care of myself—"

"From a bomb? Really? Are you that resilient, then? And what about Gracie?" He suddenly wished a thousand times over that he hadn't gone to Jenna's cabin. The moment he'd stepped into there, he'd made her and Gracie a target. *Fuck*.

Jenna's mouth tightened. "Gracie and I will be fine."

"I can't take that chance."

She stiffened. "What are you saying? Are you leaving?"

"No." He didn't miss the relief that flashed across her face, or his own heart leaping at the realization that despite everything, she didn't want him to leave. Not that it changed anything, but it felt good. A thread of hope that there was truly something decent inside him. "If we split up, I can't protect you. They'll find you, and when that happens, you need to be where I can protect you."

Jenna raised her brows. "And you can protect against a bomb?"

He felt gut punched. "Clearly not."

Jenna grimaced in visible regret. "I didn't mean it like that. I'm sorry. I just meant that we need to work together—"

He held up his hand. "I'm not soft. I can handle it."

Tears filled her eyes. "You have softness inside you, Caleb. Don't shut that down like you did before."

He was already shutting it down. "I don't have the luxury of being the guy we've both known for the last day or so. I'm going to get the rest of my guns." He turned away and pulled out his phone. "I'm calling Dylan. He knows guns. He'll help secure this place even better—"

Jenna put her hand on his arm. "Caleb."

He stopped, closing his eyes at the intensity of his body's response to her light touch. "Jenna. I'm not going to let you get killed. I need to focus."

She grabbed his shoulders and made him face her. "Listen to me, Caleb," she said fiercely. "I've seen enough in my life. I know bad people when I meet them. You're not that. You're a good man. A wonderful man."

"Jenna—"

"No. Let me finish." Her fingers dug into his shoulders, her dark brown eyes blazing. "I know you need to focus, but when this is over, when you remember everything, you hold onto the man you've been since I met you, and you come back home to him. Do you understand?"

He finally met her gaze, and he saw the absolute conviction in them. He wanted to make her that promise, but he couldn't. "I don't know what I'll find when the blinders come off my life," he said. "The person you know might not exist anymore."

"You have a choice, Caleb. We all have a choice. You made a choice when you were fourteen to throw yourself into darkness. And you kept making that choice. But life is different now. You don't need to choose that anymore." Her fingers tightened on his shoulders. "You have me, Zach, and Gracie waiting for you now, Caleb. We lost Danny to the darkness inside him and then to violence, but you taught us to trust again. Make the choice he couldn't make. For you. For us."

Her words seemed to plunge right into Caleb's heart. Swearing, he caught her chin and leaned in. "If I had a choice, I'd kidnap the three of you and the dog, take you to some remote place, and never let anyone find us again. You'd be all I need." When her face softened, he hardened his resolve. "But I don't have that choice, Jenna. And I might never have it."

She pressed her lips together. "Caleb—"

"Go upstairs. Get the kids in our room. Take your guns. I'm going to stay down here and make things more secure." He ground his jaw. "They're coming for us, Jenna. And I need to be ready."

She lifted her chin. "Fine, but before you go run off and do your I'm-an-island move, you need to know that I love you. I love you because I know who you are, and I love that man. So, go clean up this thing, and then come back to me."

He stared at her, his heart aching. He wanted to drag her

into his arms and tell her he loved her right back. But he couldn't. "Don't love me."

She ignored his great advice. "After Danny, I had no interest in loving any man again, and I don't think Gracie did either. But you broke through our barriers so quickly and so completely. So, because you're such a great guy, you are now obligated to continue to be that great guy so we don't have to doubt our instincts ever again. Got it?"

The corner of his mouth quirked. "So, it's an unspoken contract?"

"Exactly. Glad you understand." She stood on her tiptoes, brushed a kiss across his mouth, then spun on her heel and ran for the stairs, leaving him standing in the very nice living room, a gun at his hip, and a crushing need to sprint after her, drag her into their bed, and make love to her until dawn.

But instead, he turned and headed towards his guns.

Because he wasn't going to make the same mistake twice. Or however many times he'd made it.

CHAPTER TWENTY-THREE

"How long is he going to stay like that?" Gracie asked.

Jenna glanced over from feeding Zach. Caleb was by the front window, watching, texting with the Harts. He'd been pacing from room to room all day, scanning the overcast horizon, refusing to allow any of them to go outdoors. "Until he collapses, I assume. Then we'll drag him to the couch, and it'll be like when we first met him and we had to cater to his every pathetic whim."

Gracie nodded as she took a bite of cereal. "His limp is getting worse," she noted.

"I know. He's been holding his side, too. I'm guessing we have maybe ten minutes until we hear the thump of his body hitting the floor."

"Men can be so stupid sometimes," Gracie said.

Caleb turned his head to look at them. "I can hear you."

Gracie giggled. "Of course you can. You're like twenty feet from us."

Jenna beckoned to their weary guardian. "I know you have no memory of anything, but I'll let you in on a little life secret. Eating food periodically is really helpful."

"So is sleeping," Gracie added.

"And babies. Babies are helpful, too."

"And dogs," Gracie said. "Hugging a dog adds ten years to your life."

Caleb stared at all of them, his brow furrowed in confusion and exhaustion.

Jenna was pretty sure he hadn't slept all night, which wasn't going to help any of them if the bad guys came. "Caleb, get over here, sit down, and eat."

He still didn't move.

"Should I call Dylan and ask him for permission to leave the window? Is it at all possible that he'll tell you that the security system he set up is good enough that you can at least take a minute to eat? Gracie, grab me Caleb's phone. I'll call Dylan and get a hall pass for Caleb."

The corners of Caleb's mouth finally broke into a smile. "Am I that bad?"

Jenna relaxed when she saw his grin. "Always." She patted the seat beside Gracie. "Park your fanny, big guy. I made lots of yummies for breakfast."

With one last glance out the window, Caleb abandoned his post and limped over. As he slid into the seat beside Gracie, Jenna saw him wince and press his hand to his side. She frowned as she put bacon and an omelet in front of him. "Does your side need to be checked by a doctor?"

He shook his head. "It just hurts. The antibiotics are working. No infection." He took a bite of the omelet. "This is fantastic."

"My mom is a great cook," Gracie said, as she leaned on the table, watching him. "She used to cook all the time, but then she started traveling. Gram can't cook at all, so I'm basically in the middle of slowly starving to death. It's a rough life for a teenager."

Guilt flashed through Jenna at the reminder of real life

outside the bubble they were in. "That's why I learned to cook. If I relied on Gram when I was growing up, I would have wasted away to nothing."

Caleb's blue eyes studied her as she brought fresh blueberry muffins to the table. "You didn't have a mom and dad around to cook?"

"Nope. They were in the military. Gone most of the time." Jenna sat down. "It was hard when they were gone. I decided I wasn't going to do that to my kid..." Her voice trailed off at her own words, and she saw Gracie's jaw tighten. "Gracie? Am I gone that much?"

Gracie shoved her spoon into her bowl. "Yes."

Jenna let out her breath. This time with Caleb had opened her eyes to what it would be like to simply slow down and be present with Gracie. With him. With life. She realized suddenly that she didn't want to go back to her life. "I never liked being a private detective," she said softly.

Gracie looked up at her. "Then why do you do it?"

"Because it was a source of income that was handed to me. I was afraid not to do it."

Caleb nodded. "It's scary as a single mom. Taking care of your kids and yourself."

"Exactly." She'd never talked to Gracie about how freaking terrifying it was to suddenly be a single mom, but she could see that Caleb understood.

He shifted, and then she felt his leg against hers, under the table. Resting there. Providing the comfort that only another adult could provide. With Gracie, she always had to be strong, strong, strong. But with Caleb, she could lean on him, and it felt good.

Caleb was watching her with interest. "What would you do instead, Jenna?" he asked.

Jenna took a breath and laughed, a shaky laugh. "I have no idea. I've never thought about it." She looked at Gracie. "But

I want to be around. No more travel. No more playing with guns. No more spending my days following people who give me the creepy-crawlies."

Gracie pressed her lips together, and Jenna realized her daughter didn't believe her.

Jenna leaned across the table. "Gracie."

"What?" She didn't look up from her cereal.

"I mean it. I'm going to find a way."

Gracie finally looked up at her. "I want to stay here. I like this house. The Stocktons are nice. I want to meet the horses. Can you work for them? You know horses."

Jenna stared at her daughter in surprise. "Work with horses?"

"Didn't you used to ride?"

"I did." Jenna's heart started to pound. She'd been horse crazy as a kid. "I used to ride English, though. I did jumpers." She smiled, remembering. "I used to think if I could make it to the Olympics, then my parents would be proud enough to come see me." She shrugged. "But then they died, so what was the point?"

She realized suddenly that Caleb and Gracie were staring at her. "What?"

"That was pretty morbid," Caleb said.

"And a terrible example for me," Gracie added. "On a lot of levels."

Jenna laughed softly and jiggled Zach on her lap as he continued to work on his bottle. "But you love me anyway, so it's all good."

Gracie rolled her eyes. "So, we're not going to stay here, then? We'll go home and then you'll keep working your old job while you look for a new one, and then it will never change."

Jenna frowned. "It is going to change. It might take a while—"

"See?" Gracie sighed. "Forget it, Mom. Just do what you do." She pushed back from the table. "I'm done. I'm going upstairs—"

Jenna held out her hand. "Gracie—"

"No." Gracie glared at her. "Stop making promises you won't keep. It's not okay."

"Stay downstairs, Gracie," Caleb said as she started toward the stairs. "We need you within sight all the time. Just a precaution."

Gracie stuck her tongue out at him and flounced to the couch, put on her headphones, and then pulled out her phone.

Jenna sighed. "She's right about me leaving my job," she admitted softly, keeping her voice low enough that the noise-cancelling headphones would drown her out. "I don't know what I'd do, and I have to earn money." She looked at Caleb. "Maybe it'll never change—"

"No." He leaned in. "There's a fire inside you. I can feel it. It's just a matter of you listening to it and letting it guide you." He bumped his fist over his heart. "Your instincts know. You just have to hear it."

Jenna frowned. "My instincts are shouting about the bills I need to pay and—"

"No." Caleb put his finger over her mouth, silencing her. "Stop. That's cluttering your mind. Let the truth come out. Horses? Do you like horses?"

She shrugged. "Yes. But I don't want a job working with them. They're for pleasure."

He frowned. "What else do you love?"

"Chocolate."

"Brody mentioned that the Stocktons and Harts have a bakery venture."

She smiled. "I like to eat it, not bake it."

"What else do you love?"

You. The word whispered on her lips, but she didn't say it. She felt too off-kilter, and she didn't really feel like admitting it anymore. "Reading."

"So, be a book reviewer."

She started to laugh. "I'm sure they get rich off all the free books they get. Look, I appreciate it, but it's not that easy—"

"Name one more thing you love. Like really, really love. Other than your kid."

She held out her hands. "I don't know. Dogs?"

CHAPTER TWENTY-FOUR

HE RAISED HIS BROWS. "Dogs? That's not a surprise. I see the way you snuggle Simba. She melts your heart, doesn't she?"

Jenna glanced over at Simba, who was on the couch with Gracie. "I always wanted a lot of dogs. What I really want is a huge amount of acreage, and a big house, and every single rescue dog that needs a home. A rescue where the dogs sleep on my bed and hang out in my living room." She smiled. "We'd run around the country whenever people called us, and we'd go get the dog and help it heal in its heart and body."

A slow smile spread across Caleb's face. "That sounds awesome. I'd love that."

"But how do you earn money? Dogs are notoriously tight-fisted when it comes to paying room and board."

He finished his food and held out his arms for Zach. "It would have to be a charity, funded by donations."

Jenna handed Zach to him, smiling as he nuzzled the baby. Caleb was so tender and gentle, even if he didn't acknowledge it. "Fundraising is difficult. I don't have contacts."

"The Harts could fund the entire thing out of their petty cash fund."

Jenna laughed. "I'm not going to sponge off them—"

"What if they wanted to do it? Didn't Brody say that their ranch is centered on rescuing horses? Chase said that the Stocktons' ranch was as well." He raised his brows. "Maybe they like dogs, too."

A tiny bit of hope crept into Jenna's heart. "I couldn't ask them—"

"Why not? What if they want to do it, but haven't had the time to put it together? What if, by not saying anything, you're depriving both them and you of a dream?"

Jenna stared at Caleb. "I don't know—"

"Hang on." Caleb switched Zach into the other arm, and then pulled out his phone. He called someone, then put it on speaker while it rang.

"Who are you calling?" Jenna tried to grab the phone. "I'm not ready to talk about it with anyone—"

"Everything okay?" Brody's voice came over the phone. "I'm on my way there, about five minutes away."

"All's fine. I have a question for you."

"Go ahead. What's up?"

Jenna gestured at Caleb to shut up, but he ignored her. "I was just talking to Jenna here, and she mentioned that her dream was to open a dog sanctuary. Big property, big house, the dogs live in the house, sleep on the bed, and all that jazz. Obviously, it costs money. Is that something that you guys might be interested in working on with her?"

There was silence for a long moment, and Jenna felt her cheeks heat up. "Brody, it's Jenna. Caleb wasn't authorized to call you about this, so forget about it. I don't even know that I want to do it, and I'd never ask you—"

"Hell, yeah, we'd be into that."

She stopped, her mouth dropping open. "What?"

"I'm a horse guy, so I never thought about dogs before,

but hell yeah. Absolutely. Let's talk about that after this whole thing is over. I love it. Write down your ideas."

Jenna's heart started pounding. "I don't know anything about running a dog sanctuary—"

"Well, I didn't know anything about computers, but I had to figure it out to save a couple of homeless kids living with me, and it turned us into billionaires, so a total lack of knowledge and one hundred percent passion sounds like a winner to me." He paused. "It is one hundred percent passion, right?"

Jenna's throat tightened. "When I was a little girl, I found an abandoned puppy by a stream. My grandma let me keep her, and she was my best friend for the next sixteen years."

Caleb put his hand over Jenna's and squeezed. "What was her name?"

"Maggie Mutt. It was silly, but I thought she deserved a middle name that honored who she was." Every night that Jenna had gone to bed with her parents away, and then dead, it was Maggie who had curled up on her pillow, put her chin on Jenna's forehead, and comforted her.

It had been a long time since she'd had a dog. Too much travel. Too little money. Too busy to remember what a difference they could make in her life. Until Simba had reminded her.

"Maggie's Guest House," Brody said. "That's what we'll call it."

Caleb grinned. "It's perfect. Maggie can be the hostess welcoming the next generation of lost dogs into Jenna's sanctuary."

Tears filled Jenna's eyes, and suddenly, she was too overwhelmed to speak.

Caleb smiled, put his arm around her shoulders, and pressed a kiss to her forehead. "Jenna's crying right now," he told Brody. "I think that's a yes on the one-hundred-percent-passion question."

Brody laughed, his rich, deep voice echoing even over the phone. "Sounds great. Start thinking about location, Jenna. Both my family and the Stocktons have a lot of land in Wyoming, where you are, and the Hart Ranch in Oregon also has plenty of space. Let me know if either of those sounds good. Or we can look elsewhere. But let's start the dialogue. Sound good?"

Jenna finally spoke up. "I don't know if I can just start a sanctuary, Brody. I don't know anything about doing it, or where to do it, or—"

"You'll never know anything until you start. It's not a reason not to start." Brody paused. "Dylan's calling me. He's been working on trying to get access to the local security camera from that night. I need to take his call. More soon."

He disconnected, and Jenna sat back, her throat tight with emotion. "I can't do that," she blurted out. "I have no idea how to even start. I can't take money from Brody. I need to earn money and—"

Caleb put his finger against her lips. "Jenna."

She pushed his hand away. "Don't silence me."

"I'm not trying to silence you," he said gently. "I wanted to press pause on the resistance."

She stood up. "It's not resistance. It's fact. I can't move my life out to Oregon or Wyoming and start a dog sanctuary. That doesn't even make sense—" She realized suddenly that Gracie was watching her. *Crap.* She took a deep breath and tried to lower her voice and relax her body language. "I appreciate that you care, but please don't try to direct my life again."

"I wasn't trying to direct anything. I was opening doors for the direction that was calling you."

"It wasn't calling me! It was just a random fantasy! Real

life isn't sitting around some vast acreage with a whole bunch of dogs!"

"Why not?"

"Because—" She couldn't think of a reason. "Because it's not!" She took a steadying breath. "I need to get outside."

"No. It's not safe."

"No one is trying to murder *me*. It's safe enough." She grabbed her sweatshirt and grabbed her gun off the top of the fridge, where she'd stashed it while they ate. "I just need to get out of here."

She hurried toward the door and grabbed the door handle...and then she heard a tiny voice. "Mom?"

Jenna closed her eyes, trying to pull herself together. What was she doing, running out the door? She couldn't walk away. She could never walk away. She took a deep breath, dropped her hand from the doorknob, and turned to face her daughter. "Sorry, Gracie. I got upset, but there's nothing wrong. Everything's fine."

Gracie was leaning on the back of the couch, frowning. But she didn't look worried. "Did I just hear right that Brody said we could open a dog sanctuary in Wyoming?"

Jenna frowned. "I thought your headphones were noise-cancelling."

"They are, but I fake it so I can listen to conversations when I want. I want to open the dog sanctuary. That would be awesome. Can we?"

Jenna glanced at Caleb, who was bouncing Zach on his knee and not bailing her out. She made a face at him, then looked at her daughter. "Gracie, it's complicated."

"Why? Why does it have to be complicated? It's not that complicated." Excitement lit up Gracie's eyes. "It sounds amazing. I'll help. I promise I will. I can run the social media accounts. Visibility will be key for donors. I'm sure we can be influencers and get companies to sponsor our posts." She pulled out her phone and began typing. "Like assorted dog food suppliers, but also outdoor gear, because we'll be walking them outside. There are so many possibilities."

Jenna looked helplessly at Caleb, but he was grinning and no help at all. "Gracie—"

Gracie looked up. "Mom. Don't. Just don't. For once in your life, stop being a downer and live. It's *dogs*. You literally just got a billionaire to offer you money to have a thousand dogs sleep on your bed. You can't even tell me that you're going to say no."

Jenna let out her breath. Gracie was right. It sounded incredible, a dream that was so incredible it was impossible to believe in. But standing there in that beautiful foyer with a gun at her hip, she wanted to believe in it. To run toward the gift that was dangling in front of her.

But how? How did she leave her life and race toward this gift that didn't even seem like it could be real? "There's no bed that's big enough for a thousand dogs." Wow. On a scale of lamest excuses ever, she might have just hit the jackpot with that one.

"I have a bed. We'll split them. Five hundred for each of us. Gram can come live with us, and she would probably take a couple. And Caleb can take some, and Zach, too, if we get to keep him." She turned to Caleb. "Do you like dogs?"

"I love them." He answered fast, without hesitation, then looked surprised by his answer. "Yeah," he said again. "I'm pretty sure I do."

"Awesome. You can help." Gracie turned back toward Jenna. "Mom? Are you in?"

A thousand reasons to say no flooded Jenna's mind. But as she stared into the excited eyes of her baby girl, who she'd barely seen for so long, she knew that there was only one answer that she could give. She'd survived infidelity, the death of her spouse, a career she hated that involved stalking creepy men cheating on their wives, and a terrifyingly sporadic bank account.

She'd survived all that, and was still standing. "I have no idea how to do it."

"You never let me use that as an excuse not to do anything," Gracie said.

Caleb bounced Zach on his knee. "Don't underestimate yourself, Jenna. You're an amazing woman. Smart. Kind. Brilliant. You can do it. All you need to do is trust yourself and ask the right people for help."

She looked at him. "Will you help?" She blurted it out before she could stop herself.

He met her gaze, and she saw him preparing to give his little speech about how he might be a terrible person who would have to go live in a pit of doom.

So, she held up her hand to stop him. "You told me to fight for what you want. Why wouldn't you do the same?"

He met her gaze, then glanced at Gracie, then back to Jenna. "I don't want to make a promise I can't keep."

"Make the promise you want to keep. It's where you have to start."

He ground his jaw. "I won't break a promise to you. I don't know what's coming for me."

The same old story.

Jenna suddenly knew what she had to do. Caleb was reflecting herself back to her. Afraid to commit. Afraid to believe in the good. Afraid to grab hold of the goodness of life when she had a chance. If she wanted him to believe in himself, if she wanted Gracie to live a life that she loved, then she had to be the example.

She took her hand off the knob. "Gracie?"

"Yeah?" Hope was etched on her daughter's face.

"Maggie's House is on."

Gracie screamed in delight, leapt off the couch, and threw

herself into her mom's arms. Jenna held onto her daughter tightly, tears filling her eyes. Why had she waited for so long to change the song she'd strapped her life to? Saying yes felt so easy now that she'd done it.

Gracie broke free and sprinted upstairs to get her tablet to start researching options, leaving Jenna behind.

She looked across the room at Caleb. Yearning was etched on his face, a raw, naked longing that made her heart turn over. That was the man she loved. The one who had the biggest heart she'd ever met.

He met her gaze and smiled. "Best decision ever," he said softly. "I'm proud of you for making it."

Her heart tightened. "Thanks."

He tucked Zach into the curve of his arm, stood up, and walked over to her. He smiled. "You're glowing."

She grinned. "I feel like I can't sit still. This is crazy. It's crazy, isn't it? Too crazy?"

"Not crazy at all." He leaned in and kissed her, a glorious, tender, wonderful kiss that made her heart soar. "I'm super proud of you. And happy for you."

"Thanks." She beamed at him. "Thanks for making that call. I never would have." She raised her brows. "Maybe you're the good guy I think you are."

His eyes darkened. "That would be fantastic."

"Make the promise, Caleb." She grabbed the front of his shirt. "Make the promise you want to make, even if you think you can't keep it. Put it out there to the universe and give it life."

He said nothing, but he slid his hand behind her head and kissed her. It was a kiss of promise, of love, of forever. She felt all his promises in the way he kissed her, in the way his arm encircled her waist, in the way he whispered her name, heartfelt, emotional, and protective.

She leaned into him and kissed him back, accepting his promise, giving it life, allowing it to breathe and grow.

They heard Gracie's feet thundering down the stairs, and they pulled back from the kiss, but not from each other. Their faces were close, Zach tucked between them. As Jenna gazed into Caleb's eyes, she knew she'd found home. "I still love you," she whispered. "Even if you are stubborn about admitting you can't live without us."

He smiled. "I appreciate your patience."

"It won't last forever, so let's get this thing taken care of—"

At that moment Gracie ran into the room, and a truck pulled up outside, who Jenna assumed was Brody. "Mom, I have so many ideas. This is going to be great." She ran over to the kitchen table and sat down. "Come look."

Jenna smiled at Caleb. "Thanks for opening that door for us."

He smiled back. "You bet."

She squeezed his hand and then turned away, as he and Zach headed for the front door. He moved the curtain to peer out. "It's Brody and Dylan. They're—" He paused, then swore.

Jenna and Gracie both turned to look at him. "What is it?"

"There's something wrong." He opened the door, and Brody and Dylan practically sprinted inside.

Dylan was on the phone, talking urgently, and Brody had the computer open. "You need to see this. Now."

CHAPTER TWENTY-FIVE

ADRENALINE GRIPPED CALEB, and he shut the door behind them, locking it. "What's going on?"

"This." Brody started to head toward the table, then saw Jenna and Gracie staring at him. "Jenna, take Gracie upstairs."

"What? No. I know what's going on. I'm not leaving." Gracie leaned back and folded her arms over her chest.

Dylan was pacing by the front windows. "They're on the way."

"Who is?"

Brody swore. "Jenna?"

Jenna sat next to Gracie, both females stubbornly refusing to leave. "Knowledge is power. What's going on?"

Brody glanced at Caleb, and he swore under his breath. How much should he try to protect Gracie? How much could he? He looked at Jenna, and she nodded. "We'll sit here." She patted her lap, and Simba hopped up and then sat down.

"All right." He gestured Brody to the couch.

The eldest Hart immediately sat down and set the computer on the table. As the screen booted up, he handed

Caleb the broken watch. "No dice on the watch. Dylan got it to turn on a couple times, but it keeps shutting off again. It's definitely fried. I didn't know if you wanted it back."

Caleb took the watch and slipped it back on his wrist. It might be broken, but it was his, and maybe it would trigger something. As he did, the face flickered on briefly again, then went off.

"Check the computer," Brody said, turning the laptop so Caleb could see it.

On the screen was a black and white video of Jenna's cabin. Fear settled in Caleb's belly, and he had a sudden urge to grab Jenna and Gracie and run like hell with them. "What is it?"

"They tracked you there. They triggered the silent alarms. Dylan has a team on its way to the house."

"They're at Jenna's?" Tension gripped him. Hell. What if he'd left them there? He glanced at Jenna, and her jaw was jutting out. She didn't look scared. She looked ready.

He relaxed slightly and returned his attention to the screen. "What am I looking for?" The cabin looked untouched.

There was a four-way split screen showing the interior of the cabin and the exterior. Nothing was moving.

"Just watch. They're moving around in there. We didn't have time to cover all the blind spots, but we'll see them in a moment."

Suddenly, there was a shadow at the edge of the screen. Movement. A slight blur.

Caleb frowned and leaned in, watching carefully. He saw the toe of a boot come onto the screen and then off again. "Not your brother?"

"No."

He swore as a man came onto the screen. He was angled away from the screen, but he was moving fast, opening cabinets, lifting pillows. He was moving like a man who knew what he was looking for. He paused by the couch, and then went down on one knee to retrieve something. He held up a white object.

Caleb sucked in his breath. "He found a diaper. He'll know a baby was there." He stood up, gripping Zach more tightly. Restless. Needing to take action.

If they found him there that fast, they'd find him wherever he went.

He wouldn't be able to hide from them.

He needed to face them, and shut them down.

A second man came onto the screen. He had a gun in one hand, and he was heading toward the bedroom.

Fear clamped in Caleb's gut, even though he knew Gracie wasn't in the room. Son of a bitch. He was so glad Jenna and Gracie had come with him.

"It's a military grade gun," Dylan said. "These are serious fuckers."

"Six minutes," Dylan said. "My team is six minutes away."

Caleb paced restlessly, covering the space between Jenna and Gracie, and the couch. Trying to be both places. "Is your team good?"

"Ex-military. Special skills," Brody said.

Caleb glanced at him. "How the hell do you have a team like that?"

Brody met his gaze. "I protect my family, and some of them need more protecting than others."

"Don't listen to him. It's *my* team," Dylan said. "My company. I bring them in for special jobs, like this one."

Jenna put her arm around Gracie, whose eyes were wide. She shifted Simba to Gracie's lap, and the teenager hugged the dog tightly. "He'll come after you, Brody. The police will tell them that you spoke with me."

Brody nodded. "Not if we get them here, first."

Caleb paced over to Jenna and Gracie. He handed Zach to Jenna, then leaned on their chairs, one hand on each back. Looming over them. Protecting them with his body as he watched the screen.

Caleb suddenly noticed a piece of paper stashed on the windowsill. "The picture of the Stocktons," he said. "It's still there."

Caleb watched the first man pick up the paper and look at it. "Put it down," he whispered. "It's nothing."

But he didn't put it down. He held it up and showed it to the other guy, who came over. They both leaned over it, and then one of them pulled out his phone and took pictures of it.

"Facial recognition," Dylan said. "You're a decent enough artist and the Stockton bone structure is very recognizable. They'll figure it out quickly."

"And then come here."

"Unless we stop them."

As they watched, the man did something on his phone. "He's sending the image to someone," Caleb said. "Someone else knows now."

"Four minutes until my team arrives," Dylan said.

At that moment, the two men in the house sprinted for the door. Swearing, Caleb watched as they raced outside into the dark woods. "What? They're gone?" Son of a bitch. "They must have known they triggered the alarm—"

He paused suddenly, his gaze going to something on the ground by the trees. "What's that?"

Brody leaned in. "It looks like a fallen tree. A log."

"It wasn't there when we left." He knew. He'd memorized every single detail of the place, a skill/habit that he'd apparently retained after his memory meltdown. "It's something they left there. Can you zoom in?"

Dylan was in the corner of the living room, huddled with

his phone, talking fast, letting his team know that their targets were on the move.

Jenna stood up and came over for a better look, frowning as she stared at the screen. "I don't remember a tree being down."

"There wasn't one." Caleb braced his hands on the back of the couch, watching carefully as Brody toggled the screen so that one camera was the only view. He zoomed in, and it was grainy and blurry. Impossible to decipher.

"Hang on," Brody said. "I can get that sharper."

Caleb leaned in, watching as the image started to get clearer. Suddenly, he knew what it was. He immediately glanced back over his shoulder, but Gracie was still at the kitchen table, immersed in whatever she was typing on her iPad.

Jenna sucked in her breath, clearly also realizing. She met his gaze, fear etched on her features, because they both knew it wasn't a game anymore. Not that it ever had been, but the stakes had just gone up.

She also glanced toward Gracie, but the teenager was lost in her imagination. "She's working on Maggie's House," she said. "Not paying attention to us."

He nodded, tension gripping him as he waited for Brody to fix the resolution.

One second.

Two seconds.

And then it cleared.

A man came into focus. He was lying on the ground, not moving.

Caleb recognized the man's jacket, and his heart started pounding. "Can you zoom in on his face?"

"You bet."

It took another couple seconds, and then Caleb had a clear view. He swore under his breath, his fingers digging into the back of the couch. "That's the man who gave me Zach. It's Zach's dad." *Son of a bitch.*

Jenna gripped his arm, and he looked over at her, recognizing the gravity in her expression. "Maybe he's just unconscious."

He didn't answer. Because he didn't need to. She knew. He knew. Everyone knew.

"There's someone else there." Brody shifted the angle of the camera, and Caleb realized there was a woman on the ground as well, just behind the man.

Zach's mom? He bowed his head, stunned. *Hell.* If that's who it was, Zach was his kid now.

Zach was his son.

It felt right. Absolutely right. He already loved that kid completely. He'd stand by him. Be everything to him. And so would Jenna—

His gaze shot to Jenna at the thought. Her eyes were wide as she stared at the screen. She must have felt Caleb's gaze on her, because she looked over at him. "You think that's Zach's mom?"

He nodded. "He said they already had her. He was going to try to rescue her, so yeah, it makes sense."

She lifted her chin. "We're his family now, then."

Relief rushed through Caleb. He wasn't in it alone. "Yep."

"We're his only chance, not just for this, but forever."

"But I don't know where the paperwork is that his dad was talking about. I don't have anything to prove he's mine, to make him legally my son." He swore. "I don't even know what his dad's name is."

"We can take care of that," Brody said. "We faked paperwork for all of us when we were homeless kids on the street. Zach will be safe." He looked up at him. "I promise you that. We all know what it's like not to have a family to take care of us, and we won't let that happen to him, even if something happens to both of you. I promise it."

Caleb didn't like the idea of Zach being his kid by faked paperwork. It wasn't enough. Hell, for all he knew, the man might not even have been Zach's dad. "I need answers. I need names. I need proof."

Jenna put her hand on his arm. "You'll remember. You'll know."

Caleb needed desperately to know what he'd forgotten. He wanted to know for Zach's sake. Restlessness rushed through him, and he pushed back from the couch, clasping his hands on his head.

Needing to take action.

Needing to do something. What? He didn't know.

Bright lights suddenly flooded the screen, and armed men appeared.

"That's my team," Dylan said, walking over, still on the phone.

Three of the men took off into the woods, and two others squatted down by the bodies, checking them.

"Both dead," Dylan announced after his team reported in. "A man and a woman. No identification. No trail of the others. They'll keep looking, but it doesn't look good."

Caleb swore. "They'll be coming for us. Could be an hour or two. Or a day. But it won't be long." He swore. "What the hell do they want with me? With Zach?" He was so frustrated. The enemy was closing in on him and this family that he'd just found. And he had no idea what the hell was going on.

"My team is scanning the fingerprints of the couple on the ground," Dylan said. "If those two are in any system, we'll figure out who they are."

Caleb swore and looked at Jenna, who was holding Zach. Gracie was sitting at the kitchen table, her head bent over as she worked. He felt helpless, so helpless. "How do I protect you? That man was a pro, and they got him."

"You're a pro, too," Jenna said.

"Am I? I don't know—"

"You are." She jiggled Zach against her chest. "You can't deny it anymore, Caleb. That's your world. Your people."

He felt like he was breaking in two. "I don't want that world."

She smiled. "I know. You can leave it behind as soon as this is over. But right now, you need to focus on the fact that this *is* your world. If you weren't amazing at it, that man wouldn't have given you Zach to keep safe." She walked over to him. "Caleb," she whispered. "Right now, we all need you to be the man you're trying to forget. You have to become him again. For us. Or we're not going to make it."

Caleb stared at her, desperation warring in his chest. He looked at Zach, his little head leaning sleepily on Jenna's shoulder. Something soft unfurled in him. Something so soft that it had no place in the hell they were standing in the middle of. He leaned forward and lightly pressed a kiss to Zach's head, then did the same to Jenna. He brushed the hair back from her face. "I'm sorry I invaded your cabin and got you guys tangled up in this mess."

"I'm not. I wouldn't trade it for the world." She smiled. "You got me dogs."

He grinned. "I did."

She raised her brows. "So, what now?"

"I can get a team here in six hours," Dylan said. "But no sooner. They can take our second jet, but it'll take time for them to get off the ground."

"They'll be here before then." Caleb was certain of it. He didn't know how or why, but he did. *What did he know?* He needed to remember. He was desperate to remember. The threat was real, and he didn't know how to defend against it. "I'm guessing we have an hour."

Brody shut the computer. "You're not on your own. We'll stick around."

"It won't be enough. These guys are good." He needed help.

Brody leaned back on the couch. "You know, your brothers are pretty capable folk. Logan was in the CIA for a bit. They like to band together to protect each other. It's kind of their thing."

Caleb's first instinct was to say no. To refuse to bring his brothers into the danger he'd brought with him.

Then he thought of Chase. Of the way Chase and Quintin had reacted after seeing him. Going down on their knees with emotion. Grateful to be with the brother who'd left them behind for so long.

What would they do to help him?

What if they asked him for help? He'd do it. In a heartbeat. Even though he didn't remember them.

They were his family.

Brothers.

He'd left before. Why? He didn't know. What was he going to do now? Fight on his own? Keep playing the solo bit he'd clearly decided to follow for the last decade?

He looked over at the kitchen table, where Gracie was still working, Simba curled up on the chair next to her. He looked at Jenna and Zach. His family. They were already his in his heart. He'd do whatever it took to keep them safe.

Even if it meant going against the person he'd so clearly wanted to be. He pulled out his phone. "I'm calling my brothers."

Brody grinned. "That's a fine idea right there."

For better or worse, Caleb was going to reach out to them. The past didn't matter anymore. What mattered was now, and the people he needed to protect. He put his arm around Jenna and kissed her head while Brody and Dylan got on the phone and made some calls.

Chase answered on the first ring. "Hey, Caleb," he said cautiously. "What's up?"

"I need help."

CHAPTER TWENTY-SIX

The moment Chase hung up the phone, Mira smiled. "History repeats itself, I take it?"

"Yep." Chase's adrenaline was already coursing. He was ready. Willing. Able. "You being in danger started the cycle of bringing me and my brothers back together. It's only fitting that danger is what completes the rebuilding of our family."

She looked over at their boys, who were playing with Brownie, the new dog they'd recently acquired from the shelter. "Okay, so what's the plan?"

Chase pulled up the family chat. "Let's figure it out." He grinned. "This isn't going to be the call they expect today."

She raised her brows. "No, it's definitely not." She moved to sit next to him as he pressed the button for a group video call.

One by one, his brothers answered, until they were all online. Some solo, some with their wives. Laughter and joking ended the minute they saw Chase's face.

"What's going on?" Logan asked. Logan had a CIA background. He was the one Chase was counting on the most.

Chase didn't worry about how they'd react with the news.

These were the Stocktons. Family was everything to them, no matter what. "Critical situation. Just listen. Stay focused."

They all nodded, and he could see them leaning in toward the phone.

He took a breath. "Brody found Caleb." He couldn't help but pause for a moment, steadying himself as the emotions flooded the faces of his family. "He's alive, but he has total memory loss. He doesn't remember anything since he woke up in the middle of a burned-out building a couple days ago."

Stunned shock flashed across everyone's faces. Grief. Worry. Concern.

"He doesn't remember us?" Travis, the youngest, who was now a country music superstar, asked.

"Not a thing." Regret was thick in Chase's throat. "He's in danger. Brody brought him to my new guest house last night. He's there with his girlfriend, a teenage girl, and a baby—"

"His girlfriend?" Travis interrupted again. "Doesn't she know his past?"

"No. He just met her yesterday."

"And she's his girlfriend already?"

Chase grinned. "They haven't used the words, but yeah. You can see it in the way they interact. She's his person. And he's hers."

At that news, all of his brothers and their wives grinned. "That's the way we do it," Quintin said. "One day, we think we're all heroic and single forever, and then we find her."

"Or realize she's been living across the hall for two years," teased Skylar, Logan's fiancé.

Logan laughed and kissed her cheek. "Or that, yeah. Took some bullets to wake me up, but it worked out."

"Yeah, well, seems like most of the time true love in this family comes with an element of danger, and this time's no different," Chase said. "Professionals are coming after Caleb and the baby. Maybe within minutes. Hours at most. He can't remember who it is, what they want, or anything." He swallowed. "He just called me, asking for help."

"He called *you*?" Steen, who had gone to prison to protect someone he loved, sounded shocked. "He reached out?"

"Yeah." Chase looked at the faces that were so dear to his heart. "The men after him left two bodies at his girlfriend's place as a message to him. They *will* kill. No one has to help. I'm going over there now. Mira's taking the boys to the safe room in my basement—"

"Of course we're in," Logan said.

"I'll stay with all the kids and women in your basement," Zane spoke up. "I'll guard everyone who comes." He stood up, and his screen got shaky as he went on the move. "We're all heading to the car now. We'll be there in five minutes."

"I'll also stay with the kids and women," Travis said. "We're on our way."

Chase grinned. He'd known that his family would all band together to help Caleb, even after he'd abandoned them for ten years. But even knowing what their reaction would be, it still made his throat tighten.

This was what family was to them. All in. Always. No matter what.

He hoped like hell that Caleb remembered who they were...but somehow forgot the bad stuff. If Chase had to choose...which would he want for his brother? He wasn't sure anymore. Family was everything. But their past was so damaging.

"I'll meet you at Caleb's," Logan said. "I'll call Brody and see what he knows. Maybe I have some contacts that can help off the record." He was also moving already. "I'll bring extra toys for anyone else who wants to shoot people tonight."

"I'm in." Dane Wilson, the local sheriff who had married their sister, spoke up. "I'm on my way."

Everyone else chimed in with what they were going to do. Plans were made quickly, with barely a detail explained, because they knew each other so well.

In less than a minute, the call was over, and every single Stockton was in motion. Chase hung up the phone and looked at his wife. His throat was thick with emotion, and he didn't even know why.

Mira put her hands on his face. "It'll be all right," she said. "You guys will keep him safe. You've got him back, and you're not going to lose him now."

Relief rushed through him at her words. "Right. Okay." She'd known exactly what his fear was, without him even realizing it. "I'll be back. I promise I won't get shot."

"I know." She smiled. "This is how you guys do it. We'll be fine." She kissed him fiercely. "Go save your brother, and then come back home to us. We have a reunion party to plan for tonight, remember?"

"I do." Chase ran over, scooped up his boys, kissed them both, then handed them over to Mira. "Zane and Travis will be here in a few minutes."

"I know the drill. Let's go, boys! Party with the cousins in the basement!" As Mira herded the boys toward the kitchen to gather food, Chase broke into a run. First, his guns. Second, the barn to get the horses.

Third, to get to his brother.

"Chase?" Mira called out, making him stop.

He looked back at the woman he loved. "What?"

"Grab the nametags from that foster child info session we hosted a few weeks ago." She winked. "There are so many of you. It'll help Caleb keep track."

Name tags. For his brother.

Oh, hell. Why not? Humor was everything.

CHAPTER TWENTY-SEVEN

Jenna walked over and sat down next to her daughter, trying to feign serenity while the men worked the phones, brought out guns, and fiddled with the security software. "Hey, Gracie."

Gracie didn't look up. "I'm making a list of all the items we'd use at a dog sanctuary, so we can make a list of who might want to sponsor us. I already reserved MaggiesGuestHouse on all the social media platforms, so we're good there—"

"Grace."

Her daughter suddenly looked up. "You're using that voice. What's wrong?"

"The men that are after Zach and Caleb are on their way here."

Gracie's gaze swiveled to the living room, and she frowned when she saw all the preparations. "So, what's the plan?"

Jenna was suddenly overwhelmed with the need to hug her daughter. As the daughter of two private investigators, the idea of a bad guy coming after them didn't even faze Gracie. Somehow, in the midst of all Jenna's personal difficulties, she'd managed to raise a daughter who was brave, resilient, and a problem-solver. "I love you, Gracie."

Gracie rolled her eyes. "I know, but what's the plan?" Her face brightened. "Can I have a gun?"

"Heavens no." The idea...yikes. "Caleb's family is coming over to help."

"A trap? We're going to set a trap, aren't we?" She grinned. "I love traps. That'll be fun. Are we the bait?"

Jenna started laughing. "You want to be bait?"

"Sure," she said, with absolute confidence. "Caleb will protect us." As she said it, Caleb walked up to the table.

He put his hand on Gracie's shoulder. "I will keep you safe, Gracie. You're right about that." His voice was hard. Focused.

Jenna looked up, surprised by how serious he looked. There was a difference to him. An edge. She suddenly believed he was a man who could take another human's life and not look back. A part of her shivered, and she reached out to touch his wrist, to bring him back from that place.

His gaze shot to hers, but he didn't respond. Instead, he put two phones on the table. "There's the phone we promised you, Gracie. It's a direct line to me. You can call me anytime."

Gracie took the phone. "Where are you going?"

"Out."

"Out?" Jenna picked up hers. "Out where?"

"To hunt them."

The way he said it sent chills down her spine. She knew she'd told him he had to be the man he was trying to forget, but he was a little terrifying. He was like a human weapon: cold, hard, deadly. "Don't get killed," she said softly.

His blue eyes flicked to hers. "If something happens to me, Zach's your son. Brody will help arrange that. Promise me that."

Tears thickened in her throat. "Don't let anything happen to you."

"Promise me that."

She lifted her chin. "You never make us any promises. If I promise that, you have to make us a promise."

Caleb swore under his breath as a truck pulled up outside. "We don't have time—"

Jenna shrugged. "Then Zach's on his own." She put the baby in Caleb's arms and stood up. "Come on, Gracie. Let's see how we can help."

Gracie grinned as she trotted next to Jenna. "He's going to follow us," she whispered.

Jenna put her arm around Gracie's shoulder. "I know. How many seconds?"

"Three," Gracie whispered. "Three. Two. One—"

"Wait!"

Jenna exchanged grins with her daughter, and then they both turned around to see Caleb striding up to them. "What promise do you want?"

Jenna met his gaze. "What promise do you wish you could make to us?"

He swore. "Jenna—"

"Let's go, Gracie. We don't have time for this." She and Gracie had just turned away when Caleb spoke.

"I wish I could promise you forever," he said softly.

Jenna's heart turned over as she and Gracie looked over at him.

"I wish I could promise you that I would love you both, laugh with you, live with you, protect you forever. That I'd get down on one knee at some point and make it official. That we'd have the chance to become a family, the four of us, plus Simba, and I could be the guy you both deserve." His face was desperate, but his voice was soft, rough. Heart-melting.

Jenna smiled. "Gracie?"

"That works for me," she said.

"All right." She took Zach. "I promise to take care of Zach if something happens to you."

"But it won't, because you need us," Gracie said.

Caleb stood there, looking helpless, lost, and Jenna saw his torment. The man he'd just shown to them fighting with the man he had to become right now to keep them safe.

She stood on her tiptoes and kissed him. "We're fine," she whispered. "Go do your thing."

He kissed her hard and fast, pressed his lips to Zach's forehead, and then pulled Gracie into a huge, warm hug. Gracie threw her arms around him and hugged him tightly, the hug she never got from her dad before he left for the last time.

And this one, she didn't even need to ask for.

After a long moment, Caleb let go. His jaw was flexed, his blue eyes intense. He touched Gracie's cheek, then turned and strode past her to the front door.

Tears filled Gracie's eyes, and Jenna put her arm around her daughter. "He'll be back," she whispered. "I know he will." She decided she wasn't going to help the men, even though she had the skills to do so.

She was going to use her skills to surround Gracie and Zach in her own circle of protection. She had faith in Caleb to handle his end of things, so she'd take care of hers.

"I know he'll be back," Gracie whispered. "And then we get to keep him. Right?"

"Right." They met gazes, and Jenna saw the awareness in her daughter's eyes about what might happen. Danny hadn't come back. The danger was real that Caleb wouldn't either.

But together, they had hope. Hope mattered. "Let's go," Jenna said, clearing her throat. "Let's talk to Brody and find out the best place for us to hunker down."

As she spoke, Caleb opened the front door to go outside. He looked back over his shoulder at her, and they met gazes. He mouthed something, then turned and walked outside.

She was pretty sure that he'd said he loved her.

But she wasn't positive.

Maybe he'd just told her that she had spinach in her teeth.

"Did he just say, 'I love you?'" Gracie asked.

Jenna smiled. "I think he did, baby."

"He was talking to me," Gracie said. "I'm pretty sure of it."

Jenna grinned. "I'm definitely sure of it."

As she shifted Zach on her hip, Jenna knew there was something else she was sure of: that man had better come back alive. They had a lot of plans to build. And she wanted him to be a part of them.

CHAPTER TWENTY-EIGHT

Caleb's chest was tight with emotion as he stepped out the front door into the pouring rain, leaving the little trio behind.

It was hard as hell walking away from them. How had he left his brothers ten years ago? What kind of monster was he? He shook out his arms restlessly, and his watch beeped. He looked down quickly, and saw the screen was on again.

Staying on.

Time was wrong, though.

He forgot about the watch as a pickup truck pulled up and the front doors opened. He tensed as two men got out. One had his blue eyes. The other was bi-racial with dark eyes, but they both had the same facial structure as Caleb did. His brothers.

His heart started thudding as the nearest one walked up. Emotion flooded his brother's face. "Hell, Caleb. You look better than when you left."

Caleb grinned. "You look pretty unrecognizable, honestly. Did you lose weight? Shave a beard?"

"I got a nose job. I like it, but it does make it difficult to tell who I am." He held out his hand. "My name's Logan. I'm your favorite brother. You told me that you were leaving all your money to me."

Caleb shook his hand, frustrated that he could still feel nothing for these strangers. "I decided I'm leaving it to Jenna. You're out of luck."

"You chose a woman over me? I respect that." Logan shook his head. "I can't believe it's you. Where have you been?"

"No idea."

"Yeah, I heard that."

As he spoke, the other Stockton came up. This one was taller, wearing jeans, cowboy boots, and a cowboy hat. He looked like pure cowboy, like the picture Caleb had drawn. Awe shocked across his face when he saw Caleb. "Mother of hell," he said. "I can't believe it. Welcome back, bro."

The need to remember coursed even more strongly through Caleb. Who the hell were these men? He wanted to know. He wanted to remember. "Thanks."

"I'm Steen. I'm your favorite brother, not Logan. He's a liar."

Caleb felt the warmth in Steen's voice, and he knew his brothers were close. He could feel it. But he was still outside it, an observer who didn't belong. "Thanks for coming."

Steen set his hand on Caleb's shoulder. "It's what we do. If you can't remember it, we'll show it to you." He gestured behind him, and Caleb saw six horses galloping across the plains toward him, two with riders, and four without. "Chase is bringing the horses. We'll split up. Some will take the horses and patrol. Others will protect the house."

"I can shoot anything from anywhere, so I'm taking the roof," Logan said, as he reached into the back of the truck and pulled out a large, black equipment bag that contained a significant amount of hardware. Was Logan trained as a sniper? "Quintin's going to stay up there with me."

"We're staying at the house," Brody said from behind him. "We'll be monitoring the cameras and security system."

Two more trucks pulled up, and more men hopped out. One didn't look like the others, but he was wearing a sheriff's badge. "Dane Wilson," he said as he shook Caleb's hand. "I'm married to your sister. You don't know her, but I'm your best friend."

Caleb let out his breath. "So, everyone's my favorite?" He tried to keep his voice light, but the tension was palpable between all of them. He could feel these men were holding back, treating him as the stranger that they were to him. Awkward. What if it never changed?

"Or maybe none of us are your favorite." That was from a man standing behind Dane. He looked almost identical to Logan, clearly mixed race. "You did disappear, after all."

There it was. The tension Caleb would have expected from a family he abandoned. He met the man's gaze. "I did," he admitted. "I have no idea why, but maybe we'll figure it out. I apologize for that."

The man narrowed his eyes. "You really don't remember?"

"No." Caleb held out his hands. "I'm sorry for anything I did. Everything I did." And he was, but he could tell from that brother's face that the apology would mean nothing unless it came from the brother who knew what he was apologizing for.

"What the hell are you guys doing standing around, chatting?" Chase rode up on the horses, with another brother beside him, a brother who was watching Caleb with narrowed eyes. "We don't have time for a reunion. The bad guys are coming." He tossed reins to the others, and three of the brothers mounted up, leaving one horse empty. "Caleb? You want a horse? What's your plan?"

"I don't know the land." Helplessness again rushed through him.

Chase raised his brows. "What *do* you know?"

Caleb looked around again. It took a moment to shift from the long-missing, amnesic, guilt-ridden brother back into the man who knew how to hunt human beings. His heartrate slowed. His vision sharpened. His muscles vibrated with energy. Suddenly, he could hear sounds he hadn't noticed before: the shifting of the horses' hooves, Chase's breathing, the sound of talking from the house, birds chattering nearby. He could smell the rain that was roiling nearby, hidden in the black clouds that were closing in fast.

He was a predator. He knew it, suddenly, without a doubt.

He looked around, and he saw that all the Stocktons had gone silent, watching him.

"Shit, man," Logan said softly. "You're like me. You're dangerous."

"I am." Caleb stepped into the lead role, as if it was what he was used to doing. "Two riders to that butte," he said, pointing toward the southeast. "It has a clear three-hundred-and-sixty-degree view. A rider hiding in that cluster of woods." He pointed to another butte, this one rocky and steep. Whoever went up there wouldn't be able to get down in a hurry. "One rider there."

As the riders started mounting up, he surveyed again. "Two roads going in and out, right?" As he spoke, the rain intensified, drizzling down upon them, splattering on the hoods of the trucks, and sinking into the men's coats.

Chase nodded. "I have a truck stationed on each road. No one gets past without us noticing."

"Earpieces." Brody and Dylan started handing out small devices to every Stockton and Dane. While they were getting situated, Caleb continued to survey the land around them. What was the best approach? How would they come in?

It would be tough to approach unnoticed. It was rainy and gray, but still light enough that they'd be seen.

The Stocktons mounted up and headed off, talking quietly among themselves. The wall had been put up between Caleb and them, and he didn't care.

Caleb was focused now. On the job.

All that were left at the house were the Harts and Caleb, and one horse.

Brody handed Caleb an earpiece. "What are you doing?"

"I don't know yet." He felt like he was missing something. That there was a weakness he wasn't seeing.

"I'm going inside to monitor the security system," Dylan said. "I want to watch the cameras."

Caleb nodded, but he didn't move as Dylan went inside. He just scanned the gray, cloudy horizon. As he stood there, the rain intensified, pouring down harder, louder, stronger.

"What are you looking for?" Brody asked.

"I don't know." It was right there, at the tip of his consciousness, but he couldn't grab it. "The bomb," he said softly. "It has something to do with the bomb in that house two days ago."

"There's no bomb here," Brody said. "No time for anyone to plant anything."

"I know." Caleb paced away from the house and then turned to look at the building. The house was a two-story expansive, meandering home with big windows and lots of alcoves. A barn stood behind it. "Has anyone checked the barn?"

"Yeah."

"Check again."

Brody raised his brows. "I'm sure it's fine."

"Check again."

"You're kind of a dick when you're on the clock," Brody observed.

"I've heard that." The moment Caleb said that, he knew he was right. He had heard that. He wasn't a nice guy. He wasn't popular. Who the hell was he? He didn't care how ugly his truth was. He needed to know now, because unless he figured it out, they were all going to die. He was sure of it. "But I'm right."

"All right, then. I'll go." Brody took off at a sprint, heading to the barn, moving fast and easily.

Caleb was the only one outside now. Alone. How he liked it.

The rain had unleashed its wrath now. He could hear the rain hammering on the roof. On the trucks. Loud enough to drown out noise.

His phone rang, and he instinctively answered it. "Caleb here."

"It's Gracie. Just testing to see if it works. Bye." She hung up before he could answer.

Silently, he shoved the phone in his pocket. Gracie. Jenna. Zach. They were in that house with only Dylan there to protect them.

Swearing, Caleb walked over to the last horse. He swung up automatically and easily, settling into the saddle with the familiarity of a man who knew horses. He gathered the reins in his left hand, rested his gun on his right thigh, and urged her into a slow lope around the perimeter of the house.

He could see Stocktons in place on the buttes now. Silhouetted figures on the lookout.

Obvious.

Anyone would see them.

Which meant that the hunters wouldn't show themselves. The Stocktons wouldn't see anyone.

Caleb urged his mount faster, almost desperately, working his way around the house, searching for what he couldn't remember. Where would they come from? How would they approach? And *why*?

He loped away from the house up a small butte. He could

feel the eyes of the Stocktons and the sheriff on him. Why the hell were they helping him? He'd left them, and apparently been a dick about it. So, why were they all here? His mind was spinning as his two worlds began to crash against each other harder and harder.

What was Jenna doing in the house? Were they in the basement? He wanted to be in there with her, but he knew that he needed to be outside. On the offensive.

There was suddenly a piercing shriek in his earpiece, and he ripped it out, wincing at the pain. He knew instantly that it had been disabled. He looked up at the riders on the butte, and one of them was holding up his arm, signaling that they were cut off.

Shit. The enemy was close.

Swearing, Caleb suddenly heard a low, rhythmic throbbing, barely audible over the pounding rain. It took him a split second, and then he recognized it. A helicopter. Coming after the house? Bombing?

A bomb.

Suddenly, Caleb was back in those woods, running toward the house that he'd woken up in two days ago. Fear gripping him. Shouting for Maria. Maria. *Maria*.

Maria hadn't been *his* wife. She'd been the wife of a drug dealer he'd been sent in to assassinate. Instead, he and Zach's parents had decided to rescue her from a hellhole in Mexico. Two weeks ago, her husband had figured out where his wife was and who had helped her escape. One by one, he'd been hunting them all ever since.

He'd shown up to kill Maria in person. On site. He'd been on that video at Jenna's cabin. Because he wanted the pleasure of watching each of them die. Which meant he was most likely coming after Caleb right now.

Caleb suddenly remembered everything, *everything*.

Including what had happened to the house that they'd believe had exploded.

It hadn't been a bomb.

It had been a helicopter.

Like the one coming for the house that Jenna, Gracie, Zach, and Simba were in right now.

CHAPTER TWENTY-NINE

Caleb fumbled for his phone as he kicked the horse into a gallop, barreling for the house where those he loved were hiding.

The buttons didn't work. The phone was dead. They'd fried everything.

"Jenna!" He bellowed her name and urged his mount faster, racing for the house. "Get out! Get out! Gracie! Dylan! Get out!"

Behind him, the sound of the helicopter became louder. They were coming for the house. For Zach. For everyone inside. "Get out!" He shouted again, urging the horse faster and faster.

He'd never ridden so hard in his life, and he remembered every time he'd ever ridden.

No one appeared at the windows. Were they in the basement? Unable to hear the helicopter. Unaware that death was coming for them. He'd been running for the house two days ago. Screaming for Maria to get out.

Knowing he would be too late.

Not again. *Not again.*

He urged his mount onward, driving the horse as fast as she could go.

Behind him, the sound of the approaching helicopter became more distinct. He glanced over his shoulder, but it wasn't visible. At any moment, it would burst out of the clouds.

He reached the porch and vaulted off without even slowing down. He sprinted up the steps, threw open the door. "Jenna— Oomph!" He braced himself as Gracie threw herself at him. "Caleb! I knew you'd come back!"

"Always." He locked his arm around her, holding her tight.

Behind her came Jenna racing toward him, carrying Zach, while Simba clung to her heels. Behind her was Dylan, coming up last to guard the rear, even though he was much faster than the others.

"Get in the truck!" Caleb shouted, as he set Gracie down. "Go, go, go!" He sprinted after them and vaulted into the drivers' seat as the others climbed in.

"I'll be a decoy," Dylan shouted as he raced for the other truck, holding a bundle in his arms that was definitely supposed to be a fake baby.

Caleb loved that guy already.

He hit the gas and tore away from the house as the helicopter appeared over the horizon.

"Holy crap," Gracie whispered, staring out the back window as she hugged Simba. "You're a really bad dude to have that after you."

"I *was* a bad dude. Not anymore." He floored the accelerator, and the truck shot down the long driveway. He liked that house, but he really hoped that they went for the house and not the truck.

"Not anymore?" Jenna was frantically strapping Zach into the car seat. "What do you mean?"

"I remember. All of it." Jesus. There was so much flying through his head right now, but all he could focus on was that helicopter. "When I realized you were in danger, that was the trigger that broke through it all."

"You remember?" Jenna sounded shocked.

"I do." He felt like his head was going to explode, but he had to stay focused. "Watch the helicopter. Is it going for the house?"

"No." It was Gracie who answered. "It's coming after us."

He swore. How did it know which truck? How did they know?

They knew.

"They're tracking me. Somehow they're tracking me." He swore as the truck bounced over the rut. "It's me. They have me."

"Or Zach," Jenna said. "Maybe they're tracking him."

"No, it's me. That's how they found Maria. Something there..." He looked down suddenly at his wrist, at the broken watch he'd pulled from the rubble, that Dylan had fixed. The watch that Maria's husband had given him. The one that was still on. Working. *Transmitting.*

"Son of a bitch."

That was it.

The watch.

He was still alive because that watch had broken in the explosion. Until Dylan had fixed it, they hadn't been able to track him. But once they'd identified the Stocktons, they'd already been heading out there, and the watch had given them their exact target.

He knew what he had to do. He swerved the truck and bounced off the road, heading toward the rocky butte that his brothers had been on. "Get Zach out of the seat. When I say go, you guys get out of the truck, and go under the ledge."

"What?"

"Do it!"

Jenna quickly unbuckled Zach and pulled him into her arms. "You're going to get them to go after you, aren't you?"

"Yep."

"But—"

He looked back at her. "There's no point in my living if something happens to you guys. You're my world. I love all of you. You have to live."

"No!" Gracie threw her arms around his neck, pressing her face against the headrest. "Don't!"

"I have a plan. I'm very good at what I do." And he was. And now he knew. "Three seconds, and then you guys have to get out."

Jenna met his gaze in the rearview mirror. "We'll be waiting for you to come get us."

"I'll be there." And he would. *He would.* "Gracie?"

She was still clinging to him. "What?"

"I promise I'll be back for you."

"When?"

"About an hour."

"An hour? That's it?"

"Yep."

"Promise?"

"I promise." He then hit the brakes. "Get out."

They didn't hesitate for even a second. They scrambled out of the truck, and the moment Jenna shut the door, he gave her a quick smile, then hit the gas. He watched through the rear-view mirror as they ducked into a small cave, the one where he'd spent many hours hiding out when he was avoiding home as a kid.

Then he was around the corner, and they were out of

sight...but the helicopter was bearing down on him. He unbuckled his watch as he drove, and tossed it on the seat next to him.

He hit the gas, his plan to make it to the river before they blew him up. He'd dive out at the top of the riverbank, send the truck over, and then shoot out the helicopter when it came over. His watch would go down with the vehicle, and they'd realize too late that he was out.

It was risky as hell, but it was his only chance. And he was good. But was he that good?

Maybe.

But as he circled around to head to the river, he saw one of his brothers waving at him from the top of the butte pointing back at the house. Then the brother pointed at the house, too. And then another Stockton, who was on the smaller cliff pointed back to the house. All his brothers, pointing him back toward the house.

Where Logan and Quintin were waiting on the roof, armed and ready, with weaponry that had been in a very large bag. What did they have?

Did he risk his brothers by drawing the helicopter back toward them?

He was used to going solo. He'd left them to keep them safe.

But suddenly, he didn't want to be that guy. This was his damned family, all that mattered to him. He wasn't running away from them anymore.

With a loud shout, he spun the truck around and headed back toward the house, toward his brothers, toward the men he loved.

The helicopter banked and then followed him, bearing down. Caleb hit the gas, heading right toward the house. Closer and closer.

The helicopter would have him in range momentarily.

He saw a glint of light from the roof of the house.

He was almost close enough.

He might not make it out of this alive, but if they got the helicopter, then it would be over. His family would be safe.

All he had to do was hang in there another moment.

He knew the moment that the helicopter had him in range. The moment that they'd fire.

So, he hit the brakes.

The ground in front of him exploded, the helicopter zipped past, and then suddenly, it veered off to the side, smoke rising.

It spun out of control, whipping around, and he watched as it crashed to the plains, harmlessly away from any of the structures. The metal crumpled in a pile, and then it exploded.

It was over. Logan stood up on the roof and held up his arms with a shout of victory, holding up a piece of artillery that no civilian would ever own.

Caleb didn't wait to inspect the carnage. He gave Logan a salute, and then he started the truck again and headed back toward the cave.

He was almost desperate to see Jenna, Gracie, and Zach by the time he reached them. He hit the brakes, and leapt out of the truck. Gracie sprinted out of the darkness and threw herself into his arms. He caught her and locked his arms around her, holding her tight as she sobbed on his shoulder. "It's over, Gracie," he whispered. "It's over. I'm not leaving again."

Jenna came out of the shadows, clutching Zach to her chest. "Just like that, it's over?"

"Well, I have some loose ends to tie up, but yeah." He knew who was hunting him. He knew who to tell. And he knew who to give his notice to. He wasn't playing the game anymore. He was getting out.

"And you really remember?" She was still clutching Zach, her eyes wide.

"Everything. Everything that I need to remember to make this end, and to know that I'm never going back to being that guy again." He shifted Gracie to his left hip, and held out his arm. "I have so much to tell you, but the most important one is that I'm back, I'm back to who I was before my life fell apart when I was fourteen, and you're the one who saved me. I'll never let you go, Jenna. Never."

Tears filled her eyes, and she ran over to him. He caught her and Zach and drew them against him, so that all three of them were in his arms. Simba danced around them, barking until Gracie finally bent over and picked her up, bringing her into the circle. His family. The one he never thought he'd have, that he'd be worthy of.

But he'd forgotten his unworthiness long enough to find the love that would heal him.

And one more thing... "Gracie? You know how you told me you want to be a country music star?"

Gracie pulled back and nodded, tears still streaming down her cheeks. "Are you famous?"

He grinned. "No, but my brother is. He performs under a stage name. He won two Grammy's this year."

Gracie's eyes widened. "Who is it?"

"His stage name is Travis Turner."

Gracie's mouth dropped open, and then she flung herself on Caleb, screaming with teen girl hysterics. Caleb grinned over her head at Jenna, who was shaking her head, mirth dancing in her eyes. "You just keep getting better, don't you?"

"I try." He caught her hand. "And I'll keep trying. Every day. To be the best man I can. For all of you."

Her face softened. "I know. I love you."

"And I love you." He would have kissed Jenna, but a

certain teenage girl was jumping up and down between them, yanking on his arm, begging for an introduction.

Yeah. Today was a good day.

The answer to the question that had been haunting them? Yes. The answer was yes, he wanted to remember.

Hell, yeah. Because now, he had it all.

CHAPTER THIRTY

CHASE URGED his horse into a lope, riding toward the butte that Caleb had driven behind.

Smoke was rising from the downed helicopter, and his brothers and Dane were heading over to the helicopter to check for survivors.

But he didn't care about those men.

He cared about his brother.

Would Caleb leave now that the threat was over? If it was over. Or would more be coming? Would it ever be over?

Would Caleb disappear again? Exposed to enough of his past to realize he needed to keep moving?

Tension gripped Chase as he urged his mount onward. He had to keep Caleb around. He had to convince him to stay. He didn't know how, but he couldn't lose him again.

He rounded the corner and slowed when he saw Caleb hugging Jenna and the kids. His throat tightened, and he drew his horse to a halt, emotion clogging his chest at the sight of Caleb embracing them so tightly.

It had taken memory loss, danger, and desperation, but

Caleb had found love. His family. His woman. What all the other Stocktons had also found.

Chase rested his hand on his thigh as he watched. It was all he wanted for his brothers, to find the gift of love. Of finding that partner who would knit together all the gaps in his soul, filling them with love and acceptance and healing.

Caleb had been the last, and now he'd found it as well.

Even if he left now, at least Chase would know that his brother had love.

Caleb suddenly looked over at Chase. He said something to Jenna and Gracie, and they both nodded and stepped back.

Caleb turned toward Chase and began to walk toward him. "Chase." His voice was rough, scratchy. The expression on his face was full of emotion and—

Caleb remembered.

Chase suddenly knew for absolute certain that Caleb remembered.

Caleb broke into a run. "Chase!" His voice was desperate.

Tears filled Chase's eyes, and he vaulted off his horse. "Caleb!" He sprinted toward his brother, and they met halfway. Caleb grabbed him and held on so tightly, gripping him like he'd never let him go, and Chase did the same, holding onto his brother with everything he had.

The emotion was overwhelming, and he let it overtake him. The love. The fear that had gripped him for a decade, terrified that his brother was dead. Abandoned. Lost. That he'd let Caleb down by not being enough for him.

A thousand emotions and questions raced through Chase's mind, but none of it mattered.

Because Caleb was home, and all the distance between them was gone.

"I'm sorry," Caleb muttered, his voice thick with emotion. "I'm so fucking sorry I left. That I abandoned everyone. I'm so sorry, Chase—"

Chase pulled back and met his brother's blue eyes, that he'd thought he might never look into again. "No," he said fiercely. "Never apologize for who you are and what you had to do. I love you. I'll love you every single day until the end of time, no matter what."

Caleb nodded. "I love you, too, Chase. I always have. Every night I thought of you. Of the others. Of this place. I dreamed of coming home, but I couldn't."

Chase laughed through the tears coursing down his cheeks. "I dreamed of you, too. Maybe we were together in our dreams."

Caleb grinned. "And now, together in real life."

"For damn sure."

At that moment, they both heard hoofbeats, and they looked up as Steen rode up. "Everything okay?"

Caleb let go of Chase. "I'm back. I'm sorry. I love you."

Steen stared at him in shock, then leapt off his horse. "Caleb!" He threw his arms around Caleb, and Caleb did the same, holding onto each other as tightly as he'd held to Chase. Then, one by one, the others rode up, realized what was happening, and threw themselves onto the pile.

Moments later, Chase was in the middle of a reunion hug with Caleb and five of his brothers. The others would be there soon. But every Stockton was back. They were complete.

After all these years, after all the darkness that had tried to take them down and split them up, the Stocktons were back together. Forever.

Then Chase looked over and saw Jenna and Gracie watching, tears running down their cheeks as they clutched Zach and the dog. Chase held out his arm to them. "You're part of the family now, too. Come on."

Before they had a chance to respond, Caleb broke free, jogged over to them, and put his arms around Jenna and

Gracie's shoulders. "Guys, I'd like you to meet Jenna, Gracie, Zach, and Simba. Ladies..." He paused as a surge of emotion overtook him, momentarily stealing his voice. He cleared his throat and then continued, "I'd like you to meet...*my family*."

And then the hugs began again, this time putting Jenna and Gracie into the middle of the brothers.

The circle was complete.

CHAPTER THIRTY-ONE

It was almost midnight by the time Caleb had a chance to speak.

He put his arm around Jenna and walked to the fireplace in Chase's living room. The great room was overflowing with Stocktons. There were so many now. His brothers, yeah, but also a sister he'd never met. Nine spouses. A couple grandparents. Family friends. A bunch of kids, most of them not biologically related to his brothers, but family nonetheless. It was exactly how he would have imagined his brothers forming their families.

They'd all chosen incredibly loyal, strong, and admirable women who understood the Stockton hell they'd grown up with, and saw the good in every one of his brothers.

Like Jenna.

He'd hugged more tonight than he had in the entire rest of his life combined, and he knew he'd never stop. Gracie was huddled up with some of the other Stockton teenagers, giggling especially delightedly at Zane's oldest son, Luke, who was back from college for the weekend.

Jenna slid her arm around him and beamed up at him. "I love you, Caleb."

He smiled down at her, his heart full. "Is it crazy how much I love you after such a short time?"

She shrugged. "I think that when you've been through hell and back, you know when you find something good. We're not sixteen. We know."

"I do know." He drew her against him and kissed her. He couldn't wait to get her alone, to make love to her as a complete man, but tonight, right now, was about his brothers. He owed them the truth.

Jenna already knew what he was going to say. He'd felt he had to tell her first, and her unconditional support had touched his already healing heart. "I'm keeping you forever, you know."

She smiled. "Back at ya, big guy." She touched his side, where his injury was. "Are you doing all right?"

"Never been better." And he meant it. "Ready?"

She touched his jaw. "They don't need to know. They'll love you anyway, even if you never open the door to the past."

"I know." He kissed her fingertips. "But I want to share it. I think it matters."

"Okay, then." She squeezed his hand. "Go for it." She released him. "I'll be here."

He nodded, watching as she walked over to the couch and sat down next to Mira, Chase's wife, who had already swept Jenna into the circle of women who loved the Stockton men. Mira was holding Zach, getting to know her nephew. He scanned the room, his heart pounding as he breathed in this room full of his brothers.

He'd never thought he'd be back with them. Not even in passing, let alone to return forever.

Because he was back for good. Nothing would ever drag him away from this family. Not ever.

Chase caught his glance, and his oldest brother grinned at him.

Caleb smiled, and then cleared his throat. "Can I have your attention, please?"

It took a few moments for the room to quiet, but eventually he had their attention. "I know that I've talked to everyone here, and you all know that I love the hell out of all of you. Let me just say now that I'm not leaving ever again. I'm back for good, and I'm keeping Jenna, Gracie, and Zach with me. Right, ladies?"

"And Simba," Gracie shouted.

Caleb grinned at the dog sitting on Jenna's lap. "Of course Simba."

Gracie let out a whoop, and Jenna raised her hand in a fist pump.

"I wanted to explain why I left." It was time to face his past. The night when he was fourteen, gotten drunk, stolen that car so he could save a dog, and then got in the accident. How he'd left the scene, only to find out later that a girl had died in the accident. A girl he didn't even remember being in the car, because he'd been so messed up. Had she been alive when he'd left? If he'd stayed, would she be alive? Thoughts that had haunted him for years.

He was going to tell his brothers about the drug addiction that had almost destroyed him. The years he spent trying to make up for who he was, working as a private contractor hunting down drug dealers in Mexico, until he'd met Maria. How he and Zach's parents, Peter and Gabrielle, had decided to rescue Maria instead of killing her...and how that had unleashed a wrath in her husband unlike anything they'd ever expected. How Caleb had felt so dirty that he could never return to Wyoming, that he'd spent his life hoping that one of the trips into Mexico would get him killed.

Until he'd forgotten all that, and he'd faced life without

his past, and had learned that he had value. That he deserved love. That he would never let Gracie, Jenna, and Zach or his brothers go again.

Chase suddenly stood up. "Don't."

Caleb frowned. "What?"

"Don't." Chase walked to the front of the room, and he put his arm around Caleb, facing the crowd. "Look, we all went through hell as kids. It's a miracle we all survived. As I look around this room, I don't see the broken, scared, fucked-up kids we once were. I see men who are loyal, loving, and good people. Great dads. Incredible husbands. Every single one of us has crafted a life where we bring good to this world. I see it, and I know all of you do as well."

Mira clapped, and then the room joined in, cheers and clapping.

Caleb's throat tightened, but Chase kept going. "We've let Dad's shadow haunt all of us for so long, coloring our views of our worthiness, driving us apart." He looked at Caleb. "Whatever happened over the last ten years, it wasn't your fault. It was the monster who raised us."

Caleb took a deep breath, trying to contain his emotions. "It was," he said. He understood that now.

Chase tightened his arm around Caleb. "We're all heroes for the life we've created. With Caleb gone, we could never complete our healing. But now we have him back, so I think it's time to let the past go. We can spend time wading through the shadows of our past, or we can spend our energy looking forward, loving each other, our families, and all the possibilities ahead of us." He looked at Caleb. "You forgot your past because you needed to be free of it in order to heal. And it worked. So I vote that we all learn from that, and we just let it go, and focus on today. On each other. On love."

The response was instant. Zane stood first, clapping as he strode across the room. The former motorcycling rebel threw his arms around Chase and Caleb, hugging them tightly. "Yes," he said, through a choked voice. "I'm in."

"Me, too!" Travis stood up. Caleb grinned as he watched his brother approach. His little brother was a country music superstar. He loved that so much.

Travis threw his arm around his brothers. "To the future!"

"Yes!" Steen, who spent years in prison before he found his way, stood up. "To the freedom to craft our own lives." As he walked to the front, the others stood up. One by one, brother by brother, until they were all standing at the front, a unified front of nine.

Caleb held out his hand to their sister, who'd had the good luck to never know their dad, but was still part of their legacy. "Jaimi. Come on."

Jaimi smiled and jumped to her feet, jogging to the front of the room. Her brothers pulled her in. Together they clasped hands, and then as a unit, they raised their joined hands as the room cheered.

Nine brothers. One sister.

Unified in victory.

Unified in love.

Unified in freedom.

Stocktons forever.

Together forever.

CHAPTER THIRTY-TWO

Two years later.

JENNA LEANED on the rustic pine table, staring at herself in the hallway mirror.

Her eyes were sparkling. Her skin was flushed. And she couldn't keep the smile off her face.

She was so happy.

Happier than she'd ever thought it was possible to feel.

She almost couldn't believe that was her face beaming back at her. She could still remember when the eyes staring back at her had looked so scared, worried, hopeless. Almost lifeless...

Then she smiled. Chase's speech had been so powerful for all of them. Life changing. She had no time to spend looking back at the past. She had time only for living the life she was in right now, and appreciating every gift that life gave her.

Movement behind her caught her attention, and she glanced over her shoulder as two strong arms swept around her waist and dragged her into the kitchen. She giggled as

Caleb pinned her up against the center island, his blue eyes dancing with mischief.

"Hey, beautiful." He caught her left hand and pressed his lips to the sparkling diamond ring and matching platinum band encircling her finger. "I still can't believe we're married."

She grinned. "It's been eight months." It had been the most amazing wedding, shared with Quintin and Emma, who had refused to get married until Caleb had returned. Sharing the beautiful event with the couple had made them all so close. She now counted Emma as her best friend, and the four of them had many couple dates...that included their kids, of course! She loved being a part of this family-oriented family, and both she and Gracie had thrived surrounded by so much love. Even her grandma had sold her home and moved to Wyoming, because she'd fallen in love with the Stocktons as well.

A fairytale wedding, leading to a fairytale life.

"I know it's been eight months since we got married. Best eight months of my life." Caleb dropped to his knees and pressed a kiss to the barely visible bump in her belly. "And adding a little munchkin to our family is incredible."

She laughed and ran her fingers over his head. His hair was longer, no longer the rigid military haircut he'd had when she met him. "Zach won't be the baby anymore."

"He'll always be our baby. You know that." He spread his palm over her belly. "Speaking of that, Zane's going to drop Micah off for a few hours this afternoon."

Her heart warmed at the mention of the ten-year-old who was part of Zane and Taylor's summer residential horse camp for underprivileged kids. Micah was in the foster system, and he was the sweetest boy ever. She and Caleb had fallen in love with him early on, and Zane was helping them navigate the system to bring him into their family, first as a foster, and then by adoption. "We're going to keep collecting kids, aren't we?"

"Apparently, it's becoming a Stockton family tradition."

She felt a bump against her leg, and she looked down to see their newest addition staring up at them, wagging her fluffy tail. She bent down and scooped up the twelve-pound fluff ball that they'd rescued two days ago, laughing as the puppy showered them both with kisses. "Dogs and kids. It's what makes life worth living."

"And love. Love is underneath it all." Caleb rose to his feet and pulled her against him, tucking the puppy between them. "Two years ago today was the day I lost my memory. Best day ever."

Jenna set the dog down and wrapped her arms around his neck. "Best day ever," she agreed. "You gave me myself back. My daughter back. You gave me a son. And you gave me, you."

"And us. Caleb also gave you us." Chase leaned around the corner, Zach perched on his hip. "How could you forget how great the Stocktons are?"

Jenna laughed as Caleb pulled her against him and kissed her forehead. "I could never forget. I love all of you."

"And we love you." Chase came over and kissed her cheek. "Zach wanted his mama. Uncle Chase is good for only so long."

"Hey, baby." She pulled the toddler into her arms. "Thanks for watching him, Chase. We were a little crazy getting ready for the new arrivals this morning." Her heart melted as Zach giggled at Caleb's silly faces.

Caleb was the best dad. Warm. Loving. Patient. Kind.

And the best husband. Friend. Lover. She smiled at Caleb, and he grinned back, that mischievous grin that told her that the minute they were alone...

Chase grinned. "I love watching Zach. You know that. When do they arrive?"

"Soon—"

"Mom! Dad!" Gracie burst in through the open door, two massive Great Dane mixes running behind her. "They're driving up!"

Excitement leapt through Jenna as she grinned at Chase. "I guess they're coming now."

"Let's go!" Gracie raced down the hallway as more dogs joined her, barking and romping with delight. "Come on!" She flung open the front door and raced outside.

Chase nodded. "I'll go help out. I'm coming, Gracie!" He jogged after the fifteen-year-old, leaving Jenna and Caleb alone.

Neither of them moved. "Twenty dogs," Jenna said. "There are twenty dogs about to arrive." It was their biggest rescue ever.

Caleb grinned. "Good thing we finished the new fences. Five fenced acres will be plenty of room for them to run."

The fenced yard came right up to the house, so the dogs could come and go from the house. No dog lived in a crate or a cage while it was at Maggie's Guest House. They had dog beds everywhere, and they'd added couches covered with blankets.

It was a house filled with love, kids, dogs, family, hope, and new beginnings.

Jenna breathed deeply, inhaling the moment. "I can't believe we made this sanctuary happen."

Caleb held out his hands for Zach, and the toddler launched himself into his dad's arms with a round of giggles. "Together, we can do anything." He pressed a kiss to her knuckle. "You, me, Gracie, your awesome grandma, and the whole Stockton and Hart clans."

As he spoke, they heard the sound of a car engine outside.

Jenna looked out the window to see Travis, Steen, and their wives climb out of the cab of the largest Maggie's Guest House van. Gracie pulled the side door open, and Jenna saw three Stockton kids in the back, with puppies on their laps and in their arms.

She'd never dared to even dream of opening an animal rescue. But not only did she have it, but it had become a family affair that brought everyone together every day in a venture built on love.

Caleb held out his hand, and Jenna put her hand in his.

And together they walked outside to where puppies, kids, family, and love awaited them.

∼

Thank you so much for reading *A Real Cowboy Always Comes Home*. I hope you enjoyed it! Since this is the last book of the *Wyoming Rebels* series, you might be wondering what to read next! If so, keep reading. I've got you covered!

What to read next?

If you are new to the *Wyoming Rebels*, start the series from the beginning with *A Real Cowboy Never Says No*.

If you want more cowboys, try the spinoff *Hart Ranch Billionaires* series. Preorder the newest book, *A Rogue Cowboy's Christmas Surprise* (Coming Nov. 2022), or start with the prequel, *Her Rebel Cowboy,* or first book in the series, *A Rogue Cowboy's Second Chance*.

If you want more small-town, emotional feel-good romances like the *Wyoming Rebels*, you'd love my *Birch Crossing* series! Get started with *Unexpectedly Mine* today!

Are you in the mood for some feel-good, cozy mystery fun that's chock full of murder, mayhem, and women you'll wish were your best friends? If so, you'll fall in love with *Double Twist!*

Are you a fan of magic, love, and laughter? If so, dive into my paranormal romantic comedy *Immortally Sexy* series, starting with the first book, *To Date an Immortal*.

Is dark, steamy paranormal romance your jam? If so, definitely try my award-winning *Order of the Blade* series, starting with book one, *Darkness Awakened*.

SNEAK PEEK: DOUBLE TWIST

Mia Murphy Mysteries (Book One)

A SHADOW MOVED across my fifth-floor window.

Assassin.

I yelped and launched myself out of bed. My foot caught in the sheet, and I crashed to the floor. I rolled onto my back, frantically kicking to get free. I scrambled up and lunged for the doorknob—

Then I heard a meow.

I whirled around and saw King Tut, my neighbor's rude and massive black cat, staring at me through the glass, with his unblinking yellow eyes, thick gray mane, and unruly tufts of fur in his ears.

A cat. Not a hit man. *I wasn't going to die tonight.*

My legs gave out. I landed hard, and then pressed the heels of my hands to my eyes, trying to slow my frantic heart rate.

Breathe in. Breathe out. Breathe in. Breathe out. *I'm not going to die tonight.*

It was hard to believe I used to be fairly chill. Relaxed. Resilient.

Being raised and trained by a con artist mother had made me pretty unflappable, even after I'd ditched that life when I was seventeen.

Now? A grumpy *cat* had sent me running for my life. Two years being undercover against my drug lord ex-husband, Stanley Herrera, had totally screwed with my tolerance level for stress.

I'd made one little anonymous tip to the FBI hotline after finding bags of white powder in our china cabinet. One tiny, socially conscious gesture. That was all it had taken to get me dragged into a two-year sting run by an FBI control freak I'd nicknamed Griselda.

Agent Straus didn't appreciate my pet name for him, which made me call him Griselda as often as I could. I'd needed to find some way to amuse myself, because spying on the man I was sharing a bed with had been surprisingly stressful, especially once I learned how much he liked to have traitors chopped up into little pieces and used as an example to others.

Con artists were non-violent. Non-confrontational. Clever law-benders who delighted in the artistry of deception. My childhood hadn't prepared me for thriving in a world of hit men, murder, and violence.

The night Stanley had figured it out and pointed a gun at

my forehead? If Griselda hadn't been literally breaking in the front door at that second—

But he had. So it had worked out fine.

Except for the apparent wee bit of lingering jumpiness on my part.

King Tut meowed again, tapping his left paw impatiently on the glass.

I took a deep, calming breath, and rolled to my feet. "All right. Cool your jets."

I walked over to him and fought with the window until I was able to get the crooked casing to move. As soon as it was open, King Tut hopped off the sill and strolled into my cardboard-box-sized bedroom, the one I'd been stashed in during Stanley's trial so a hit man couldn't keep me from testifying.

I'd always thought it would be fun to have my ex sending killers after me. Childhood dreams right there, right?

Tonight, no FBI agents were lurking in my hallways, and no one cared what I did. Why? Because ten hours ago, Stanley had been convicted, and he was now heading off to his new home behind bars.

Since I had nowhere else to go, Griselda had let me stay in the safe house for one more night, which gave me a chance to say good-bye to the cat who had been my only decent company for months. My only friend, actually, but who wants to sound like a loser?

The FBI had offered me witness relocation, but I'd turned it down. The last thing I wanted was to turn my life over to yet another person. I'd been forced into crime by my mother. I'd been tangled up with Stanley for years. And then I'd been used by Griselda as his little spy.

I was done letting someone else control me.

No more. Never. Ever. Again.

Tomorrow, I was packing up and moving on. To where? I

had no idea. But I had about twelve hours to figure it out, so plenty of time.

The air drifting through King Tut's window was cold and crisp, an early May chill that made me shiver. The spring air felt alive and clean, like the fresh start I was claiming for myself. I braced my hands on the window and leaned out, inhaling the night air.

My next-door neighbor's window was open, and I marveled once again at how King Tut managed to jump the gap between our windows without being fazed by the five-story drop to the unforgiving pavement. Granted, I'd met my very sketchy neighbor a couple times, and if I lived with him, I'd probably risk plummeting to my death to get away from him, too.

The sound of a police siren drifted up from below, and I leaned out to check the street. It looked more like Griselda's ride than a Boston police car.

It stopped in front of my building as the theme from *The Greatest American Hero* burst from my phone.

Habit borne from two years of taking every call in case Griselda had news that would save my life made me hurry over to the nightstand and check the screen. *Griselda.*

This was supposed to be over. He wasn't supposed to call me in the middle of the night anymore. Ever again. Alarm prickling at the back of my neck, I hit the send button. "What's up?"

"Mia! Assassin. Get out!" he shouted. "Now!"

Terror shot through me, and I grabbed King Tut. But just as I started to run for the front door, I heard the whoosh of a silenced gun, and the lock on my front door exploded.

I skidded to a stop, scrambling backwards as I gripped the phone. "He's at the door!" I whispered. "He's here!"

Griselda swore. "Hide in the bathroom. Lock the door and get in the tub. I'm on my way up."

The front door splintered, and King Tut yowled in fury and tried to leap out of my arms.

Struggling to keep my grip on him, I raced into the bathroom, locked the door, and then dove into the tub, clutching the wriggling feline in my arms. I yanked the mildewed shower curtain closed, and then curled onto my side in the fetal position so all my body parts were below the rim.

The floorboards creaked outside the door, and I tried to hold my panicked breath, but it echoed off the yellowed tiles. Loud. So freaking loud. I really had to learn how to stop breathing in times of crisis.

I couldn't believe this. After all I'd survived for the last two years, *now* I was going to get whacked in a tub?

There was so much indignity in being murdered in a bathtub.

King Tut purred and began kneading my chest, through my tank top. I bit my lip and slid my hand beneath his claws to protect my skin.

His purring got louder, and the footsteps paused just outside the bathroom door.

Seriously? I was going to get busted by a cat?

I raised my head enough to peer around the edge of the curtain at the door. The wood was so flimsy there were already cracks in it. Literally one bullet is all it would take to get in. It probably would take no more than a gentle nudge with a pinkie finger, actually.

I was pretty sure my late-night visitor could muster up at least that much force, which meant I had maybe a millisecond at most until the only thing between me and a hired killer was a moldy shower curtain.

Griselda was, at that very moment, sweating his way up four flights of stairs. He was almost as fit as he liked to tell everyone he was, but he wasn't *that* fast.

In retrospect, maybe it would have been better to lock

the bathroom as a red herring, and then hide somewhere else, like hang out the window by my fingertips. I would admire myself so much more if I died that way, instead of cowering in a tub.

My mom would be so disappointed in me for cowering in my last moments of life.

Truth? I would also be disappointed in myself for cowering in my last moments of life. I needed to die as more than a bathtub victim.

My phone rang again, but it was outside the bathroom. I must have dropped it during my sprint for safety. The floor creaked, and I heard my personal Grim Reaper move away from the door in pursuit of my phone.

Frantically, I scanned the bathroom for a weapon. Toothbrush? Towel? Mascara? Hairdryer?

Hairdryer.

I tucked King Tut under my arm, scrambled out of the tub as quietly as I could, and climbed up onto the sink. I tucked myself up against the corner closest to the door, set King Tut on my lap, and picked up the hairdryer.

I tested the weight of the hairdryer, swung it from the cord, and then heard the creak in the hall again, outside the bathroom.

I went still.

My assassin waited.

King Tut purred.

My quads started to cramp. My arm ached from holding up the hairdryer. Sweat dripped down my eyebrow and stung my right eye.

The doorknob rattled.

Fear shot through me, obliterating all thought of leg cramps.

The gun fired, and then the door handle exploded. I leapt back and my foot slipped on the porcelain. King Tut dug his claws into my thighs for balance, as I grabbed the towel rack to keep from tumbling off my perch right to my assassin's feet.

Two more shots and the door drifted ajar while I perched precariously, clinging to life by one old towel rack and a stained sink. I'd never wanted to see Griselda as badly as I did in that moment.

But he didn't show up.

Instead, the gleaming barrel of a gun poked through the gap in the door and then bullets flashed out of the end of it, right at the tub. Where I'd just been. Because that had clearly been a great place to hide. *Thanks, Griselda.*

A man moved into my line of vision. He was angled away from me, his gun and his attention focused on the tub. His all-black attire and ski mask escalated my terror level to near-debilitating heights.

He fired several more shots into the shower curtain, then reached out with his gun to push the shower curtain aside and inspect the bullet-ridden body he wasn't going to find.

This was it. My chance.

I braced myself, then tightened my grip on the cord. "Hey!" As I shouted, I swung as hard as I could.

He spun around just as the hairdryer smashed him across the face, shattering his nose with a loud crunch. He dropped like an old lady shocked by her first sight of porn.

I leapt over him, landed on the hall floor, and then raced for the front door. I ran out into the hall corridor, and then something hit me between the shoulder blades and flung me forward. I hit the carpet and dropped King Tut, who yowled with protest as he landed gracefully on his feet.

I scrambled up, but before I could get off my knees, something cold and hard pressed into the back of my head. A gun?

I froze.

"Mia Murphy. You two-faced, lying, little snake."

I blinked at the sound of my ex-mother-in-law's voice. "Joyce?"

The gun pressed harder into the back of my head. "We took you in as family. We loved you. I called you my daughter. And then you turned on my son and ripped him from me. And now you want to steal his business."

"Steal his business?" If I hadn't been so stressed about the gun pressed up against the back of my head, I would have started laughing at the ridiculousness of that idea. "There's literally nothing I want less than becoming a drug lord—"

"For that, you die." Joyce kicked me in the hamstring, and my leg immediately cramped, making me lurch to the right.

Except dying. *That* was something I wanted less than running a major drug operation.

"Turn around," Joyce snarled. "I want to watch your agony and pain as the life drains from your pathetic, unworthy body."

Wow. That was alarmingly sociopathic.

I slowly turned, frantically trying to figure out how to get out of this one. Then I saw her face. It was bright red. Twisted with rage. Mottled with anger. Her eyes were almost glazed. Crazy eyes. And she was aiming a machine gun at my face.

She met my gaze with unflinching hatred. "Without your testimony, Stanley won't get convicted on his appeal."

Witness protection? Who needs witness protection? Clearly it had been a great choice to turn that down. "Listen, Joyce, there's been a misunderstanding." I tried to summon the quick-thinking that had saved me so many times as a kid, but the assault weapon aimed at my face was making it difficult to concentrate. "I'm not going to testify against Stanley again or take over his business."

"Exactly. You'll be dead." Her flushed face twisted into a triumphant grin. "Say good-bye, you snot-nosed, thieving rat."

"Wait!" I held up my hands, which were shaking so badly I could practically feel the breeze on my face. "If you shoot me, you'll go to prison. Put the gun down. We'll both walk away and pretend we never met—"

She called me a name that would have had nuns fainting (or cheering, depending on the nun), and then her finger moved on the trigger.

I had no time to duck before the deafening sound of gunshot exploded in the hallway.

I yelped, but I didn't collapse in a bullet-ridden death.

Her mouth opened in surprise, a red stain blossomed on the front of her shirt, and then she toppled over. She hit the floor with a thump, and behind her stood Griselda. He was dripping with sweat, panting, and aiming his gun right where she'd been.

Like it? Get it now!

SNEAK PEEK: A ROGUE COWBOY'S SECOND CHANCE

★★★★★ *"Wonderfully written, lots of heart."*
-*Candy G. (Five-Star Amazon Review on* A Real Cowboy for Christmas)

BRODY HART RAN his hand over the gleaming chestnut hair on Stormy's neck, pleased by how well the horse was doing. She'd been in such rough shaped when he'd rescued her, and now her coat was gleaming. Her dark brown eyes now had that sparkle he always fought to rekindle when he brought a new horse to the Hart Ranch. "Glad you found your way home," he told her.

Stormy snorted and swished her tail, impatient to get released from the cross-ties.

"I know. I'm almost done." Whenever Brody was in town, he did the shoeing for the horses who needed extra care. He'd made a study of farrier methods and honed his skills to best help the animals they rescued and brought onto the Hart Ranch.

He trusted no one else with Stormy's feet, and his care had made a difference. She'd barely been able to walk when she arrived, afraid to put weight on her broken hooves.

Now she galloped through their extensive pastures, tail held high, the purest freedom of spirit. She was why he had this ranch. She and all the others like her.

He ran his hand down her back leg and leaned his shoulder into her hip, shifting her weight off her hoof so he could lift it and work on it. He was humming quietly to himself when he heard footsteps behind him.

He didn't have to look up to know who it was. He recognized the gait of all eight of his brothers and sisters. He'd trained himself to do that back when they were homeless kids, hiding under the bridge in the dark. It had been imperative that he knew who was coming, so that he would know how to keep those under his care safe.

The habit remained today even though they were all adults, and no one was after them, trying to drag them back into foster homes, or worse. "Hey, Keegan."

His brother spoke without preamble. "Did you sleep last night? At all? Your light was on all night."

"You stalking me?" Brody set the lightweight, high-tech shoe on Stormy's foot to test the shape. Most horseshoes were steel. A few racehorses used aluminum. He'd experimented on a lightweight, durable plastic compound. It was too expensive to ever become popular, but he didn't care about money.

He cared about his horses. And his innovations had saved Stormy's feet.

"No." Keegan leaned against the wall, his booted feet in Brody's line of vision. "Just keeping an eye on my bro." He let out his breath. "Did you find anything?"

"Nothing new." Brody lined up a high-tech nail and tapped it through the shoe and the outer rim of Stormy's hoof. "It was a false trail." Only nine of the homeless kids who'd been living under a bridge together so long ago had stuck together, taking the last name of Hart and claiming legal status as a family. But a number of others had gone through their pack during the five years Brody had held them together, not sticking around long enough to become a Hart, but always leaving behind an imprint that the rest of them never forgot.

After one of those who'd moved on had been murdered a few years ago, Brody had made it a point to track down everyone he could find and make sure they were alright. He'd located most of them, touched base, and helped out where he could. But there were a few he couldn't find, and he wasn't planning on resting until he found them all. He thought he'd located one of the women, but he'd run into a dead end last night.

Keegan sighed. "We're all adults now, Brody. It's not your job to continue to hold us all together."

"It's what I do."

"I know. But you don't need to be the guardian of everyone anymore."

Brody finished securing Stormy's shoe and set her hoof down. He stretched his back as he turned to face his brother. Keegan was wearing a dusty cowboy hat, faded jeans, and a loose flannel shirt. His short blond hair was neat, and his blue eyes blazed with the warmth that was a hallmark of every Hart.

Keegan looked like a dusty cowboy, not one of the Hart billionaires who had gotten lucky with security software when they were teenagers. The world saw his family as billionaire celebrity recluses. Brody saw his family as the only people who mattered to him, real people who were all still fighting to escape the childhoods that had sent them running for their lives to hide out under a bridge as kids.

The shadows still ran deep for all of them. But the family they had formed had given all of them the safe space they needed, no matter what demons crawled out of their pasts after them. The Harts had a rule, which Brody had made when they were all under the bridge, that no one could hold out. Emotions had to be shared. Secrets had to be revealed. No one carried their burdens alone.

It was why they'd survived, and why the Harts were thriving now.

Which was why he answered Keegan's question. "Every night I go to bed, I see Katie Crowley's face. I wonder what I could have done to save her. If I hadn't let her go to Boston—"

"Stop." Keegan held up his hand. "You have to stop that shit. You're not a god, Brody. You never had the right to tell any of us what to do or how to live. Those of us who stayed chose to stay. Those who chose to leave were following their paths. However it turns out isn't your fault."

"But she's dead—"

"Yeah, it was shitty. You don't need to tell me that. I think about her, too. But she died years after leaving us. I hate to tell you this, bro, but you aren't responsible for the entire lives of every person you've ever met."

Brody scowled at him. "She's *dead*."

"And the rest of us are alive." Keegan put his hand on

Brody's shoulder. "We're all here, Brody. Eight of us, plus you. More, if you include the Stocktons, now that Hannah married into their family. Katie was Hannah's sister, but Hannah has fought to find a life again, happiness, and a family. Learn from her. Let yourself be happy, Brody. That's what you're always telling us."

"I know." Brody shoved his cowboy hat back from his head and wiped his wrist over the perspiration beading on his brow. "It's different for me. It's my job to hold everything together."

"Yeah, well, not if it wrecks you." Keegan lightly punched Brody in the shoulder. "Family meeting tonight, bro. You're the topic. I just thought I'd warn you."

Brody frowned. "Why me?"

"Because we all think you're turning into an old shit, and you need to get a life." Keegan grinned and ducked when Brody tossed a rag at him. "Seriously. You better come in your party pants or you're going to get your ass kicked. We're tired of your crap, old man."

Brody laughed, his spirit already lighter. "Who's house?"

"Bella's hosting tonight."

Bella was the older of the two Hart sisters. She was the chef for the part of the Hart Ranch that provided high-end, rustic vacation packages for big spenders who wanted to experience the cowboy life on a dude ranch. "Is she cooking?"

"She is."

"Well, damn. I wouldn't miss it if she's cooking."

"You wouldn't miss it anyway." Keegan tossed an envelope at him. "By the way, this arrived this morning by personal courier. Looks important so I opened it."

Brody took the envelope, which was, indeed, torn open. He didn't care. He had no secrets from his family. "What is it?" As he asked, he noticed the grin on Keegan's face. He stopped. "What?"

"Open it."

Brody shot Keegan a suspicious look, then slid his fingers into the envelope and pulled out a small white envelope with his name on it. That envelope was also open. He lifted the flap and saw it was a concert ticket.

Covering the name of the performer was a yellow sticky note. Someone had jotted in purple pen, "Personal invite from Tatum Crosby. She hopes you'll come."

He froze. "Tatum?"

"Tatum," Keegan confirmed.

Brody ripped the sticky note away and saw Tatum Crosby listed as the headliner for the concert. His seat was row one. Behind the ticket was a backstage pass. "The concert's tonight in Portland," he said, scanning the details.

"I saw that. You can't go, obviously. Family meeting and all."

Brody couldn't take his gaze off the ticket. Tatum Crosby. She'd swept through his little group when she was seventeen, a brilliant flash of fire, passion, and energy. She'd stayed for a summer.

A summer he'd never forgotten.

And then he fucked up, she'd left, and she'd never spoken to him again. He'd kept track of her, though. Watching her ascent to the realization of her dreams. "This can't be from her. She'd never invite me."

"Is it her writing?"

"No." She'd left Brody a note when she'd taken off. A note he'd kept for a long time as a reminder of how badly he could screw up if he wasn't careful. A reminder that had helped keep him focused on being the protector that all those in his care had needed.

He shoved the ticket back into the envelope and held it out to Keegan. "Toss it. I'll be at the family meeting tonight."

Keegan didn't take it. "I can't. I texted the Hart chat. We

think you should go to the concert. See her. Family consensus."

"No." Brody tossed the envelope into a nearby trash can. "It's not from her."

"What if it is?"

He paused and looked at his brother. "She's married."

"Divorced. You know that."

Brody let out his breath. "Our fling was a long time ago."

"It wasn't a fling, and it might have been a long time ago, but she still haunts you. She's the reason why you've never met anyone else. We all know it." Keegan plucked the envelope out of the trash. "You're always telling us we deserve love. You're the one trying to marry all of us off because we all deserve the family we didn't have. But you're the one who won't even try. Because of her."

Brody walked to the end of the aisle and stared across their expansive ranch at the sun quickly rising in the sky. Tatum Crosby. Keegan was right. She had become his world fifteen years ago, and that hadn't ended when she'd left.

"You have to go, Brody. You always say that the universe hands you what you need, not necessarily what you want. Well, guess what?" He shoved the ticket back into Brody's hand. "You got handed a ticket, so you gotta go."

Brody scowled at his brother. "Why do you remember the things I tell you only when it's convenient?"

"Because I'm smart. I booked the penthouse at the Ritz in Portland for you already. They're delighted Brody Hart will be gracing them with his presence this evening." He grinned. "We're still going to eat Bella's dinner, but we're doing it without you, so you better have a good time, or you'll miss her dinner for nothing."

Brody grabbed a brush and began working on Stormy's neck. "I'm not going. It's not from Tatum."

Keegan laughed. "Of course you're going. There's no way

in hell that you could possibly walk away from this invite without knowing that for sure."

Brody ground his jaw. "I fucked up. She was right to leave."

"Yeah, an eighteen-year-old, homeless, runaway trying to keep a bunch of kids alive and together made a mistake. He definitely deserves to pay for that for the rest of his life, right?"

Brody looked over at his brother. And said nothing.

"How many of her songs do you know every word to?" Keegan asked.

Brody replied without hesitation. "All of them."

"Then you need to go see her, or you'll never be free."

One-click now to get started!

A QUICK FAVOR

Did you enjoy Caleb and Jenna's story?

People are often hesitant to try new books or new authors. A few reviews can encourage them to make that leap and give it a try. If you enjoyed *A Real Cowboy Always Comes Home* and think others will as well, please consider taking a moment and writing one or two sentences on the eTailer and/or Goodreads to help this story find the readers who would enjoy it. Even the short reviews really make an impact!

Thank you a million times for reading my books! I love writing for you and sharing the journeys of these beautiful characters with you. I hope you find inspiration from their stories in your own life!

Love,
Stephanie

BOOKS BY STEPHANIE ROWE

MYSTERY

MIA MURPHY SERIES
(COZY MYSTERY)
Double Twist
Top Notch (Sept. 2022)

CONTEMPORARY ROMANCE

WYOMING REBELS SERIES
(CONTEMPORARY WESTERN ROMANCE)
A Real Cowboy Never Says No
A Real Cowboy Knows How to Kiss
A Real Cowboy Rides a Motorcycle
A Real Cowboy Never Walks Away
A Real Cowboy Loves Forever
A Real Cowboy for Christmas
A Real Cowboy Always Trusts His Heart
A Real Cowboy Always Protects
A Real Cowboy for the Holidays

BOOKS BY STEPHANIE ROWE

A Real Cowboy Always Comes Home
SERIES COMPLETE

THE HART RANCH BILLIONAIRES SERIES
(CONTEMPORARY WESTERN ROMANCE)
A Rogue Cowboy's Second Chance
A Rogue Cowboy's Christmas Surprise (Nov. 2022)

LINKED TO THE HART RANCH BILLIONAIRES SERIES
(CONTEMPORARY WESTERN ROMANCE)
Her Rebel Cowboy

BIRCH CROSSING SERIES
(SMALL-TOWN CONTEMPORARY ROMANCE)
Unexpectedly Mine
Accidentally Mine
Unintentionally Mine
Irresistibly Mine

MYSTIC ISLAND SERIES
(SMALL-TOWN CONTEMPORARY ROMANCE)
Wrapped Up in You (A Christmas novella)

CANINE CUPIDS SERIES
(ROMANTIC COMEDY)
Paws for a Kiss
Pawfectly in Love
Paws Up for Love

SINGLE TITLE
(CHICKLIT / ROMANTIC COMEDY)
One More Kiss

ABOUT THE AUTHOR

N*EW* Y*ORK* T*IMES* AND *USA* T*ODAY* bestselling author Stephanie Rowe is "contemporary romance at its best" (Bex 'N' Books). She's a Vivian® Award nominee, and a RITA® Award winner and five-time nominee. As the bestselling author of more than fifty books, Stephanie delights readers with her wide range of genres, which include contemporary western, small-town contemporary romance, paranormal romance, and romantic suspense novels.

www.stephanierowe.com

ACKNOWLEDGMENTS

Special thanks to my beta readers. You guys are the best! Thanks to Kelli Ann Morgan at Inspire Creative for another fantastic cover. There are so many to thank by name, more than I could count, but here are those who I want to called out specially for all they did to help this book come to life: Alyssa Bird, Ashlee Murphy, Bridget Koan, Britannia Hill, Donna Bossert, Deb Julienne, Denise Fluhr, Dottie Jones, Heidi Hoffman, Helen Loyal, Jeanne Stone, Jeanie Jackson, Jodi Moore, Judi Pflughoeft, Kasey Richardson, Linda Watson, Regina Thomas, Summer Steelman, Suzanne Mayer, Shell Bryce, and Trish Douglas. Special thanks to my family, who I love with every fiber of my heart and soul. Mom, I love you so much! And to AER, who is my world. Love you so much, baby girl! And to Joe, who teaches me every day what romance and true love really is. I love you, babe!